USA TODAY BESTSELLING
AUTHOR OF *VIKING HEAT*

SANDRA HILL

DARK VIKING

ISBN 978-0-425-23740-3

5 0 7 9 9

continued . . .

Praise for the novels of Sandra Hill

"Exciting, unexpectedly erotic, and entertaining . . . Another winner."
                                    —*Booklist* (starred review)

"Wickedly funny, deliciously sexy . . . Loved it!"
        —*New York Times* bestselling author Karen Marie Moning

"Smart, sexy, laugh-out-loud action, Sandra Hill always delivers."
        —#1 *New York Times* bestselling author Christine Feehan

"Wildly inventive and laugh-out-loud fabulous . . . Once again, the talented Sandra Hill proves that a real hero isn't stopped by any obstacle—not even time."
            —*New York Times* bestselling author Christina Skye

"Hill writes stories that tickle the funny bone and touch the heart. Her books are always fresh, romantic, inventive, and hilarious."   —*New York Times* bestselling author Susan Wiggs

"Some like it hot and hilarious, and Hill delivers both."
                                    —*Publishers Weekly*

"Another wonderful story that includes action, adventure, passion, romance, comedy, and even a little time travel."
                                    —*Romance Junkies*

"A perfect ten! . . . A must-read for everyone who loves great romance with heartfelt emotion."   —*Romance Reviews Today*

"Only the mind of Sandra Hill could dream up this hilarious and wacky scenario. The Vikings are on the loose once again, and they're wreaking sexy and sensual fun."
                                    —*Romantic Times*

"Feeling down? Need a laugh? This one could be just what the 'dock whore' ordered."   —*All About Romance*

Berkley Sensation Titles by Sandra Hill

ROUGH AND READY
DOWN AND DIRTY
VIKING UNCHAINED
VIKING HEAT
DARK VIKING

Dark Viking

Sandra Hill

BERKLEY SENSATION, NEW YORK

THE BERKLEY PUBLISHING GROUP
Published by the Penguin Group
Penguin Group (USA) Inc.
375 Hudson Street, New York, New York 10014, USA
Penguin Group (Canada), 90 Eglinton Avenue East, Suite 700, Toronto, Ontario M4P 2Y3, Canada
(a division of Pearson Penguin Canada Inc.)
Penguin Books Ltd., 80 Strand, London WC2R 0RL, England
Penguin Group Ireland, 25 St. Stephen's Green, Dublin 2, Ireland (a division of Penguin Books Ltd.)
Penguin Group (Australia), 250 Camberwell Road, Camberwell, Victoria 3124, Australia
(a division of Pearson Australia Group Pty. Ltd.)
Penguin Books India Pvt. Ltd., 11 Community Centre, Panchsheel Park, New Delhi—110 017, India
Penguin Group (NZ), 67 Apollo Drive, Rosedale, North Shore 0632, New Zealand
(a division of Pearson New Zealand Ltd.)
Penguin Books (South Africa) (Pty.) Ltd., 24 Sturdee Avenue, Rosebank, Johannesburg 2196,
South Africa

Penguin Books Ltd., Registered Offices: 80 Strand, London WC2R 0RL, England

This is a work of fiction. Names, characters, places, and incidents either are the product of the author's imagination or are used fictitiously, and any resemblance to actual persons, living or dead, business establishments, events, or locales is entirely coincidental. The publisher does not have any control over and does not assume any responsibility for author or third-party websites or their content.

DARK VIKING

A Berkley Sensation Book / published by arrangement with the author

PRINTING HISTORY
Berkley Sensation mass-market edition / October 2010

Copyright © 2010 by Sandra Hill.
Cover art by Dan O'Leary.
Interior text design by Stacy Irwin.

ISBN: 978-0-425-23740-3

BERKLEY® SENSATION
Berkley Sensation Books are published by The Berkley Publishing Group,
a division of Penguin Group (USA) Inc.,
375 Hudson Street, New York, New York 10014.
BERKLEY® SENSATION and the "B" design are trademarks of Penguin Group (USA) Inc.

PRINTED IN THE UNITED STATES OF AMERICA

10 9 8 7 6 5 4 3 2 1

This book is dedicated to Hazel Green Brungard, an old classmate of mine. Hazel has long been a vocal and appreciative fan of everything I write, no matter the genre. She generously supports the Ross Library in Lock Haven, where we both learned to love books in its Victorian nooks and crannies. And most of all, she has an enthusiastic sense of humor when it comes to reading. Bless you, Hazel, for sharing my belief that the best books make you smile.

One's self only knows what is near the heart.
Each man reads but himself aright.
No ailment seems to a sound mind worse
Than to have lost all liking for life . . .
That I saw for myself as I sat in my keep,
Awaiting a maid to woo . . .
For I did think, enthralled by love
To work my will with her.

—FROM "HÁVAMÁL" ("THE WORDS OF ODIN THE HIGH ONE")
OF *POETIC EDDA*, EARLIEST ORAL VERSIONS, CIRCA 800 AD

Chapter 1

Double or nothing ...

With a loud whoosh, Rita Sawyer's body went up in flames, and she prepared to catapult through the fifteenth-floor window of the burning skyscraper. The whole time she pondered whether she'd have the time or the inclination to shave her legs before her date this evening with her ex-husband's brother.

Darron, who was suffering major post-divorce guilt ... on his brother Scott's behalf, of all things ... had made it his mission in life to find her a mate to make up for his hound dog brother's betrayal during Scott and Rita's short-lived marriage. As a result, he was bringing along the "perfect man" for her. His words. Presumably heterosexual with a job. Absolute essentials for her as a twenty-nine-year-old veteran in the dating wars.

To be honest, she was still raw and angry over Scott's infidelity, whether it was one time, as he outrageously claimed, or dozens, as she suspected. She'd seen what adultery had done to her mother, as well.

Having known Scott since kindergarten, she'd seen him at his worst, and it wasn't even when she'd caught him in bed with a fellow physician. Think seven years old and green snot. She shouldn't have been surprised when he'd turned out to be an adulterous snot when he grew up.

She had an ulterior motive for meeting with Darron tonight. He was a top-notch financial advisor, and Rita was facing monumental money problems since her mother had died, leaving her with medical bills out the wazoo. It wasn't the long bout with cancer that caused all the problems, but the experimental treatments not covered by insurance, for which Rita had gladly taken out loans, and the year as a caretaker when she'd had no income. Unfortunately, all in vain. Collection agencies now had her on speed dial.

"Scene Three, Take Two. Lights! Camera! Action!" Larry Winters, the director of this latest spy thriller starring Jennifer Garner and Hugh Jackman, shouted through his bullhorn.

Whoosh! Bursting into a ball of flame, Jennifer went sailing through the glass and the air with expertise, landing on a trampoline that looked like the roof of another building, from which she then front flipped onto yet another rooftop, aka a padded platform. Of course, it wasn't really the fifteenth floor, but the third, and it wasn't really a skyscraper, but a set prop, and it wasn't really Jennifer Garner, but her, Rita Sawyer, stunt double.

"Cut!" the director yelled. "That's a wrap! Great job, Rita!"

Immediately, a technician began hosing down her flames while others were peeling back her flameproof wig along with the tight cap that protected her short, spiky blonde hair à la the singer Pink, two Nomex jumpsuits, and gloves. Still others wiped the retardant gel off her face.

"Hey, Rita. Got a minute?" The producer, Dean Witherow, called out to her. "I have a couple gentlemen who'd like to meet you."

Noticing the two military types in the visitors' area, probably consultants on the film, she sighed with resignation. Folks were fascinated with her after witnessing some of her stunts, especially men who fantasized about what she could do in bed. Being a proud lady of the SWAMP, as in Stuntwomen's Association of Motion Pictures, she'd heard it all. One lawyer from Denver once asked, before they'd even gotten to the entrée in a fancy L.A. restaurant, if she could do any kinky stunts during sex. Jeesh! And, yes, she could, actually. Not that she'd told him that.

After a quick shower in the doubles' trailer and a change of clothes to jeans and an Aerosmith T-shirt, she walked up and let Dean introduce them. "This is Commander Ian MacLean and Lieutenant Jacob Mendozo. They're Navy SEALs stationed at Coronado."

Like many others in this country, she had a proud appreciation for the good job SEALs did in fighting terrorism.

The one guy . . . the commander . . . was in his early forties with a receding hairline that didn't detract at all from his overall attractiveness. He was too somber for her taste, though.

Lieutenant Mendozo on the other hand, was whoo-ee sex personified. From his Hispanic good looks to his mischievous eyes, he was eye candy of the best sort. And she'd bet her skydiving helmet that he knew his way around a bed, too.

Rita Sawyer, get your mind out of the gutter.

Maybe I am suffering from sex deprivation, like Darron thinks.

"Were either of you among those SEALs who got in trouble for riding horseback into Afghanistan a few years back? I saw it on CNN."

Both men's faces reddened.

"We don't talk about that," the commander said.

Which means yes. "Why so shy? It was really impressive."

"The Pentagon didn't think so," Lieutenant Mendozo explained with a wink . . . a wink his superior did not appreciate, if his glare was any indication.

"Heads rolled," the commander agreed with a grimace. "With good reason. Necessity might be the mother of invention, but in the case of SEALs, they better be private ones."

"What he's trying to say is that a SEAL scalp is a coup for many tangos . . . uh, terrorists. It's important that we stay covert. That episode in Afghanistan was a monumental brain fart."

"Well, it's been nice meeting you. Maybe you can—"

"We have a proposition for you," Commander MacLean interrupted.

Gutter, here I come. She laughed. She couldn't help herself.

"Not that kind of proposition."

"Oh, heck!" she joked.

"I'm a happily married man. In fact, my wife would whack me with the flat side of her broadsword if I even looked at another female."

The lieutenant smiled in a way that indicated *he* wouldn't mind that kind of proposition.

But wait a minute. *Did he say broadsword?*

"Can we go somewhere for a cup of coffee?" the commander suggested.

Or a cool drink to lower my temperature.

Soon they were seated at a table in the commissary.

"So, what's this all about?" she asked, impatient to get home if she was going to make her "date." Now that her initial testosterone buzz had tamed down to a hum, she accepted that these two were here on business of some sort, not to put the make on her.

"How would you like to become a female SEAL?"

She choked on her iced tea and had to dab at her mouth

and shirt with the paper napkins the lieutenant handed her with a chuckle. "You mean, like *G.I. Jane*?" she finally sputtered out.

"Exactly," Commander MacLean said. "It's a grueling training program. Not many women . . . or men for that matter . . . can handle the regimen."

What a load of hooey! "Why me?"

"The WEALS program . . . Women on Earth, Air, Land and Sea . . . needs more good women who are physically fit to the extreme. With terrorism running rampant today, Uncle Sam needs more elite forces, and our current supply of seasoned SEALs are deploying on eight to ten combat tours. Way too much! So, we're recruiting special people under a mentoring program. Bottom line, we need a thousand more SEALs over the next few years, and a few hundred more WEALS."

"But why me?"

The commander shrugged. "We want the best of the best. Men and women who are patriotic . . ."

I do get teary when the National Anthem plays.

". . . extreme athletes,"

You got me on that one.

". . . controlled risk takers,"

Stunts R Us.

". . . skilled competitors who enjoy challenges and games,"

Does he see "Sucker" tattooed on my forehead?

". . . people who love to travel."

Yeah, like downtown Kabul is my idea of a Club Med vacation.

"Only one in a hundred applicants make it through Hell Week, you know."

And you think I want to put myself through that? "You've gotta be kidding."

Both men shook their heads.

"Each WEALS trainee has a mentor to get her through the process," Commander MacLean added, as if that made everything more palatable.

"And my mentor would be?"

The sexy lieutenant gave her a little wave.

Okay, I'm officially tempted.

But not enough. She'd read about Hell Week. She'd watched Demi Moore get creamed in *G.I. Jane. Who needs that? No. Way.* She started to rise from her seat. "I'm flattered that you would consider me, but—"

"Plus there's a sizeable sign-up bonus," Lieutenant Mendozo added.

Rita plopped back down into her chair. "Tell me more."

And she could swear she heard the cute lieutenant murmur, "Hoo-yah!"

I'm in the mood for . . .

Steven of Norstead, proud son of a Viking prince, handsome as a god, far-famed in the bedsport, well-tested in battle, was bored. Actually, more than bored. In truth, he was in a black, nigh unbearable mood and had been for some time.

"Who ever heard of a depressed Viking?" Oslac, his friend and comrade-in-arms, inquired, followed by a loud belch.

He belched, too, just to be friendly.

They were both deep in the alehead following a full day and night of debauchery . . . or at least multiple partners in his bed furs, if he recalled correctly. Not all at once, praise the gods. Not this time anyway. But that other time! By the runes! Father Christopher had suffered a foaming fit when he caught him in the bathing longhouse with . . . well, never mind.

Vikings often practiced both the Christian and Norse religions, but it was no great loss when Father Christopher left them for an extended monastic retreat, leaving behind Father Peter, who was less inclined to foaming fits, leaning more toward foaming ale.

But that was neither here nor there.

"I am not depressed, precisely. More like I carry a huge weight on my shoulders. All the time."

"Well, 'tis no small feat managing two vast estates. Norstead and Amberstead." Amberstead was a large, self-sustaining estate that included a castle keep, outbuildings, and farmsteads, but Norstead was four times its size, and it also included a military garrison and armory, more skilled workmen and craftsmen, such as a blacksmith, weavers, cobblers, cattle herders, shepherds, stable hands, and a much larger timber castle. There was no way Steven could handle both estates without help. "And a fine job you do for me at Amberstead."

It was difficult running the two estates that were adjacent but separated by rocky, mountainous terrain. If only Oslac would take over the much smaller Amberstead on a permanent basis, but he had property in Norsemandy that would be his on his father's death. Still, for now, 'twas good to have a friend at one's back. "Nay, 'tis more than that. I am only twenty and nine, and yet I have lost my zest for life. I can scarce get up in the morn, with naught to look forward to."

"And your people are aware of it, too," Oslac pronounced, squeezing his forearm in warning.

A serving maid, Asabor, stepped forward to refill their horns from a pottery jug in her hand. He could guess from the flushed expression on her round cheeks what was about to come.

"Did ya hear 'bout the woman who buried her husband twelve feet under?"

"Nay, Asabor, I did not." *Spare me, Lord.*

"It was 'cause deep down he was a good person."

That was not even funny. "Ha-ha-ha! Very good, Asabor."

When she left, he rolled his eyes at Oslac. His people had taken of late to telling lackwit jokes in hopes of garnering a smile from him.

First of all, to say that the people of Norstead and Amberstead were "his" people struck an odd chord with him. He still thought of his home as Norsemandy, where he grew up. When he and Thorfinn had come to Hordaland, it was Finn as the older brother who had ruled. He did not want nor need that role. Alas and alack! He was stuck being a jarl in a country that was not even his own.

Second, it was beyond distasteful that the common folks were not only remarking on his moods but attempting to do something about them.

"I do not seek pity from anyone, Oslac."

"'Tis not pity, my friend. Everyone shares in your grief. They speak in general of a gloom that pervades this valley."

"Oh," he exclaimed, "now I know what you refer to. It is those damn witches, Kraka and Grima, who continue to spread their prophecies of a great light coming to brighten all the world."

"Not all the world. Just Norstead." Oslac's lips twitched with amusement.

"Have you e'er met these two sisters, Oslac? Living in some mountain hut as they do, they are enough to scare the braies off a priest with their wild white hair and incessant cackling. I swear, they are older than time. I know they were here when my grandsire ruled Norstead, and that was some fifty years ago."

"Mayhap you need to wed. Mayhap that will be the light they speak of. Get yourself a wife and start breeding sons. King Olaf still claims you were betrothed at birth to his third daughter, Isrid."

He shot a glower at Oslac.

"What? She is not so bad."

"Oh, she is comely enough, but she talks constantly. About nothing. Blather, blather, blather. I would have to put a plug in her mouth afore tupping."

Oslac suggested something about the plug, which Steven should have expected. He had stepped into that one like a boyling unused to male jests.

"Whether Isrid or someone else, you must wed at some point. Heirs are needed for Norstead and Amberstead."

He shrugged. "Isrid or some other, it matters not to me at the present. Time enough later."

"It's your brother then," Oslac guessed.

He nodded. "Yea, ever since Thorfinn disappeared two years past—"

"Disappeared?" Oslac scoffed.

"Ever since Finn died, then." He cast a scowl at Oslac for the reminder. "We were in Baghdad. One moment he was laughing and telling me to meet him at the ship, warning me not to purchase any harem houris, whilst he conducted a final meeting with the horse breeder. The next he failed to appear, and all we found was a pool of blood and his short sword lying beside the road. Mayhap he is still—"

Oslac put up a halting hand. "Nay, Steven. You searched for sennights. Two years have passed. He would have let you know."

"But there was no body," he insisted.

"The miscreants who took his life no doubt dumped his body elsewhere. Accept that he is gone and move on with your life. I know how close you were, but he is in Asgard now, my friend."

Steven sighed and drew another long slurp of ale from his carved horn cup.

"I must say, though, that Finn was always the serious one, especially after his wife left him, taking their infant son. And you were the lighthearted one, always up for a good time."

"Are you saying I have lost my sense of humor?" he inquired, not at all offended, though Viking men did prize their ability to laugh at themselves and all of life's foibles.

"Hah! You have lost more than that. Remember the time you and I fought off a black bear with our bare hands? Remember the time you tripped Balki the Bold when he was being particularly arrogant, and he fell into Mathilde Wart-Nose's big bosoms? Remember the time you brought that ivory phallus back from the Arab lands and talked Maerta into inserting it whilst we watched? Remember the time we drank so much mead we decided we could jump off the roof of the keep into a hay wagon? Remember the time you tupped six women in a row and could still rise to the occasion?"

He just sighed deeply again.

"Mayhap you should go a-Viking."

"I did that last month. Brought two shiploads of plunder back from the Saxon lands."

"Boar hunting."

"Boring."

"Amber harvesting."

"I have too much amber already. That reminds me. We must needs send several chests to Birka for trading afore the winter freeze over the fjords."

"Visit King Olaf's royal court."

"I will be going there for the Yule season. A man can stand only so much of Olaf's bad breath."

"What we need is a good battle. Why is everyone so bloody peaceable of late?"

"I know. My broadsword will get rusty from lack of use. Many thanks for reminding me. I will have the armor boy oil it and my brynja on the morrow." In fact, now that he thought on it, it was time for the yearly cleaning of all the metal armor, putting the pieces in a barrel of sand and vinegar that was rolled around to shake and remove the rust. Later, they could be polished with bran.

Oslac poured them both more ale. "There are those pirates who are getting more daring of late."

"Or desperate."

"That, too."

"Especially Brodir the Bold. What have he and his outlaw band against you? He targets your ships more than any other."

Steven shrugged. "Some grievance he has against my family. I have met him in person only a handful of times, and never in recent years."

"You should post extra sentries lest they strike afore winter."

Steven nodded. "'Twas a time when they only attacked longships that were poorly armed and usually those farther south. Now they even stalk the inland fjords."

"Brodir has set an example for other outlaw Vikings, giving pirating a good name. If a Norseman of noble birth can pirate, why not them, too? Truly, they are becoming a menace as their numbers increase."

"Yea, 'tis a waste, too. Brodir was once a fine warrior, and respected even when he went rogue, but then he and his men raped those novices at a Sudeby abbey and put a blood eagle on the mother superior, for sport. Now he is a *nithing*, using his fighting skills to organize the pirates and train them to attack in fleets."

"Ah, look. Here comes Lady Thora, Rolfgar's widow. Mayhap she can lift your spirits . . . or leastways your staff."

"She already lifted my staff. Three times last night she let me swive her. Or rather, she swived me, to be more accurate."

"Are you sure? I swived her three times last night."

He and Oslac exchanged looks of incredulity, then burst out laughing.

"Dost think she would consider joining us in . . ." Oslac then suggested something so outrageous that Steven, who

thought he had tried everything that involved his cock,
solitary or otherwise, was shocked.

But only for a moment.

Suddenly, Steven's enthusiasm gurgled back to life. Not
his mood. But then, when had a good mood been required
for a zesty bout of bedsport? A man's enthusiasm for sex
play was a constant, especially the perverted kind.

"Oh, Thooor-aaaaa?" Oslac drawled out.

But in the end, Steven went to his bed alone. Turns out,
he was not in the mood, after all.

Chapter 2

The only easy day was yesterday . . . or was that yesteryear? . . .

Rita was hot, sweaty, tired, and smelly, and having the time of her life.

She was one of fifty WEALS candidates still surviving the yearlong training program out of the original seventy-five, many of whom had "rung out" going DOR, dropped on request, which meant they'd volunteered out of WEALS. Or they could have "rolled back," giving them the opportunity to try again for the next session, having sustained some injury or personal crisis that prevented their going on.

While her teammates groaned and moaned about the difficulties, Rita was finding many of the exercises easy, and those that weren't posed welcome challenges.

Their day started with an 0500 muster, followed by a dip in the pool, fully clothed, including boots, then a jog to the chow hall for breakfast. After more running, at least twenty miles per day, they headed to the O-course, or obstacle course, that was often referred to by others as the

Oh-My-God course. To Rita, it was the Oh-Boy course. It was located on the Grinder, an asphalt square surrounded by buildings on four sides, much like a penitentiary exercise yard. The Slide for Life. *Whee!* Log rolling. *Just call me Twinkle Toes.* The monkey bars. *Anyone got a banana?* The Tire Sequence. *Dance, baby, dance!* The tower! *King Kong couldn't climb any better.* The Cargo Net. *Hey, I did scarier things when doubling for Julia Roberts in her last film.*

Of course, they hadn't started Hell Week yet. That would come in just a few days. Then they would get their gaudy Heineken pins, a mocking copy of the Navy SEAL trident pin, better known as the Budweiser. But that didn't mean their training would be over, oh no. SEALs and WEALS continued to train for years after graduation to keep in shape and up to date on new technology.

Rita had been an only child, so it was hard to understand why she had such a competitive nature. Her inclination toward physical activities was more understandable. Genes, pure and simple. Although he had divorced her mother when Rita was a toddler, her six-foot-three father had been . . . aside from a blatant womanizer . . . a twice silver-medaled Olympic runner and later a professional golfer of some note before his early demise in a car accident. Her diminutive mother had been an Olympic gymnast. Rita had been a gymnast, too, until by age twelve she was already growing too tall and big to excel in that sport . . . eventually reaching five nine and a curvy, muscletoned hundred and thirty. Picture backflips on the parallel bars with that body. Ouch!

Later she had tried figure skating, and while she'd become proficient, she hadn't excelled to the national level. Then, of course, there had been her marathon running, sky diving, mountain climbing, kayaking, cliff diving, NASCAR racing (okay, only one week of that before being booted off the track for recklessness), skeet shooting, and alpine skiing. All that was before discovering stunt work, which combined many of those skills. And now rigorous military training, of course.

They were jogging along the shore of the Pacific Ocean now.

"Haul ass, sweet cheeks!" Master Chief Frank Uxley, best known as F.U., yelled out to her bunk mate, Wendy Patterson, when she lagged behind. Never let it be said that Navy SEALs were politically correct. The elite troops, when not on active duty or between assignments, were often assigned TDY, temporary duty, as instructors for BUD/S, the Navy SEAL training program, and for WEALS.

Jogging backward beside the group, he then homed in on her. "Ya ain't in Hollywood now, are ya, Mz. Stunt Woman. What are you, some kinda Six-Million-Dollar Woman, or somethin'? Why dontcha just give up now, and I'll walk you to the bell myself?"

When she refused to react to his needling, he added, "Ya think yer gonna find some kinda Brad Pitt here, honey? No? Some folks say I resemble Matt Damon."

She flashed him a look of disbelief. And saw his grin. When she shook her head at having risen to his bait, he winked at her and moved on to taunt some other poor trainee.

F.U. was the most arrogant, offensive, politically incorrect of all the SEALs she'd met, and she suspected it was a deliberate pose he put on to annoy one and all. It worked.

It was their second five-mile run of the morning on the Coronado beach, the early haze now replaced by a brutally scalding sun. As usual, there was sand everywhere. In their mouths, buttocks, ears, hair, eyebrows, and noses. And inside their heavy boondockers, which weighed them down even more. At the end of the day, that weighted jogging, plus long swims with web fins, caused their feet to ache painfully. She couldn't remember the last time she'd worn a pair of high heels. Nor did she want to.

"Okay, ladies, gimme some sugar."

They all grimaced but didn't dare voice their objections. When he said "sugar," he meant sugar cookies. As in rolling their wet bodies in the sand, following a quick dip in the waves, then resuming whatever evolution was called for next, uncomfortably coated.

They followed orders, then heard, "Fifty push-ups, grunts. Come on, come on, work 'em out, work 'em out."

"We're working, we're working," several of Rita's teammates muttered.

For that infraction, they were all required to do twenty more, at the end of which F.U. ordered, "Now lean and rest." That meant putting the body parallel to the ground, without sag, held up on extended arms and the tips of their boots.

"Stand!" Once they came to their feet, he added, "Brace."

They all tucked their chins in, backs straight, shoulders thrown back. Then, "Stand easy. Let's take a water break." The trainees carried two canisters of water tied to their web belts at all times and were told to "Hydrate!" often.

The class was divided in half, with the first group going with F.U. to the pool for advanced drownproofing lessons, where they would be bound, hands and feet, then tossed into the water to "bob for life." The rest of the group were assigned to Lieutenant Mendozo or JAM, the nickname for Jacob Alvarez Mendozo, who had just come on duty.

All the SEALs and WEALS were given nicknames. Hers was Spider because of her agility in climbing impossible places. It could be worse. Wendy's nickname was Windy. Not a play on her name, unfortunately. Nope, Wendy had accidentally farted one time during strenuous PT, and the SEAL instructors thought it was funny to embarrass her in that way. They'd been instructed by their XO to cease and desist, which they skirted by continually addressing her as "Windy . . . oops, Wendy."

In any case, JAM was looking hot today . . . and she wasn't referring to the temperature, which was blazing . . . in a New Orleans Saints baseball cap, drab green shorts, a white SEALs T-shirt, boondockers with socks rolled over the tops, and mirrored aviator sunglasses.

They were similarly attired, except their shirts said WEALS, and their caps had the logo, Navy Scruffies, which just about said it all. Rita's hair was in its easy-to-manage short spiky style, now plastered to her head with sweat, while many of the WEALS had long hair pulled back in ponytails that hung out the back hole in their caps so that they resembled horses' tails when they ran. Like they cared! Physical appearance lost meaning for women when they were dripping with sweat and often puking out their guts from overexertion.

"Up boats!" JAM yelled.

This was one exercise she did hate. They all did.

At the sound of their groans, JAM quipped that old SEAL motto, "Pain is your friend."

And you're the Marquis de Sade, I suppose. That's what she thought but didn't dare say aloud.

The smaller of the ugly rubber boats, known as an IBS, Inflatable Boat, Small, weighed almost three hundred pounds. It was twelve feet long and six feet wide. Trainees were required to carry the boats on their heads almost constantly, even as they ran. An equal number of trainees were on each side for balance. After a while, the three hundred pounds felt like a thousand, and the boats did irreparable damage to a lady's hair. That's why some of them began to don helmets, which would make them even hotter. Better hot than bald, though, knowing that some SEALs developed permanent bald spots on top of their heads. Sometimes they were told to carry the boats up on extended arms, which was almost worse, since muscles were soon screaming with pain.

JAM had become a friend and mentor since he was at

least partially responsible for her being here. She reminded him of that fact every chance she got, like when she was crawling in mud or covered with sand fleas. He winked at her, as if reading her mind.

Rita stuck out her tongue.

He arched his brows, as if she'd issued some sexual invitation.

"I think he's got the hots for you," Wendy commented at her side.

"Nah! He's just teasing. He used to be a priest, you know."

"You're kidding!"

"Well, he was studying to be a Jesuit. Not sure he ever took vows."

"Same as."

They took their positions under the boat, opposite each other with two WEALS in front and two in back of each of them. Then they all began a synchronized, slow jog.

"He's a friend. In fact, he's taking me to a party at the commander's house tonight as a fake date," Rita continued her conversation with Wendy.

"Huh?"

"The commander's wife, Madrene, is always trying to fix JAM up, usually with one of her Viking extended family."

"Whaaat? Vikings? In California? Are you sure you don't mean Minnesota? Ha-ha-ha! How come I've never met any?"

"There's a whole bunch of Magnussons here, from Norway, a lot of them associated with SEALs. Anyway, I'm to be his buffer."

"So you're not coming to the Wet and Wild with the gang tonight?"

"Nope." The Wet and Wild was a bar that catered to Navy personnel, including SEALs and WEALS. Its claim to fame was the wet T-shirt spray at the door, plus its hot wings and Friday night band. Missing a night out with the girls would be no great hardship.

"Would you two shut up before you get us all in trouble?" Louise "Loozie" McKay remarked from behind her.

They ignored her. Loser Loozie was such a goody-goody.

"Maybe he's gay." Wendy never skipped a beat, continuing her conversation about JAM. "Maybe that's why he's not interested in any of the Viking babes. Maybe that's why he's friends with you . . . a smoke screen. Maybe he's just not into you because maybe friends with benefits doesn't fit his agenda, if you get my meaning."

"There are a lot of maybes in there." She chuckled as she glanced over at a scowling JAM.

Wendy didn't realize that JAM had come up and was jogging beside them. "*Maybe* you'd like to do a week of Gig Squad, Patterson. I'm thinkin' you're a tadpole with too much attitude."

Gig Squad was the SEALs method of torture . . . uh, punishment. It involved doing various embarrassing, muscle-wrenching exercises after dinner in front of the officers' quarters while everyone passed by on their way out of the chow hall. Like duckwalking in a squat position.

Wendy jerked with surprise, then turned red with embarrassment. "Ooops!"

Rita was laughing so hard she almost lost her balance under the boat.

"You, too, Sawyer. I'm thinkin' your butt muscles need a workout." JAM gave her behind an exaggerated survey.

"My butt is just fine, thank you very much," she muttered under her breath.

"What did you say, Spidey?"

Bite me.

"What?"

"Nothing, sir. Not a thing. Sir."

"Be careful, newbie," JAM said to her. "You're still working off punishment for last week's stunt. Only an idiot would hand walk on the parallel bars."

She couldn't help but grin. She had been unabashedly showing off at the end of a day that had seemed like endless harassment from their instructors.

"Boats down," JAM hollered then. Instructors always hollered, even when they were right in your face.

When the two boats were lowered to the ground, and twenty women were bent over at the waist, trying to regain their collective breaths, JAM jerked his head toward the next evolution, the Dirty Name, which prompted a collective groan.

Rita had had problems with this one in the beginning. There was a series of three horizontal logs, the first one foot off the ground, the second, six feet high, and the third, twelve feet, all of them six feet apart. The trainees needed to climb to the top without ever touching the sand. Every muscle in the body was stretched at the end, including the buttocks, which was clearly JAM's evil intent.

She mouthed to him, "Rat!"

He just grinned. As she hung back while the others began the new evolution, he asked, "Pick you up at seven?"

She nodded. "What should I wear? It's a barbecue, right?"

"Stilettos, garter belt, thong, black stockings, spandex dress with a plunging neckline, and, oh, yeah, red lipstick, the glossy screw-me-silly kind."

"Are you pulling rank on me, sailor?"

"You bet your ass," he replied. "Don't forget the thong."

"Dream on," she replied with a laugh. "How about shorts, a tank top, and sandals?"

"Works for me."

Yeah, but where's MY love connection? . . .

She didn't wear shorts and a tank top, after all. Instead, she opted for a strapless sundress with bright Hawaiian flowers. Fitted to the waist with a wide straw belt, then flaring down to the knees. Flat-heeled sandals, not stilettos. And no red lipstick, either. Just pink lip gloss.

Even so, JAM whistled when he picked her up. "Methinks the lady is lookin' to get laid tonight."

She laughed. "Maybe the lady is just looking. Period. And, hey, you don't look too shabby yourself."

He was wearing khakis, a black T-shirt, and loafers without socks. His designer stubble highlighted his dark blue eyes. Too bad he didn't turn her on. He certainly had all the ingredients.

When they arrived at the party, they found that the rest of the company was already there. About fifty people. Half couples. Most of the men sported high and tights, the traditional military haircut, except for some of the SEALs, who weren't required to adhere to that standard. They often had to infiltrate foreign countries and needed to blend in.

People were standing about in small groups on the wide, low veranda of the huge oceanfront home of Commander MacLean and his gorgeous wife, Madrene, or were down on the beach playing volleyball. What had started out as a cottage a few years back, according to JAM, was now a palatial, three-story, glass-and-cedar mini-mansion, as befitted their growing family. Apparently, Madrene's father had money, lots of it. No way could a Navy man, even an officer, afford digs like this.

Sipping a sour apple margarita and listening to the sound system playing an old Beach Boys song, she watched, bemused, as JAM, at her side, kept casting hungry looks at Kirstin Magnusson, a professor at San Diego State. So much for his avoiding the Viking women thrown his way! He was the one looking to make a Viking connection, if the sizzle these two created was any indication.

"We know each other from way back," JAM offered defensively when she elbowed him in question. "We're just . . . uh, friends."

"Yeah, right. You two are so hot for each other you put this steaming California sun to shame." She motioned with her margarita to the evening sun that continued to warm them all.

"Do you really think she's attracted to me?"

"Blind! Men can be so blind."

He blushed. JAM actually blushed. "I've been kind of in love with her for a long time."

She rolled her eyes. "Kind of?"

He shrugged.

"How long?"

He muttered something.

"What?"

"Five years."

"Unbelievable! Does she know?"

He looked horrified. "Hell, no!"

"It's obvious she feels the same way about you."

He turned to look at the woman, who was blonde, in her thirties, pretty, but nothing spectacular . . . except to him, apparently. Rita noticed immediately that Kirstin's lower lip was trembling, and her expression said "crushed."

"She thinks you're with me," she deduced.

"I *am* with you."

"You are an idiot. You're not with me *that way*."

"Oh. Right."

"Go over and talk to her. Her feelings are hurt."

"By me? No way!" He studied Kirstin, who studiously avoided his gaze. "What if she's not interested? What if she cuts me off at the knees? What if I make a fool of myself?"

"You're making a fool of yourself by not trying. Go ahead, sailor, make your moves. You do have moves, don't you?" When he hesitated, she asked, "You're not a virgin, are you?"

"I'm thirty-five frickin' years old!" He gave her such a blistering glower you would have thought she'd asked if he was an axe murderer. Putting his beer down on a table, he stomped away toward Kirstin, whose heart was in her pale blue eyes as he approached.

Good for him, she thought, not at all offended by his deserting her. She was comfortable in this crowd, and it was true, as she'd told Wendy earlier, JAM was just a good friend. In the year and a half she'd known him, this was the first she'd seen him exhibit any real interest in a woman. Obviously because it was this particular one he'd had in his sights all along.

"Hey, darlin'." Justin LeBlanc, a SEAL best known as Cage, drawled in his deep Cajun accent as he looped an arm over her shoulder and gave her a light kiss on her cheek. "You are lookin' good, *chère.* How come yer standin' here all alone?"

"JAM went over to try his moves on the Viking chick." She motioned with her margarita across the veranda.

"About time," remarked K-4, Kevin Fortunato, another SEAL who had been following Cage but had stopped at the bar to get them both longneck bottles of cold beer. "He's been crazy in love with her, like forever."

"You noticed?" she asked.

"Everyone noticed," K-4 replied, while he gave her a slow head-to-toe survey, then grinned his appreciation.

K-4 had asked her out on a date several times, but somehow their schedules always conflicted. Maybe it was time. Oddly enough, she couldn't garner any great enthusiasm, despite his being an attractive man, and nice, too. Maybe that was the problem; he was too nice.

No, it was something else that kept her from forming any relationships, and not just her disillusionment with two-timing men in the vein of her father and ex-husband. It was as if she were waiting for something to happen. As if her body and her heart were in a self-enforced limbo. A holding pattern, waiting for the big bang.

She smiled to herself. Big bang? The last time she'd been

banged, it hadn't been all that big of an explosion. Maybe she should lower her expectations to a soft ooomph.

"I'm intrigued by your work as a stunt double, Rita," said Sly, another SEAL, who just joined the group.

She shrugged.

"Lots of SEALs and Special Forces guys go into private security when they leave their teams. Like Blackhawk," Sly continued. "But being a stunt double sounds kind of cool."

"A lot of it is just boring, but, yeah, it can be cool on occasion."

"Like?"

"Being set on fire."

"Whaaat?" all three men exclaimed.

"There's a special retardant gel, but it dries quickly, so you have to complete the scene in less than five minutes, or you really will go up in flames. Plus, the Nomex suits are kept in a freezer to withstand the heat. You'd shiver to death if you had it on too long."

"Still sounds dangerous," K-4 said, taking a long draw on his beer.

"It isn't if all the precautions are followed."

"I like to see those car chases," Cage remarked. "Ever done those?"

"Yep. And crashed against a concrete wall. Or so it would appear. It's all in the training."

"Can anyone apply for those jobs?" Sly wanted to know.

"They can apply, but they won't get them. It takes a special kind of highly skilled person. Most of the men and women I've worked with, the top-of-the-line stunt doubles, are unusual, and I don't just mean their extreme athleticism. They have to be able to perform dangerous things under pressure, and have trained over and over to master a particular feat. No fear, or being able to do the stunt despite the fear. It takes a hell of a lot of courage to do some of the dumb-ass things we're asked to do. Persistence, too, if you want to make it in the business. And discipline. Always, always, honing your craft."

The guys all looked at each other, then said as one, "Sounds just like SEALs."

They all wanted to know about some of the stars she'd worked with. As old as she was, compared to the younger sexy starlets, Demi Moore got high marks with the SEALs. Probably because of her portrayal of G.I. Jane.

Soon the guys went off to join the volleyball game, K-4 promising to be back soon, but Rita realized that she wasn't really in a party mood. Setting her empty glass down onto a low table, she drifted through the crowd, stopping to talk occasionally to folks she knew, then found herself in front of the house, wondering if she could call a taxi to pick her up. JAM was clearly on a roll with Kirstin, and she didn't want to stay and cramp his style.

A woman she'd met before was getting into a car out on the street, along with her husband and young son. It was Lydia Denton-Haraldsson, who owned a dance studio in Coronado.

"Hi, Rita," Lydia called out. "Do you need a lift?"

"Could you? I would really appreciate it."

Before she got in the backseat, Lydia introduced her. "Have you met my husband, Thorfinn Haraldsson? And my son, Michael." Michael, about six years old, whose grayish blue eyes were already fluttering sleepily, was strapped in the car seat next to where she would be sitting in the back. "Finn, this is Rita Sawyer, she's a WEALS trainee."

Rita shook hands with Finn and noticed his heavy gold ring etched with writhing serpents or dragons or something. Although they'd never actually met, she recognized him from the SEALs training compound. He was a new SEAL, still in training, but having graduated recently into the teams. Thus far, he hadn't been assigned instructor duty.

He smiled at her from his great height. She was tall for a female, but this guy had to be six foot three, at least. His black hair was longish, and his eyes were the same compelling shade of silvery blue as his son's.

"Thorfinn Haraldsson, huh? Another Viking!"

"To the bone," Lydia agreed with a smile at her husband, who didn't appear to appreciate her remark about "another" Viking.

"Are you one of the Magnussons?" she asked.

"Nay, I am not," he snapped, as if that were an insult. Then he softened and conceded, "Magnus is my uncle."

As they were driving along, Rita asked, "When is the baby due?"

Lydia, who had a nice-sized bump sticking out from her maternity top, put both hands over her tummy and looked lovingly at her husband before revealing, "Babies, not baby. We're expecting twins before Christmas."

"How nice!"

Finn took a hand off the steering wheel and squeezed one of his wife's hands.

"How's the WEALS training going, Rita?"

"Grueling but fun. I might change my mind after Hell Week, but for now, I enjoy working my body to the max."

Finn made a snorting sound of disagreement.

"What?" she asked. "You don't think physical training can be fun?"

"Nay, I do not think for females there is any enjoyment to be found in muscle-punishing exercises. Holy Thor! The only way a woman's body should be worked *to the max* is beneath a man. Women in this country do not know their proper place."

Lydia made a choking sound.

"Oh, and where do you think a woman's place is?" Rita asked, not at all surprised by Finn's attitude. Lots of SEALs . . . heck, men in general . . . believed that women in the military was an oxymoron.

"In the bed furs with her man and in the birthing hut providing a husband with heirs."

Lydia's choking sounds turned into groans.

Bed furs? Birthing hut? What century is this bozo from? "Is he for real?" Rita asked Lydia.

"Oh, yeah. My very own male chauvinist Viking."

Finn glowered at his wife.

She patted him on the arm, then told Rita with a wink, "My Finn gives male chauvinism a good name."

If you say so, Rita thought, but what she said was, "Isn't that nice?"

"I saw that wink," Finn said. "You will pay later for making mock of me, sweetling." Then he was the one who winked. At his wife. And flashed her such a hot look the air practically sizzled inside the car.

Rita couldn't help but be a little envious of the loving relationship these two clearly shared. Maybe she should look for her very own Viking.

Then, reminding herself of the dinosaur attitude this man displayed, she immediately corrected herself. Maybe not.

Chapter 3

Hell Week was hell!...

Hell Week began with a bang. Literally.

It was almost over now, and it had been Satan's playground, to be sure. Just one more day. In the midst of a heat wave, the scorching California sun beat down on them like the devil's own barbecue pit. Not surprisingly, Satan's minions had been a bunch of Navy SEAL instructors who were surely descendants of Lucifer himself.

There were thirty-five helmets lined up starting at the bell sitting on the corner of the Grinder. Ten more WEALS trainees had dropped out this week. That left only forty of them to complete the course, God willing. A nice even number to fill five IBSs.

The week from hell had started with Breakout while it was still dark on Monday. The women in the barracks were awakened by loud shouts from bullhorns in their faces, men clanging trash can lids together, the sounds of AK-47s firing blanks, and what appeared to be actual explosions outside.

Once mustered on the Grinder, which resembled an eerie horror movie set with its dull lighting and colored smoke and constant loud noise, she saw a scene of orchestrated chaos meant to intimidate the trainees into quitting. While male SEAL trainees might not mind having no showers or change of clothing since Hell Week started, the women did not like reeking, not one bit. To them, that was as painful as the muscle-wrenching exercises.

While the goal of Breakout had been to scare the crap out of them, the goal of the entire week was to make them as wet, cold, exhausted, and miserable as possible. And smelly.

JAM had told them at one point, "Eventually you'll be able to recognize the distinctive body odor of your teammates."

To which one astute woman had replied, "Oh, that's something to look forward to. I much prefer Obsession."

"News flash to swabbies. While you're out on a black op, perfume attracts gnats . . . as well as tangos. You wanna be bug . . . or bin Laden . . . bait, that's fine with me."

The trainees had become used to instructors being bent over, in their faces, shouting orders. And they never referred to them by name. It was maggot, or swabbie, or tadpole, or newbies, or slugs, usually preceded by the F-word. Or sometimes it was the colorful, "You pukes!" Speaking of which, they'd also become used to puking their guts out in the sand and water when pushed to their limits.

"Surf Appreciation, ladies," F.U. yelled, now that they'd completed a round of Helen Kellers, the politically incorrect name for a particular rotation. The SEAL instructors rarely called them ladies, and when they did, it usually presaged some form of torture in the name of exercise, which Surf Appreciation was.

"Come on, come on, drag your sorry asses out into the water, darlin's," Cage prodded in a slow Cajun drawl.

They knew the drill. Their sorry asses, covered by filthy

BDUs, stomped out into the pounding surf in heavy boon-dockers and sat down with their arms linked together. In the cold, cold water of the Pacific, they faced the shore where the Marquis de Sade's men stood watching them with arms folded across their chests. While waves as high as ten feet broke over their heads, their bodies kept being sucked backward. Teeth chattering, it was a constant fight to hold their ground, and the rotation lasted until they were almost at the point of hypothermia.

After that, as a way for them to warm up, they were told to run. Of course!

Pain, pain, pain, that was the name of the game, all to condition their bodies to the horrors they might face on a real mission.

Following a brief lunch in the chow hall where some of them fell asleep over their trays of food, they were told to prepare for Rock Portage, one of the most dangerous tests a SEAL or WEALS candidate faced. It was so dangerous that the ratio of instructor to trainee became one to one. The women geared up in wet suits with Nomex hoods and flippers, then walked to the hated IBSs.

Before they left, Commander MacLean came over and told them, "Remember, it's all a case of mind over matter."

"Yeah," Wendy whispered to her. "They don't mind, and we don't matter."

"That's for sure," she agreed.

"Good luck!" the commander added.

Now in the water once again, they climbed into their IBSs, eight each, and paddled to a count shouted out by the coxswain, which was Wendy, over to the smooth area beyond the breaking waves facing the Hotel del Coronado shore. On arriving, they paddled in place, waiting, about a hundred yards from the shoreline, where jagged black rocks stood up like sentinels of death.

The goal was for each boat, one at a time, to make a

safe surf passage, riding a wave, through the treacherous rocks, without breaking a limb or drowning. At least they were performing this operation in daylight. In BUD/S the SEAL trainees went out at night. The Hindenburg factor was multiplied dramatically in moonlight. Not that this wasn't bad.

Rita was going to be the bowline man for her team . . . or was that bowline woman? Whatever. Once a perfect wave . . . *please God, let there be a perfect wave* . . . rose behind them, they tossed their paddles aside and lifted themselves to straddle the tubes on both sides, Rita at the forefront on her side. One of the women let loose with a rebel yell when Commander MacLean, on the shore, raised his hand. "Go, go, go!" a SEAL instructor from a nearby boat shouted.

In they went, way too fast, like a giant surfboard, except not so fun. At the last moment, Rita jumped into the water and found a secure spot between two rocks. "Take a bite! Take a bite!" someone screamed into a bullhorn.

"I'm biting, I'm biting," she muttered to no one in particular as she wrapped the bowline around her waist. A few seconds later, the boat came closer on a second wave, and she reached for the stern line.

But it was a rogue wave and it twisted in on itself, overturning the boat. So powerful was the force that it snapped her bowline and hurled her up into the air. She heard shouts of alarm and screams before she came down, striking the back of her head on one of the rocks.

Then everything went blank.

Men! Clueless through the ages . . .

"I can get a tongue thickening."

Steven and every sailor within hearing distance turned to stare at Oslac.

They were on Steven's favorite dragon ship, *Wind*

Breaker, on the return trip from Birka . . . a very successful trip, by the by, in which they had traded amber for fine
Frisian wine, pottery from the Rhineland, oats and barley,
samite silks, iron kettles, swords, bows and arrows. Ells
and ells of Northumbrian wool to supplement the lesser
quality Norseland fleece to make clothing for one and all
at Norstead and Amberstead over the winter months. Six
horses, a goat, and three cows to be serviced by their randy
bull Ornulf, best known as Ornulf the Ornery. Ornery had
no finesse in the bedsport . . . or was that pasturesport? As
a result, after a few tries, the female cows ran when they
saw him coming.

"That is naught to brag about, Oslac. My tongue thick-
ens, too, when I am *drukkinn*, and it grows a fuzz, as well,"
Steven said, leaning on the rail beside him.

"Not that kind of thickening, lackwit. The other kind.
The good kind. Besides, I was not bragging. 'Tis no great
feat."

"You mean, it hardens, like your cock when it readies
to tup?"

He nodded.

"That for damn sure *is* a great feat, if you really can
do it." Steven arched his eyebrows with disbelief. "Show
me."

"You must be daft. Nay, I will not."

"Next you will be telling me that you can lick your own
balls."

Oslac just grinned.

"Oslac!"

"What male has not tried such?"

"A boyling, mayhap, but not a grown man."

"Pff! I did not say I tried it recently. Besides, there is
that age-old question: Why does a dog lick his ballocks?
The answer: Because it can. I say, if a dog can do it, why
not men?"

"Dogs are so lucky in that way," a nearby seaman

shouted out above the roar of the waves slapping against the longship and the rhythmic dip of the oars in the water.

"Me wife Mary refuses, sayin' no way is she puttin' her tongue anywhere near those hairy buggers," another sailor contributed.

"Yea, betimes a man has just got to do a job himself," a third sailor added to the barmy discussion.

"I would wager that Adam of biblical lore could pleasure his own ballocks," Oslac added defensively since everyone within hearing was laughing at him.

"Before or after he ate the apple?" Steven asked, his lips twitching with mirth.

They both burst out with laughter, that they were reduced to this type of conversation. It was a warped kind of stress reliever after having spent the past night and morning outrunning Brodir the Bold and his pirate crew. There had to have been more than two hundred outlaw Vikings in the six pirate ships.

If they had been traveling with more than three longships, they would have stopped and fought to the bloody end, but it had been pointless with Brodir's six ships against their three. In retrospect, it had been foolhardy of Steven to have sent his other supply ships up ahead. After Brodir had been exiled from his homeland, he had developed some kind of plot against those at Norstead for unnamed past crimes. Steven knew without a doubt that he and Brodir would meet again. Hopefully soon.

Thank the gods, they were almost home now. Of course, he would probably be subjected to one joke after another from his people, as he had been before departure, in their halfbrained attempts to raise his spirits. Mayhap he would issue an edict: No more jokes!

As if reading his mind, Aghi, the helmsman manning the rudder, said, "Why do men die before their wives?"

"I am not going to participate in any of these word jests."

"Because they want to," Aghi said with a whoop, laughing at his own joke.

Steven just shook his head. "Oslac, I have been thinking about that conversation we had sennights ago," Steven began.

Oslac cocked his head to the side in question.

"When you suggested that it is time for me to wed." The almost-battle with Brodir had brought home to him that if he died, Norstead and Amberstead would be left without any of his blood in charge.

"Aaaahhh! So you have picked a bride. Isrid?"

"Nay, what is it with you and King Olaf's daughter? Mayhap you should take her yourself."

Oslac looked horrified now that the tables were turned on him. His good friend had been married at one time to the most disagreeable woman that ever was born. Girda drowned one day, two years past, whilst nagging Oslac as he'd prepared to board a longship. Yea, it was wrong to take pleasure in anyone's death, but really, Girda had been beyond shrewish. One time she had even carped at Oslac to help with the laundry, and when he refused by laughing at her, she had attacked him with a broom. Imagine that!

"By the by, do you know why men fart more than women?" Oslac asked of a sudden.

"Oh, please, Oslac, not you, too!"

"Because women do not shut up long enough to build up wind in their bellies."

"You should know, having been married to a talksome woman," he remarked.

Oslac nodded vigorously.

Steven once again picked up on the thread of their previous conversation. "I have not chosen a bride, and in truth it matters not to me whom the woman is. As long as she is of child-breeding years, passably fair, and biddable."

"And passionate? Do you not want a woman with an enthusiasm for the bedsport?"

Steven shrugged. "There are bedmates aplenty. Wives are for popping out heirs."

"I thought you were Christian."

"I have been raised in both the Norse and Christian religions. I was not thinking of the *more Danico*. Only one wife will I ever take."

"So you are Christian when it suits you, and Norse at other times."

"Precisely."

Oslac laughed. "I would like to be a fly on the wall of your great hall when you make this proposal to your prospective bride."

"Oh, my gods and goddesses! What is *that*?"

Steven's longboat was riding low in a course close to the rocky shore as they approached Ericsfjord, the waterway that led to Norstead. There was something crumpled atop the stones.

"What *is* that?" Oslac repeated Steven's question back at him. "'Tis a body, but is it man or animal?"

"It has seal-like skin with breasts. Leastways, those two bulges appear to be in the right places. And its feet . . . unbelievable! It has webbed feet. 'Tis a monster, for a certainty. A female monster." Steven raised a hand for his archers and lancers to ready their weapons as the rudder master steered the vessel landward.

"Too bad it is not a mermaid. I have heard they are incredible sex partners."

"You have not. You are making that up," Steven said, as he lowered the rope ladder over the side. They were in the shallows now, and the anchor had been thrown. Although longships were built to ride low waters as well as the high seas, maneuvering any closer in the midst of the rocky landscape posed peril to the ship. Sharp rocks could cut through the seasoned oak like a hot knife through butter.

"Truly. Mermaids have no nether channel for a man's cock." Oslac was still blathering on about mermaids. The lackwit! "So he must put it in their sucking mouths."

They both looked at the creature, which appeared to have no place for a woman's parts, like a mermaid, which was half fish. But, nay, it had no mermaid tail. Just the webbed feet.

"I swear you have been listening overmuch to the old ones who speak the ancient sagas of giants and trolls and dinosaurs and such." He was already halfway down the ladder, his small sword unsheathed, but he kept his head turned toward shore. He had to admit, on closer scrutiny, that the mouth *was* lush and sensual. Good for sucking, to be sure. Unless it had teeth. They would have to check.

"Have a caution, Steven. There may be others." Oslac had his sword drawn from its scabbard as well. "Ahoy there, monster! Stand slowly and raise your hands."

At first the monster did not obey. Mayhap it did not understand words. But wait. Slowly it rose to its webbed feet, fighting for balance. Then it raised its head and stared directly at him.

What an ugly beast! Its face was an odd mixture of brown and green and black, and it had no hair, just a black sealskin covering its head and neck.

"Where am I?" it squeaked. "Where are the instructors?"

"Huh?"

"The instructors. The SEALs."

He and Oslac exchanged glances at the mention of seals. So it was a water creature after all. A talking one, no less.

"I have an idea," Oslac said. "Let us put this creature in a cage and set it upon the dais of your great hall. Think of the fun it would provide."

"We have no cages at Norstead."

"How about those large crates used to take geese to market . . . the ones that fit in the hold of a knarr?"

Steven was not so sure how much entertainment he would get from a seal creature. Mayhap they could sell the creature to some wooly-witted Saxon, if worst came to worst. The Saxon kings were wont to keep bears in cages at their royal courts . . . a practice he had always abhorred . . . but they enjoyed taunting them to snarl and shake their bars.

He shrugged his approval.

"What shall we call it? Oh, oh, I have an idea. How about Siren? A jest. Because, of course, this she-creature is far from tempting."

Steven smiled at Oslac's ever constant humor. "Sea Siren it is then."

Even mermaids get PMS . . .

Rita blinked groggily through a mist of confusion.

She must have blacked out after the IBS overturned during Rock Portage and struck her head on one of the breakwater rocks. She didn't even know if she'd completed the exercise, or . . . God forbid! . . . would be rolled back and have to do it all over. This Rock Portage rotation, the culmination of Hell Week in WEALS, was not as demanding as a BUD/S Hell Week for SEAL trainees. Still, this was worse than the time she'd crashed her motorcycle after a triple wheelie over a California freeway in *Die Again 5*. Hellish, for sure. She'd broken both legs and three ribs.

Her head pounded with pain. Her throat and chest burned from all the water she'd swallowed and then up-chucked. Nausea churned inside her stomach. And she was about to get her period. She was not in a good mood.

Trying hard to focus, she recalled what felt like gallons of murky water spewing out of her mouth, hurling onto a size thirteen boondocker that probably belonged to one of the SEAL instructors. Oddly, the man had exclaimed, "Holy Thor! There is vomit on my best boots." Must be that ridiculous Viking Thorfinn Haraldsson. Good! The chauvinist deserved a bit of humbling puke.

Slowly her vision started to clear and her senses to focus. That's when she realized that she was lying down. And that there were bars in front of her. Wooden bars. On all four sides of a space that was no more than six by six.

Whaaaaat?

She immediately launched to her feet, not an easy task when she was still wearing flippers, and her head skimmed the roof. Was she in the brig? No, how could she be? Even if she'd failed the Rock Portage rotation miserably, the worst that could happen would be her being dumped from WEALS or forced to repeat the exercise. Besides that, what kind of brig had wooden bars?

"The Sea Siren awakens."

Rita's eyes shot to the right where a man stood, a man with compelling silver gray eyes. He of the size thirteen leather boots, she presumed—not boondockers after all—was tall, with black hair down to the shoulders and braids framing either side of his face. Braids that were intertwined with colored crystal beads. What kind of man wore beads in his hair? A hippie? No, she couldn't see this brute singing "Kumbaya." A rock star? Hah! He didn't look even a little bit like Steven Tyler. He was too big. Too masculine. Too menacing. *And, whoa, check out that gold-embroidered tunic he's wearing, held together at the waist with a gold-linked belt worth a king's ransom.*

But the clothing and braids were nothing compared to his facial features. Holy cow! He looked like a bigger, darker, younger version of George Clooney in some period costume. But definitely not George himself.

"What sea siren?" Rita asked, turning to see who was behind her, where there were only more bars.

"You."

"Huh?" She shook her head to clear it, which caused her brain to practically explode. "Why am I in this cage?"

"Protection."

"I don't need protection."

"Not yours. Ours. You are dangerous."

"Are you crazy?"

He shrugged.

"I don't even have a weapon on me."

"Do you usually carry a weapon?"

"Of course."

"Of course," he repeated, as if she'd just confessed some great crime.

She realized then that he had been speaking to another man who'd come up to stand beside him, handing him a horn of what she assumed was some alcoholic beverage. Whereas the first guy was dark and dangerous, this guy was blond with whiskey-colored eyes. A blond Adonis. Brad Pitt. Yep, she was locked in la-la land with George Clooney and Brad Pitt look-alikes.

She licked her dry lips and said, "I'm thirsty, too."

Both men were staring at her lips in the oddest way.

The blond not-Brad god handed her his horn and jumped back as if he expected her to pounce on him right through the bars.

She took a sip, then grimaced. "What is this?"

"Mead," the frowning not-George replied, still staring at her mouth.

"Mead? Is that like beer?"

Not-George nodded his head. "Mead is a honeyed ale."

After emptying the horn, she wiped the back of her hand across her mouth, just realizing that she was still cammied up. "So, who are you two jokers?"

Not-George hesitated, then disclosed, "I am Steven Haraldsson of Norstead and Amberstead. This," he waved to his friend, "is my comrade-in-arms, Oslac. And, believe you me, sea wench, this is no joke."

"I'm Petty Officer Rita Sawyer. U.S. Navy WEALS."

"Ree-tah," Steven sounded out her name as if it was an uncommon one. "Where are you from, Ree-tah?"

"The United States. I told you I'm with WEALS."

"I do not see any wheels on her. Do you, Steven?" Oslac asked.

Rita threw her hands up with frustration.

Apparently tired of standing, they pulled over a bench and sat down, continuing to study her intermittently as they chatted with each other in low voices.

Rita was beginning to think this was all a hallucination. She was probably in the Coronado Special Forces medical center, being treated for a concussion. Hell, maybe she was even in a coma, and she was imagining this whole scene. Hopefully, she would awaken soon and laugh over her crazy dream. Hopefully, she was not dead.

In the meantime, she said, "So, Steve, what do you plan to do with me in this cage?"

"I have not decided yet, Ree-tah. And my name is Steven. Master Steven to you."

Yeah, right. "Okay, your lord and master Steven, where am I?"

"The Norselands."

"And you two are Vikings, I suppose."

"We are."

"Steven . . . that's not a Viking name, is it?"

"My mother was half-Christian through her mother, a Saxon lady."

She looked at the well-muscled men and herself in a prison of sorts, and an uncomfortable idea came to her. "You're not planning on making me a sex slave or something, are you? Because I've gotta tell you, it's not gonna happen."

"We are not so randy or perverted that we would tup an ugly creature like you," Steven scoffed.

"Ugly, am I? I'll have you know, I have no trouble attracting men. Oh, good Lord! I can't believe I'm defending myself to you two dunces. In a dream, no less. By the way, you're not nearly as good-looking as George Clooney up close." Which was a lie. He was better looking by far.

"George who?" Steven asked. "The only George I know is a Saxon lord who resembles a toad."

"There you go!"

"Are you calling me a toad?"

"If the shoe fits . . ."

"What shoe?"

"Aaarrgh!"

Meanwhile, Oslac was tuned into his own agenda. "You have no nether cleft, far as I can see." He craned his head to the side to see better.

"I swear, I must have landed in some loony bin, and you two are candidates for Dumb Men of the Year . . . heck, Dumb Men of the Ages. By the way, have you heard why doctors smack babies' butts right after they're born?" When neither of them answered, she said, "To knock the penises off the smart ones."

Steven turned to Oslac, and, instead of laughing, said, "Did you put her up to this? Even a stranger now tells jokes to make me smile."

Oslac put up both hands. "Not me."

Dumb, dumb, dumb. "Am I a prisoner of war, or something? If so, there are military codes of conduct, you know."

"You mention military . . ." Steven narrowed his eyes at her. "Why did you come to our land? Are there others waiting to attack? Are they all sea people like you? Or do only some take human form? Why do you not have scales like a mermaid? Why are you not dying here out of the water, like a fish?"

"Whoa, whoa, whoa! So many questions. But first, I have to pee. Unlock this cage and point me to a bathroom."

"Pee?" The two lunkheads stared at Rita in question, then at each other.

She crossed her legs to emphasize what she meant.

"Dost mean piss?" Steven asked.

"Yes!"

"And you mean to piss in my bathing pool?"

"No, you idiot!"

"How do you piss?" the blond idiot asked in a confrontational manner, as if he'd caught her in some trap.

"The same way you do, buddy. In a toilet."

"The same as . . . you have a cock?" Steven asked, staring at her even harder, especially her lower region.

"This is a ridiculous conversation, and it's hotter than hell in here. Can't you open a window or something?"

"We are in a weaponry room. There are no windows," Oslac pointed out, again as if he had been testing her, and she had failed.

She glanced around, and, sure enough, it was some kind of weapon storeroom. Ancient weapons. Swords, shields, maces, battle axes, bows and arrows, lances, chain mail, leather and metal helmets with nose and eye guards.

"Okay, no windows then." As she began to peel off her Nomex hood, she felt a lump the size of a goose egg on the back of her head. "Ouch!"

Both men gasped. "She is pulling off her scalp," Oslac said to Steven.

"What alien world do you two bozos come from?" She tugged off the tight cap, then fluffed out her blonde hair, which was damp with sweat.

"You have hair," Oslac remarked with wonder.

"No kidding, Sherlock. Jeesh!"

"And it is short, like a boyling," Steven added.

"Hey, it's just like Pink's, and no one says she looks like a boy. Besides, it's more convenient for doing stunts and military maneuvers."

They didn't pay a bit of attention to what she'd said, too engrossed in their own conversation.

"Mayhap she is a mermaid, after all," Oslac said to Steven.

"Or a merman," Steven opined.

They watched as she toed off her flippers, then wriggled her feet to ease the kinks. Swimming with fins was hard on the tendons.

"You have feet," Steven observed.

"Yeah, and I have hands, too. Big whoop!"

"Your sarcasm ill suits, sea wench." Steven stood, folding his arms across his chest in an intimidating manner. "Mayhap we will make a tasty fish stew of you. What think you of that, Ree-tah?"

She was exhausted from the SEAL evolution from hell. She was depressed over having probably failed the exercise. She was standing in a cage in some kind of medieval fortress in a dream-nightmare so vivid she could even smell the straw on the floor. And two dingbats were grilling her like she was the crazy one. But she was not intimidated. In fact, she was about to tell them exactly what she thought of them when she noticed something about Steven. "You look like someone I know. Similar facial features. Same height. Same silvery eyes. Same male chauvinist pig attitude. You're even wearing an identical ring. Yep, you could be a doppelgänger for Thorfinn. And he was a Viking, too. Small world, huh?"

Steven stiffened with some kind of outrage, and before she realized what he was about, he opened the cage door and yanked her out. Lifting her by the upper arms with her feet dangling above the floor, he shook her, the whole time asking her questions. "Thorfinn? Praise the gods! You have seen my brother Finn? Where? He is alive? Thank heavens! When did you see him last?"

"If you'd stop rattling my teeth and put me down, maybe

I could answer you," she complained once he paused to draw a breath.

"There is just one question I have for you," Steven said as he lowered her to the floor but still held onto her arms with a viselike grip. "Is he a prisoner in your sea world?"

"Give me a break! The sea jokes are getting old."

"I am not the one telling jokes around here."

Enough of this nonsense! Dream or no dream . . . coma or no coma . . . Rita was tired of this game. And she had to pee.

With a quick jerk of her elbows to either side, she surprised the brute into loosening his hold on her upper arms. Taking that advantage, she head butted his solar plexus, causing him to let out a whoosh of air. Then, while he was still off balance, she turned quickly, putting her back to his front and, although he had a good seventy pounds on her, she was able to flip him over her shoulder and onto the floor.

He just lay there, flat on his back in the straw, staring up at her and her bare foot pressed onto his chest.

"M'lady Fish, you are in such big trouble," he said, not at all amused. Most men weren't when they'd been bested by a woman.

"Oh, yeah?" She pressed her foot closer to his throat.

"Oh, yea!"

She heard a rustling sound and belatedly noticed at least a dozen men, including Oslac, surrounding them. Uh-oh! They all carried deadly swords. They all looked like they knew how to use them.

She turned her attention back to the jerk on the floor.

He brushed her leg aside and stood in one fluid motion, remarkable for a man his size. Then he told her in no uncertain terms, "I have a sword with your name on it. Dost prefer a stab through the heart or a head lopping?"

Before she had a chance to respond, a bearded man

wearing a vast amount of furs, resembling a bear himself, and smelling like one, too, raised his sword and, thank you, God, did not separate any body parts. Instead, he whacked her on the back of the head with its flat side. Just before she fell into another pit of blackness, she thought with hysterical irrelevance, *Another goose egg. I am going to have the mother of all headaches.*

Chapter 4

Peg legs, cutlasses, wenches, and booty, oh, my! . . .

After months of mind-numbing peace, trouble was flaring all around Norstead, and only a small part of it due to the odd sea creature who'd knocked him to his arse. An embarrassing happenstance she would pay for, in good time.

She . . . it . . . was now dead to the world, in Thorfinn's old bedchamber, sleeping off Bjarni's sword blow to her head. A tap, really. If Bjarni had actually hit her with any force, she would be well and truly dead.

He had just sat down at the high table, awaiting dinner, and was about to raise a horn of ale to his mouth when his steward, Arnstein, walked up and shifted uneasily from hip to hip.

"What is it, Arnstein? Some problem with the household?"

Arnstein's old face flushed. "I lost the wager, m'lord."

"Which wager would that be?"

"The one to tell you a funny rhyme."

"Oh, good gods, more attempts to make me smile," he

commented in an undertone to Oslac. "Am I really that bad?"

"Worse," Oslac answered with a grin.

"Go ahead, Arnstein," he said on a sigh. "Tell me your rhyme."

"There once was a Saxon from Kent
Whose manroot was so long it was bent.
He got into trouble
When he folded it double.
So, instead of coming, he went."

Oslac was bent over double . . . with mirth. Steven's men closest to the dais laughed uproariously as Arnstein ducked his head and scooted away. Steven could only stare, agape, at the lengths his people would go to in order to cheer him up. Was he really that pitiful?

He was saved from further consideration of that distasteful subject because just then, he heard a ruckus outside, getting closer. He and Oslac both stood.

Housecarls half carried a man into the great hall. When the man, whose sodden garments dripped into a pool beneath his feet, was able to speak, he identified himself as Skeggi, oar master on a longship sent by his mother from Norsemandy. News to him, by the by, that his mother's ship had been on the way here.

Steven clapped a hand over his heart. "Please tell me that my mother was not on your ship."

"She was not."

Steven released a sigh of relief. "Did your ship wreck?"

"Not precisely." Skeggi ducked his head sheepishly. "Pirates."

Steven and Oslac looked at each other.

"Brodir the Bold?" Steven inquired, his voice dripping ice.

Skeggi nodded. "Our longship got separated from its sister ship in a storm outside Hedeby. I know not where it is now. But on our longship . . ." Skeggi gulped. ". . . all but six of us gone. Five they took captive, but they sent me on. We were . . . um, ill-prepared, m'lord."

Steven was not a lord; he was a jarl, comparable to an English earl, but this was no time to correct the man. So, Brodir wanted him to know of his perfidy. "I still don't understand. Why would my mother send a longship here?"

Skeggi's eyes darted left and right before he mumbled something.

"What did you say?"

"Your sister," he said, then recoiled as if he expected to be struck.

The hairs stood out on the back of his neck. "My sister was on that ship? What sister?"

"Disa."

"*What?*" he hollered.

"Disa and her maid Sigvid."

He barely stifled a groan. Disa was the youngest of his four sisters, a year younger than himself. His favorite, truth to tell. Childless, she'd been widowed two years past when her husband had gone off to fight in Frankland. "Why was my sister coming here? Never mind. The why is not important. We must make haste to rescue her."

"Ten longships," he ordered Oslac to prepare from both Norstead and Amberstead. "Three hundred fighting men, fully armed. Food, drink to last a sennight or more, although I am hoping it will not come to that. Twenty horses with feed in case we must fight on land."

For the past two years, Brodir had been pricking at him, like a needle here and there. Naught to overly concern Steven. But when one of his family . . . and his mother's seamen . . . were attacked, action was essential.

With Mjöllnir, Thor's mighty hammer, at his back, he

vowed to personally put a blood eagle to the pirate's treacherous back whilst he still lived. A fitting death for a *nithing* who attacked women.

But first, he had another task to complete.

"I will be right back," he told Oslac. "I must needs check on our Sea Siren to see if she still lives. If she is dead, and we leave the body untended until we return, we will ne'er get the fish stench out of the bedchamber."

"And if she does still live, will you drop her back into the sea?" Oslac's question made sense, since entertainment from a caged sea creature was of no importance now . . . or in the near future.

Steven shrugged. "Mayhap."

He wanted to see her tail . . .

Rita awakened in a strange room.

Without moving, she let her eyes rove the perimeter, sensing she was in some kind of hostile environment. She had no clue how that could be when her last base of operation had been the beach in Coronado, California, but she was going to find out. Soon.

She was lying on a crude bed, raised a couple feet off the floor. The walls were wood, like the interior of a cabin . . . but not exactly. More like horizontal planks. There was straw on the floor as there had been in the weapons room. Rushes, she thought they were called in some societies. The only light came from an arrow slit window up high. Easing herself carefully off the bed, she checked the door, not surprised to find it locked from the outside.

Then she did what she'd been dying to do for what seemed like ages. Going behind a screen, she found a chamber pot and relieved her bladder with a long sigh.

Noticing a table with a pitcher and bowl and a pottery jar of soft soap, she decided to wash the camouflage off her face, soon turning the water grimy. She needed to get out of her wet suit, which was starting to itch. If only she had clean clothing to wear! Ah! Spotting a chest at the foot of the bed, she opened it to find male garments. Tunics. Slim pants, resembling tights. Belts. All of such fine cloth, they must belong to someone wealthy. Or a theatrical company. Working in the industry, she knew how authentic some period costumes could be. Holding up one of the tunics and noting its considerable size, she decided it must belong to the Viking Jerk of the Month, Steven.

Without hesitation, she peeled off her wet suit and was about to raise the tunic over her head when the door swung open. The man who stood there . . . Steven, of course . . . froze in place, stunned, and gawked at her like she was the third wonder of the world. Or an alien from outer space. Hard to tell if he was good stunned or bad stunned.

"Oh, my gods!" He stepped over the threshold and slammed the door behind him.

For a blip of a second, Rita had forgotten she was naked, although luckily he only got a side view, no frontal full monty.

Yikes! Quickly, she put the tunic and pants on. Her fingertips came to the inside elbows on the sleeves, and the bottom hung down to her calves. The neckline exposed one shoulder. "Hope you don't mind. I had to borrow your clothing."

He shrugged. "'Tis Thorfinn's."

"Ooookaaaay!"

"You are a woman," he declared, stepping forward as he recovered from his shock.

She backed up. "No kidding. What did you think I was?"

"A sea creature."

Now it was her turn to gawk. "Like an icky giant squid? Be careful, I might squirt some ink at you."

He ignored her attempt at humor. "Do you often knock men to their arses?"

"Often enough."

He arched his brows in question.

"When they need to be put in their place."

"And that place would be?"

She grinned. "Under a woman's foot."

"Surely you jest."

She shrugged. "Women need to be able to defend themselves."

"From what?"

"Terrorists, tangos, bad guys."

"You consider me a bad guy?"

"Putting a woman in a cage . . . that definitely qualifies as bad in my book."

"What book would that be?"

"Picky, picky, picky! It's just a saying. I meant that putting a woman in a cage is barbaric."

"Even when the woman is not really a woman? How do I know your sea comrades do not plan an attack on Norstead and that you were sent ahead as a trick to lull our senses?"

"That's ridiculous."

"How did you shed your black skin?" he asked, changing the subject abruptly as he stared at her crumpled wet suit on the rush-covered floor. "I thought snakes were the only ones who shed skin."

"Uh, I took it off." For every step forward he took with seeming casualness, she took one back. Meanwhile, she searched for a weapon. Could she reach that poker by the small fireplace?

"Magic, that must be it. Are you a sorceress?"

"Not last time I checked."

"Have you forgotten that I do not like your sarcasm? And do not even think of picking up that poker lest you want to taste the flavor of my wrath. A cage will be the least of your complaints then, believe you me."

She nudged the wet suit with a toe. "Look, this is just a wet suit. A garment worn in deep sea diving and other underwater work. Anyone could put it on."

"Anyone? Me?"

"Well, you're a bit too big for this one."

And, boy, was that the truth! This Viking was one tall drink of water. At least six foot three. And, okay, she'd seen her share of hunks, both in the movies and SEALs, but this guy was a match for any of them. Etched silver armbands emphasized muscled biceps. Wide shoulders, narrow waist and hips, long legs, all pointed to one fine, physically fit specimen of masculinity, all encased in attire that befitted a Norse nobleman.

A Norse nobleman about to go to war.

Okay, this was something new.

He'd changed from his earlier garments to battle gear . . . long-sleeved leather tunic over slim pants made of brushed hide tucked into tall boots. A thigh-length, short-sleeved suit of armor made of metal links was half fastened up the front. From a wide leather belt, there hung two scabbards, one holding a short sword on one side and a broadsword on the other. A metal helmet with nose guard rested in the crook of his elbow.

Most impressive, though, were his almost too-pretty facial features with their compelling silver eyes framed by lush black eyelashes. It would be hard for most women to resist. Except that he was also morose and annoying. And menacing, as well, suited for battle, as he was.

But back to the wet suit. "You'd need a bigger size. Way bigger."

"Likely story!"

"And it would never fit over that . . . tin shirt." She waved a hand at his armor.

Looking down, he said, "Brynja."

"Huh?"

"'Tis called a brynja, not a tin shirt."

"Whatever. Listen, I know that Navy SEALs are big on simulated terrorist exercises, and, whoo-boy, this one is certainly authentic. So, game over. I surrender."

"You surrender?" he inquired with sudden sexual interest, deliberately misreading her words. "How . . . intriguing! I have ne'er had sex with a fish afore."

"Just sheep?"

"Insults like that gain naught, m'lady."

"Sorry. Anyhow, it's been swell chatting with you and all that, but take me back to the commander."

"I *am* the commander." And it was about time he exerted some authority, too. This woman . . . and, yea, she was a woman, all right. Not to his taste, of course, with that ridiculous boyling haircut, being taller than the average female, with more muscles than any woman should have, and a tongue that was way too sharp.

She was rolling up the sleeves of the tunic when he made that statement. "Is this place on the Special Forces site in Coronado, or out on San Clemente Island? We've done survival training on the island, but I never saw anything like this. The detail is remarkable."

"I have no idea what you are talking about. And by the way, you speak the oddest form of English."

"Hah! You think I talk funny. You're the one. What nationality are you, anyway? Oh, that's right. You're a bleepin' Viking. Ha-ha-ha!"

"Blee-pin had best be a compliment."

"It is, it is."

He narrowed his eyes at her, not convinced. "In any case, I speak Norse, which is very similar to Saxon English. Really, I have no trouble understanding the merchants in the Saxon market towns, but they use none of those odd words you do on occasion. Which leads to the most important issue betwixt us. Where in hell is my brother?"

"Thorfinn?"

"Of course Thorfinn."

"Last I saw him was this morning, on the beach at Coronado."

Steven gasped. "Last I saw him was in Baghdad two years ago. Is Coronado in the Arab lands?"

She frowned her confusion. "Coronado is in the United States."

"Is the United States an undersea kingdom?"

"Enough with the undersea, mermaid, merman, siren, sorceress, snake nonsense. I'm a human being, just like you."

"I doubt that. If you are indeed human and you have seen my brother, take me to him."

"I would if I knew where I was."

"I have told you, this is Norstead, my estate in the Norselands."

"Where exactly is the Norselands?"

"Across the sea from Britain."

"Do you mean Norway? That's impossible. I was in the United States earlier today, and that's oceans away from here."

"Then it must be magic. Can you transform yourself into a mermaid at will?"

"Oh, God, we're back to the sea creature business."

"Take off my brother's tunic."

"Huh? No way. Not unless you have some other clothes for me. I am not going to prance around bare naked in a room with some Viking warlord."

"Prance around? Warlord?" He almost grinned at her. Almost.

"You're as grumpy and dour as your brother."

"Not so! I am the lighthearted brother."

"And I have a bridge to sell you in the Sahara desert."

"Do not try to distract me. Take off that tunic, or I will."

"Why?"

"I did not look closely enough when I first came in. I need to check if you have a tail." *And there are some other bits I want a better look at, too.*

"If you think I'm gonna let you check out my behind, you've got another think coming."

Argue, argue, argue! Must she gainsay me at every turn? Truly, this woman is as bad as Oslac's dead wife. "What? Are you going to flip me over your head again? Have a caution, sea wench. I am wise to your ways now."

"Is that so? Well, this time I might aim a knee to your precious jewels."

It took him a moment to understand what she meant, then he winced. She would not dare! Well, mayhap she would if he let her, which he would not.

"Or I could do a karate chop to your Adam's apple." She demonstrated with a hand motion to her own.

"You would be the one flipped over my head if you ever attempted such. Better yet, you would be flipped onto your back, thighs spread, awaiting a good swiving." Too late, he realized what mind image he'd inadvertently planted in his head. Where had such a ludicrous idea come from? Hah! He knew exactly where it came from. That momentary glimpse of her naked body when he'd entered the room.

"You would rape me?" she asked, incredulously.

"Never! I know more ways to bring a woman to peak than there are hairs on your body. When . . . if . . . I choose to tup you, it will be with you begging for my favors."

"Better men have tried."

He arched his brows at her, but then the door swung open. Oslac's gaze swung to him, then to the woman, and back to him again, as surprised as he was to see that the sea wench was actually a person . . . for the moment, anyway . . . even if covered by Thorfinn's tunic.

"The boats are ready. The troops from Amberstead are on their way and will be here within the hour."

Steven nodded.

"What will you do with her?"

"I cannot leave her here in this room when we might be gone a sennight or more. With her skills, she could easily overpower one of the maids bringing fresh water and food."

Before he had a chance to discuss other alternatives, the woman . . . Ree-tah . . . remarked, "I notice you two yahoos are dressed for battle. What's up?"

He thought about ignoring her question. What was it to her, after all? Unless . . . nay, surely sending this sea woman was not a ploy of Brodir the Bold. Was she?

Steven and Oslac's eyes met as they shared the same inner question.

Choosing his words carefully, he said, "Pirates have taken my sister Disa. We go to rescue her."

"Pirates? Oh, this is too much. Johnny Depp is going to join this dream adventure. What next? Mel Gibson in a kilt?"

"Your chatter is beginning to annoy me," Steven said.

"Big whoop! Listen up, Mr. Macho Man, I'm in an elite military unit, with fighting skills. I could help."

Steven laughed. "You? A soldier? Females do not go to battle."

"This one does. I told you, I'm a female SEAL. Oh, I get it. You think I mean SEAL like an animal seal. Nope. SEALs are a Special Forces fighting group in my country."

"Like Jomsvikings or Varangians?" Oslac asked.

"Um, I guess so."

"I could lop off her head for you," Oslac offered.

Steven knew that Oslac was only half serious, but the woman did not even flinch. Why was she not fearful of them?

"So, can I come, too?"

"Nay," Steven said.

"Just like that, no? No explanation?"

"I owe you no explanation." He turned to Oslac. "I cannot chance her escaping until I learn more of Thorfinn's whereabouts."

Oslac nodded.

"The cage, then."

"She will create mischief, even in the cage," Oslac warned.

He shrugged. "There is no other choice."

"No way! You are not putting me in that cage again. Go away. Don't touch me." She swatted at him with her hands. She attempted to kick him in the genitals with the heel of her bare foot. She danced around in ridiculous defensive moves, hoping to evade him.

She screamed when he tossed her over his shoulder and let her pound at his back, while Oslac led the way through the upper corridor down to the great hall, drawing the attention of one and all. When she continued to screech, nigh making his ears bleed, he smacked her on the rump. When that did not work, he slid a hand under the tunic and up her bare legs. Only then did she still when he cupped one of her buttocks in his big hand. *No tail,* he noted, by the by.

"I am going to kill you, the first chance I get," she hissed out.

"I look forward to your trying." With one last squeeze of her bottom, he put her in the cage and locked it. He almost felt sorry for her as she sat, back against the bars, knees drawn up to her chest, glaring at him . . . in silence now.

Ah, well, he could handle only one problem at a time.

As they walked off, Oslac said, "It is so much fun being around you, Steven. What will you do next?"

Steven had no idea.

Chapter 5

Turns out it was all the witches' fault . . .

For the first hour, Rita sat in her cell, fuming. And she said a few bad words. Okay, a lot of bad words.

During the second hour, she was still fuming . . . and swearing, so she took a nap. Not an easy task, considering the pounding headache she had from her giant goose egg. Two goose eggs, actually.

Third hour, fuming and swearing and napping doing her no good, she tried yelling for help. Then she tried yelling for an aspirin. No response. Though she could hear voices in the distance, the heavy door of the weaponry room had been closed. Alarming thought: who would come into a weaponry room when all the soldiers were off to war, or wherever they had gone? Heck, she might be in here, forgotten, for days.

During hours four and five, all of which were guesstimates, of course, not having a watch, her headache became one continuous throb of pain. She plotted ways that she would repay the despicable commander, who surely exceeded his orders in the treatment of prisoners . . . even fake prisoners.

The problem was . . . one of the many problems, actually . . . that she kept vacillating between that scenario and this being a dream or some far-out SEAL simulated mission. None of those was proving very viable. But what else could it be? Maybe it was tied to Steven's connection with Thorfinn. She would have to address that when he came back.

If she wasn't dead by then.

"Okay," she finally told herself, "the only person you can really depend on in life is yourself. I know that better than most. So, what am I going to do now?"

Come up with a plan, that's what, she decided.

On her hands and knees, she examined each of the rough-hewn bars of the cage. Too bad she had no sharp object on her! Deciding she had to find the weak natural bend in the wood, she studied and studied until she found one that might suit. But she couldn't do it barehanded or barefooted; so, she took off her tunic and examined the garment carefully. The seams were weakest at the shoulders. In quick time, she had both sleeves ripped off and put the sleeveless garment back on. Now her problem was getting leverage in such a small space. Making a quick sign of the cross, she wrapped one sleeve around her hand and let loose with a quick karate chop.

The wood bar was still intact.

But it was a little loose. Just a tiny bit.

Over and over and over, Rita performed her karate chop, the kind that in some cases could split concrete blocks. She alternated between both hands and feet. She even considered using her head to butt it, but with the lumps she'd already scored today, that probably wasn't a good idea.

Finally, finally, finally, she was able to break through the one bar and split it in half. What to do now?

Rita laughed with a sudden inspiration. She had two

sticks to make a fire and plenty of tinder . . . straw. Voilà! It was almost laughably easy . . . but ingenious, if she did say so herself. She couldn't wait to tell her commander back at Coronado. And the arrogant, full-of-himself commander here, too.

Once she was fully free, holding the tunic sleeves over her face to shield her from the smoke made by the little fire in the cage, she did a little Snoopy dance of glee. Actually, she had hoped to just weaken the wood when she'd made it hot, but this worked just as well. Miraculously, her headache was gone.

That was when she glanced up and saw that she had an audience. About a dozen men and women in homespun-type clothing in the Norse fashion . . . men in belted tunics over tights and women in long gowns covered by long, open-sided aprons. They appeared to be servants or household help of some type. They had been attracted by the smell of smoke, no doubt. They gawked at her as if she was a lunatic.

It was probably the Snoopy dance.

Or the fire. Of course they would be upset about fire in a wood building.

"Oops!" When that didn't draw any reaction, she said, "Hi! My name is Rita Sawyer. Can you help me put out this fire?"

"'Tis the fish woman," one man said incredulously.

"Is she dangerous?" another asked.

"How could she be?" still another spoke up. "She has no weapon."

"Mayhap she spits venom."

The group stepped back a few paces, beyond the range of her spit, she supposed.

"Listen, people, I mean you no harm. I'm just a visitor here. I'll be on my way now."

At first no one moved, but then an older woman smacked a boy on the shoulder. "Move yer arse, Haisl. And you, too,

Moddan. Get buckets of water to put out the rest of that fire. Vindr, find a shovel and wheelbarrow to clean up the mess."

"Ain't ye a prisoner here?" one man yelled out, pointing to the cage, which was pretty quickly becoming a pile of cinders.

"Me? Nah! That was just a game to see how quickly I could escape."

A young girl, not more than twenty, dressed in the same ankle-length, open-sided apron over a long gown, stepped forward. "My name is Sigge. My aunts sent me ta be yer maid."

Several of the men snickered and made laughing remarks, which caused Sigge's face to bloom with color, but she stepped forward, chin high.

At first, Rita wanted to laugh, too. Her? With a maid? But then she decided she could use all the friends she could get in this strange scenario. With a smile, she asked, "Any idea where a girl could get a bath and clean clothing around here?"

Sigge nodded eagerly, and the crowd parted a path for them as they walked through. In fact, she noticed some of them jump away from the girl as if they were afraid of her. Hmmm. She would have to check it out later. Once they reached the great hall, however, a woman, better dressed than the others, informed her icily, "They are mine."

"Who?"

"Steven and Oslac."

"Good Lord! You're married to both of them? I've heard that ancient Vikings often had more than one wife. But . . . eeeew!"

"Of course I am not married to both of them. Or either of them, for that matter. I am Lady Thora, still in mourning for my husband Rolfgar, chief hirdsman at Norstead." She blinked several crocodile tears in a manner that would do any Hollywood actress proud.

"You have my sympathies."

Sigge giggled behind her hand, which gained her a sharp look from the uppity lady. "Best you get yourself back to the kitchen garden, witch girl." The lady stared pointedly at the pentacle-shaped, raspberry birthmark . . . Or was it a tattoo? . . . on the side of Sigge's neck, which Rita had failed to notice before. "Do not think I have forgotten that spell you put on Alfr's goat. The smelly creature follows me about like a lovesick lover."

Sigge blushed. "'Tis not my fault that the spell went astray. The goat and the master were both standing in the same spot when I cast the spell."

"Just do not do me any more witchy favors. And best you be careful," Lady Thora warned Sigge. "Some say you are the devil's spawn. If you sport hooves one full moon, your master will kill you on the spot."

Sigge gasped with outrage, and she sputtered to the lady, "I am not that kind of witch. I have no ties to the black arts. You, on the other hand . . . some say you would spread your thighs for Lucifer himself if he had a big enough manpart." Sigge ducked when the lady attempted to slap her.

Rita stepped between the two, managing to catch the slap intended for Sigge on her shoulder. "So, if you're a grieving widow, what's this about owning Steven and Oslac?"

Lady Thora raised her chin haughtily. "I did not say that I *own* them."

"Oh? That's what I thought you said. Didn't you hear it that way, Sigge?"

Sigge nodded vigorously.

"Your impudence knows no bounds. Both of you. Why are you not still in your cage, by the by?" Her outrage was now directed at Rita.

"Because it was a mistake, the cage door being shut on me. I was just testing the bars," she lied, but then she quickly added, "Personally, I wouldn't take Steven or Oslac if they were handed to me on a silver platter. They're all yours, sweetie."

With a huff, the lady swanned off.

Rita arched her brows at Sigge.

"Thora will be wife to Jarl Steven or Karl Oslac when cows with crowns start jumping across the fjord. 'Tis just that the men will be men when boredom overrides good sense."

"There's a lot of boredom here at Norstead, I take it."

"You have no idea, m'lady."

Rita recalled something Lady Thora had said, and she asked Sigge, "What did she mean by referring to you as witch girl?"

Pink patches colored the girl's cheeks. "My aunts are witches, and I am a witch in training, when I am not tending the herb gardens here at Norstead. I do not have the witchy arts perfected yet." She let her words sink in, then added with disgust, "I cannot even raise a stick, let alone levitate myself."

"And levitation is something to be desired?"

"Oh, definitely. Lady Thora and the others look down on me 'cause I carry the blood of witches in my veins, but we do no evil. More good than harm."

They walked in silence for a bit, heading toward a storeroom where she could get soap and towels for bathing. Several people along the way cast surly looks toward them or went out of their way to avoid their path.

"What is that all about?" Rita asked.

"Ulf wanted to get rid of the bald spot on his head. My spell worked, but the hair grew on his backside, not his head."

Rita put a hand over her mouth to stifle a laugh.

"And Sela was flat-chested. Wanted big bosoms, she did."

"And the problem with that was?"

Sigge held her hands away from her chest, far away.

"So big they are that she nigh needs a harness to keep them from hanging down to her belly." She sighed deeply. "Some of my spells do work, especially those dealing with herb remedies. Unfortunately, folks only remember the bad ones."

"Honey, if people know you're a witch in training, and you've made a few mistakes, they can't really complain."

All of a sudden, Sigge burst out, "I am so glad that you have finally arrived. My aunts will be pleased, too."

"Your aunts, the witches?"

Sigge nodded vigorously.

"Let me get this straight. You and your two aunts practice witchcraft here, and nobody objects?"

Sigge nodded. "Because we are good witches. Some are more cautious with me, however, since I sometimes make mistakes."

"You said you're glad that I *finally* arrived?"

"My aunts predicted your coming months ago. That is why I was able to arrive in time to offer my services to you."

Rita put a hand to her head where the two lumps were starting to do a drum duo. Da, dum! Da, do. Da, dum! Da, do! People were staring at her in her strange attire . . . sleeveless man's tunic and tights, bare feet, ashes marring her arms and probably her face, sweaty hair plastered to her head. Why Lady Thora would think any man would want her was beyond Rita.

"For sennights now, they have spoken of the bright light of the future melding with the blue shadows of the past," Sigge blathered on. "Opposites will meet and explode, creating a new life for Norstead, which has been like a barren woman for many a year. Beautiful but empty."

"And I'm supposed to be that light?" She laughed, too tired to cry. "Well, I better go take a bracing bath so I can be ready for the explosion."

The explosion didn't come for another week.

She'd done some crazy stunts before, but this was ridiculous...

With Sigge introducing her as the "light" everywhere they went over the next few days, she was welcomed as some kind of savior, rather than the sea monster pariah the Lord of Norstead had deemed her before his departure.

Not that Norstead needed a savior far as she could see. It was a well-run, prosperous Viking-style estate. A wooden fortress castle, but more than that. The landscape was dotted with well-tended farmsteads and longhouses with thriving fields of oat and barley, fat cattle, poultry, sheep, and goats, all within a valley. Through this valley, and over one palisaded rise, a road led down to the massive Ericsfjord with its wharves, docks, and places for beaching the watercraft over the winter months. You couldn't see the water when at the castle, but Rita could smell its fresh semi-saltiness, the fjord being one of thousands of tributaries to the North Sea.

This settlement was unusual for the Norselands, apparently, which was not conducive to farming with its rocky landscape and harsh climate. Someone had worked diligently over the centuries to make this place hospitable for sustenance. Not self-sufficient entirely because they couldn't raise their own produce in great quantity, but still pretty damn impressive.

In outbuildings there was a blacksmith, carpenter, cobbler, weavers, dairymaids, sheep shearers, and God only knew what else. Not to mention an impressive stable. The men of Norstead were expert amber harvesters, and once a year they traveled to the Baltic, where they gathered and brought back a shipload of the stones to be marketed in trade for all the goods that could not be produced in the cold Norse climate.

The surly Steven apparently ran a well-run ship, and that didn't just refer to longships, of which there were twenty, not including the dozens he had taken with him off to battle pirates.

Largely, he relied on well-placed, designated people to carry out his orders. Arnstein, the steward who ran the keep—that's what they called the huge fortress-type home in this neck of the woods—like clockwork, with every single person having a job from chambermaid to raker of hearth ashes. Brighid, the no-nonsense head cook who had a staff of two dozen to help in preparing and presenting the vast amounts of food needed for such large numbers . . . three hundred when all were at home. The castellan Geirfinn made sure there was plenty of weaponry on hand and that fighters were constantly kept up to par with exercise, even those left behind. She and Geirfinn had become great pals once he learned of her WEALS service. Then there was Farli, who took care of anything dealing with horses, and Haisl who worked with the cotters in making sure all the farmsteads were operating properly. Skar organized hunters, fishermen, and trappers who brought back boar, bear, deer, rabbits, ducks, geese, and every type of fish imaginable. And so many others . . . tanners, seamstresses, a scissor, knife, and sword sharpener, and a cheese maker . . . yes, they had a person whose sole job was to make cheese. Even the children had to work, gathering both chicken and seagull eggs, checking the wicker traps and the nets in the fjord for fish, picking berries, and slopping the pigs.

It was all efficient and tidy and all that, but it was rather sad. No running children within the castle walls. No shrieks of laughter. The people were right. It was kind of dreary here.

The question was: Where did Rita fit into this picture?

Well, as far as the people were concerned, she was here to bring light, however the hell she was supposed to do that. That did not mean they were not wary of her. The original picture of her in the wet suit lingered, and they weren't entirely convinced that she wouldn't one day suddenly turn into a sea serpent, or at least a mermaid.

Her short hair bothered them, too.

"Are you a harlot?" Geirfinn had asked on first meeting her.

The curious manner in which he had asked the question had saved him from being belted a good one. "No, why do you even ask such a question?"

Geirfinn shrugged. "Women convicted of adultery often have their heads shaved when ordered by the shire courts in Saxon lands or Althings in this country."

"And the men who commit adultery . . . do they have their heads shaved, too?"

Geirfinn laughed, understanding perfectly what she meant. "Nay, they do not, but best you do not ask that question of the wrong person."

"Like one carrying scissors and a shaving mug?"

"Precisely."

They'd shared a grin after that.

Still others harbored entirely different reasons for why she'd needed to cut her hair. The cook, Brighid, had put a halting hand up when Rita had approached her kitchen. "Do not enter if you are diseased."

"I beg your pardon. I'm no more diseased than . . . than you are." The cook, in fact, kept an immaculate kitchen, and she, as well as all her helpers, wore pristine, open-sided aprons of various colors, often with embroidered edges, over their long gowns. The front and back of the aprons were held together at the shoulders with brooches. In the case of Brighid, her brooches had a chain connecting them like a necklace from which hung the keys to various valuable storerooms. Some of the women had their hair pulled off their faces into a bun; most covered their hair with a kerchief that tied at the nape. Young women had long single braids hanging down their backs.

"Why else would ye cut yer hair if it weren't fer fleas or lice or other vermin?"

"For comfort," Rita had answered, and explained that

with the hard work she did as a female fighter, short hair was easier to handle.

Her answer alleviated their concerns about disease but raised all other kinds of questions.

So Rita moved freely about the estate, with her sidekick Sigge at her side. People gave them ample room as they passed by, mostly fearing that Sigge would inadvertently cast one of her spells and turn them into toads or dancing pigs, both of which had presumably happened in the past. Cook wouldn't allow the girl in her kitchen, because one time beans suddenly started jumping out of the companaticum, the stockpot of thick broth that was always simmering in the huge cauldron inside a hearth big enough to fit a whole cow. Unfortunately, the pot was rarely cleaned . . . new meat and vegetables were just added to the existing liquid, so at some point beans might very well want to jump out.

Rita wore lady's gowns when inside and a boy's tights and tunic when outside. She slept in Thorfinn's old room. She could have fled, she supposed, but where would she go when she wasn't sure where she was? No, she was in a sort of limbo, waiting for the master to come back and, hopefully, help her get back to Coronado.

If he could.

And that was her biggest problem of all. While she bided her time, she'd been able to examine her surroundings in detail. They were too authentic to be modern re-enactments, and there was not one little bit of evidence of modern times. Not a speck of paper, not a factory-made nail, not a tampon or sanitary napkin, not even toilet paper, nothing.

That must mean she was in the Norselands, or long ago Norway. How long ago she feared to find out. Seriously, by some twist of science or celestial destiny, she had traveled back in time. It was impossible, of course, but what other explanation was there?

This was something she had to discuss with Steven, along with a million other things. She couldn't wait. Not!

So, while all the folks around her expounded on her being the light, she wondered what the Prince of Dark, aka Steven the Surly, would think about her being sent here from the future to lighten him up.

Even she had to smile at that.

Home from the wars ... sort of ...

Steven was about to return to his keep at Norstead after being gone for a sennight. If his mood had been dark before leaving, it was pitch-black now.

And he hadn't even lost a man.

Helvtis! Damn! The only way they would have been able to die was of boredom, since there had been nary a battle waged.

And he still didn't have his sister.

On the other hand, he did have her maid, Sigvid, who was the most irksome, weepsome, noisesome woman he had e'er met. She hadn't stopped crying since they'd found her standing alone on the shore of one of the islands Brodir had been reputed to use ... a living, speaking message left there for him.

But that wasn't the worst of it. She had developed a bad case of the hiccups. Constant, never-ending hiccups. So that every sob and every word she spoke were punctuated by the grating noise.

Neither Sigvid nor his sister Disa had been harmed in any way, apparently. In fact, "We were—*hiccup*—treated like—*hiccup*—princesses," according to the wailing maid.

"Then why in Freyja's name are you crying?" he'd demanded.

Staring at him as if he were barmy, she had sobbed out, "'Cause we were—*hiccup*—captured by—*hiccup*—pirates."

So, if they'd been kidnapped by Saxons, or Huns, or Arabs, it wouldn't have been so bad? That's what he'd wanted to ask, but he'd shut his teeth, lest he prompt more wailing . . . and hiccups.

Then she'd added some alarming news. "Lady Disa insults—*hiccup*—the pirate at every—*hiccup*—turn."

"Brodir?"

Sigvid had nodded vigorously. "And he laughs—*hiccup*—and insults her right back." She then burst into another bout of sobbing.

They'd tried everything to help her get rid of the hiccups, and wasn't that a lackwitted picture? Grown men jumping up and down attempting to scare the hiccups away. Forcing her to drink cup after cup of water, sometimes whilst her forefingers were plugging her ears, hadn't worked either; it just caused her to have to piss every other minute. Making her swallow a palmful of salt had been Oslac's opinion, which resulted in a pile of vomit on the ship's deck. Even throwing a burlap bag over her head . . . one seaman's mother's remedy . . . had accomplished nothing, except more weeping and hiccupping. Another seaman suggested that she bend over at the waist and touch her toes, then slowly raise her arms upward until she stretched to the skies. While that gave his men an appreciative view of outthrust bosoms, it did naught for the hiccups.

In the end, Steven and twelve of his hersirs took horses ashore at the joining of the North Sea with Ericsfjord and took a blessedly silent shortcut through the woods. The ships would blow horns to announce their arrival when they approached the keep, but Steven figured the horsemen would gain hours on them.

"I've been worried about something," Steven confided to Oslac.

He arched his brows.

"I forgot to tell Arnstein, or anyone else, to feed and water the sea woman."

Oslac winced as if that was not good news. As if he didn't already know that.

"What if she died in the cage?"

"Would it matter?" Oslac asked.

"Yea, it would. She has much to tell me about Thorfinn."

Oslac was still convinced that Steven's brother was long dead and said only, "Aaaah."

"Well, what will be will be."

"And the other . . . the message carried by Sigvid . . . will you agree to meet with Brodir?"

"I have not decided." He shrugged. "It leaves a bad taste in my mouth to negotiate with *nithings*. But my sister's life could be at stake."

"The maid says that they were not hurt, and she believes Brodir, for some reason, when he promises that Disa will continue unharmed."

"Disa is a sharp-witted woman. She is no doubt pulling a flummery on Brodir."

"I had not thought of that."

"Still, his idea of harm may be different from mine, if you get my meaning." Enough thinking for now. He kicked his horse to a gallop and rose to the top of the crest where he could look over the valley . . . all that encompassed Norstead. He reined the horse in for a moment, just gazing downward, and his heart swelled in his chest. It really was beautiful here.

For the first time, Norstead began to feel like home to him . . . even without Thorfinn. And he was beginning to understand what Oslac and others meant about the gloominess here. In truth, he knew exactly when it had started: seven years ago when Thorfinn's wife, Luta, left him, taking their newborn son, Miklof, with her. Thorfinn's rage and sorrow were like a living shroud about Norstead. It had been deemed that Luta and her merchant lover, along with the infant, had died in a shipwreck. Not that Thorfinn hadn't continued searching, and in fact, Steven and Thorfinn had been in Baghdad five years later on another futile search. That had been two years ago, and the time and place where Thorfinn had disappeared.

So, yea, there had been a cheerlessness about Norstead caused by Thorfinn's loss of Miklof and Steven had no doubt carried on the sense of despair for these two years hence, in his case mourning the loss of his beloved brother.

But enough of dwelling on the past. Steven was home, and despite the worry over rescuing his sister, he looked forward to a warm bath, a cold ale, and a soft bed, in that order.

But wait . . . what was that? "Do you see what I see?" he said to Oslac, who came to a halt beside him. On the exercise fields, far below, a barefooted youth in a leather tunic belted over slim braies was engaged in teaching a half dozen young boys how to shoot an arrow good and true.

Oslac nodded. "I wonder who the youthling is. He is really good. Mayhap Geirfinn recruited him from a neighboring clan to join forces here."

"'Tis not a he. 'Tis a she. And not a youthling, either. Do you not recognize the short blonde hair?"

"Oh good gods!" Oslac looked at him with disbelief.

"Leastways I do not have to feel guilty about having left the woman . . . or creature . . . or whatever the hell she is, untended in a cage."

"You were feeling guilty?"

"Just a mite. But, Oslac . . . Holy Thor! Did you see that? She just hit the target head-on, then immediately nocked another arrow and split the first arrow in half."

"Well, this is good news, right? A skilled bowman is always welcome."

"Nay, it is not good news. Can you see my men fighting alongside a woman? But worse than that, a stranger . . . perchance one sent here by Brodir to spy . . . has had access to all the weapon stores and layout of Norstead's defenses for the past sennight."

Steven kicked his horse into a gallop, but not before noticing something else. With her legs spread for balance, the fabric of her braies pulled taut over her rounded buttocks and with sunlight creating a sort of glow about her short golden hair . . . well, he had to admit to being aroused.

Dangerous, dangerous, dangerous! A sly woman could use a man's lust against him.

Best I be careful. No touching. No kisses. No bedplay.

He could swear he heard laughter in his head . . . or was the laughter coming from that other portion of his body? The one with not a jot of sense.

Chapter 6

Flip that, bozo! . . .

"You need to keep your eye on your target, Naddod," Rita told the boy, who was only twelve years old but deemed of sufficient age to begin military training. "Forget about watching your bow or arrow. Remember what I said: eyes straight ahead, on your target."

Naddod did as she instructed, and while the arrow didn't hit the center of the bale of hay they were using for a target, it was close. The boy jumped up and down and whooped his superiority to his friends, who would take their turns next.

"When can we learn to hit moving targets, like birds?" Naddod wanted to know.

"Or runnin' Saxon bastards?" another boy added, and his friends agreed.

"Bloodthirsty little buggers, aren't you?" But to Naddod she said, with a laugh, "Slow down, kiddo. You have to master one skill before you move onto another."

Rita, bored with having nothing to do these past few

days, had convinced Geirfinn to let her teach the boys weapon skills. His only condition was that Sigge stay away. Apparently she'd once caused all the arrows in the archers' bows to go wild, with several men shot in the butt and legs, one even in the penis, which had to be removed *very* carefully.

Obviously, they had no guns to demonstrate here, but archery Rita could handle just as well. This afternoon, she was going to teach them, and any girls brave enough to join them, how to use karate moves, even in battle.

Just then, someone let out a shout, "Master is back, Master is back!"

Yep! A dozen horses were riding toward Norstead, led by the "master" himself. She hadn't heard the horns that she'd been told would announce the ships' approach, ten blasts on a horn, marking the return of each of the ten long-ships that had left a week ago.

People scattered like sand in the wind, some rushing to greet the horsemen, others getting wagons ready to go unload the longships when they arrived, and still others going to designated jobs required when the soldiers came home. And, suddenly, there she was, all alone, with just one of the horsemen trotting toward her.

Nervous, she began to gather up the bows and arrows and stack them on a wagon, which would take them back to the weaponry room in the castle. The whole time she kept glancing sideways to see Steven dismount from his horse and walk toward her in a menacing way.

"Hi!" she said, giving him a little wave. "Hope you had a good mission."

Nothing. Not a reply. Not a crack of a smile. *Here we go again.*

She sighed deeply. "Okay, what's got your knickers in a twist this time? I got rid of the wet suit. I've been a very polite guest while you've been gone. I even . . . oh! It's about the fire, isn't it? Honest, I never meant it to spread . . ."

Steven jolted to a stop. "There has been a fire here at Norstead? And you started it?"

She waved a hand dismissively. "Just a teeny tiny little fire." She held a thumb and forefinger about two inches apart. A bit of an exaggeration, but who was measuring? "I needed to do something to get out of that cage."

Steven's eyes widened with astonishment. "You set fire inside my keep? Have you no sense, woman? A wood castle would go up in flames as easily as the wind blows."

He was not going to be reasonable.

He took one step forward.

She took two steps backward. She had to admit he was one prime specimen of hunkiness. He'd ditched the mesh shirt thingee for a belted leather tunic and slim pants, which outlined wide shoulders, narrowed waist, and muscular thighs leading down to knee-length boots. There was a week's growth of hair on his cheeks. Not exactly designer stubble, but not unattractive. And the silver gray eyes! They were more compelling, more piercing than any she'd ever seen, and there were some incredible contact lenses used in Hollywood these days.

The question remained: Why, after years of working in the movie industry, after a year of working with some very virile SEALs, was she suddenly finding herself drawn to a Viking Genghis Khan? With the face of a younger George Clooney, she immediately amended.

She licked her suddenly dry lips.

"Why do you look at me like that, Ree-tah?"

Ah, so he remembers my name. One point in my favor. "How was I looking at you?"

"Like you would enjoy making a meal of me."

She shrugged.

"What? Your continually flapping tongue has naught to say about that?"

"What's to say? You know how good-looking you are without one more woman telling you."

"I swear, I have ne'er met a woman who speaks so boldly."

"Maybe you need to widen your circle of . . . friends."

"And you are offering to be my . . . friend?"

"Sure. Why not? Unless friend means something different to you than to me. Anyhow, if you weren't all scowly faced over the fire when you got here, what were you so angry about?"

"Scowly faced? You try my temper beyond the bounds of good sense," he said, shaking his head with disbelief. "You are perchance a spy for our pirate enemy, and you had the gall to not only assess our store of weapons but the layout of our fortifications."

"Me? A pirate spy?" She laughed and took another two steps back, now that he was once again piercing her with his icy silver eyes. "Listen, you and I have a lot to talk about."

He moved quickly to the right.

She dodged to the left, leaving the wagon between them.

"Come here," he ordered, beckoning her with a forefinger, "if you want to talk."

"Not a chance!"

"'Twill go easier on you if you come willingly."

"Said the spider to the fly."

His lips actually twitched with humor at that picture.

"What will you do if I come?"

He shrugged. "Throttle you? Blister your arse? Torture you on the rack?"

"Do you have a rack?"

He smiled then. A full-blown, I-can-seduce-you smile that hit her tummy like an erotic punch. "Nay, but mayhap I could borrow one from your pirate friends."

"Enough with the pirate crap! I am not here to spy."

"Prove it. Come to me." He held out a hand.

Oooh, boy, was she tempted! But he wasn't offering

what she wanted, unfortunately. "What will you do? Tie me up? Put me in that cage again? Lock me in a bedchamber? I'll surrender if you promise to let me go free after we talk."

"You do not dictate terms to me."

"Your loss, buddy! You'll never learn anything about your brother."

"Tell me one thing about Thorfinn to show good faith."

She hesitated. "I'm pretty sure that he time-traveled."

Steven let loose with a roar, like a bear she'd once seen on one of her wilderness sets. "You play with me when it comes to my brother? I really will kill you for that."

"Here's the thing, Steven. I'm not playing games. Thorfinn traveled forward in time to the year two thousand and ten, and I traveled back from there. At least that's the only explanation I can come up with. I know, I know, it's hard to take in, but after we've talked, maybe you'll understand."

"Time travel?" He rubbed a hand over his face, clearly losing patience.

She backed up a few paces, planning her strategy for when he made his lunge for her . . . something he most definitely would be doing any minute now.

"You better not hurt me, or you'll be sorry." *Did I actually say such a wussy thing? Jeesh!* She now had enough space between her and Steven. All she needed to do was wait for the right moment.

There it was. He rushed forward.

She took a running leap, grabbed the side of the wagon 'til she was standing on her hands, and then, without pause, turned, and used that impetus to propel her into a backflip over to the other side of the wagon where she faced the other side. Without hesitation, she made a long jump and began to run for her life.

Steven's jaw dropped, and he just stared at her for a moment.

She headed toward a wooded area. She'd never escape totally, but it would give him time to cool down.

But Steven was something else again. Using the bottom of his boot, he shoved the back of the wagon so it moved away, then he ran after her, making a final lunge, like a football player, which brought her to the ground with him on top.

"Move, you big oaf," she huffed out when she could breathe again. "You're crushing me."

He raised himself enough to turn her on her back, then arranged himself on top of her once more. She didn't fail to notice that he had both of her hands held in one of his above her head, or that his you-know-what was pressing against her you-know-what. With a growing interest she might add.

Then he did the unexpected. He smiled down at her and said, "Well, well, well. What shall we do now?" The whole time he was running the fingers of his free hand through her hair, with a kind of wonder softening his face. Then a forefinger was outlining her lips. The wonder was replaced with lust, pure and simple.

But who was she kidding about *him* being in lust mode? The whisper of a touch affected her like an electric shock to everything sexy in her body. She had to restrain herself from licking the finger or taking it into her mouth.

What was happening to her?

He murmured against her lips, "Ree-tah," and kissed her. It was like no kiss she'd ever experienced before.

Hard for her brain to comprehend in this haze of growing arousal, both hers and his by the size of the bulge between her legs. While she lay there, like a stunned cat, failing to kick and scream and attempt escape, she was being very skillfully and very thoroughly kissed by Genghis Viking.

And she liked it!

How to seduce a seductress? . . .

Steven had been practicing the art of seduction since he was fourteen. He knew all the cues and nuances of how to touch the soft skin on a woman, knowing precisely when and where to the best effect. There was an art to it. There was also a line some women needed to be convinced to cross.

This woman crossed the line and then some.

It was now a question of who was seducing whom.

Somehow she had loosened her hands and had her arms wrapped around his shoulders. She even spread her thighs wider and drew her knees up to cradle his hips. Without a doubt, his cock was riding her woman channel like a rudderless longboat.

All this within moments. All this out in the open for one and all to see. All this with so much exquisite pleasure he wanted it to last forever.

I have to stop.

Now.

Soon.

"You taste so good," she murmured.

She must be referring to the mint leaves he'd been chewing.

She licked his lips from side to side before dipping her tongue inside his mouth

His eyeballs probably rolled back in his head.

Then he murmured back, "You taste good, too," and used his tongue to show her exactly how good things could be betwixt them. "I have ne'er kissed a mermaid afore," he mused aloud.

"You still have never kissed a mermaid," she pointed out.

He arched a brow at her. "So, you are all woman?"

"You would know better than most." The saucy wench then wriggled her body beneath his for emphasis.

"Definitely all woman," he gurgled out, then kissed her again, putting a hand behind her waist and lifting her up to better rub their nether parts together.

She groaned.

He grinned.

"You're laughing at me," she accused.

"Nay, I am enjoying myself. There is a difference."

He was finally able to draw away, bracing himself on his elbows, when he heard Oslac calling him from a distance.

She looked stunned. Her eyes, as clear a blue as a summer sky, glazed with arousal. Her mouth swollen from his kisses.

"You know, Steven, if you would stop growling and stomping around making demands, you would gain the information you want. Be nice."

"Really? Have I not been very nice the last few moments?"

"It was interesting."

"Interesting? That was more than interesting."

"Okay, it was more than interesting, it was . . ."

"Incredible?" he finished for her.

She nodded, as if she didn't quite believe it herself.

He tilted his head to the side. "If I play nice, you will tell me all your secrets?"

"Well, some of them," she conceded with an impish grin.

"Give me one."

"Your brother got married."

Steven shot to his feet. "How can that be? Finn swore he would never wed again."

"Love happens sometimes."

"Love!" he scoffed.

"Seeing is believing. If you could see him and Lydia together, you'd believe. They adore each other."

"Two things you have told me, and both are equally unbelievable."

"What two things?"

"Finn is a time traveler and he has married again."

"I admit the time travel is a stretch. I'm finding it hard to accept that, too. But your brother is definitely married to Lydia Denton, owner of a dance studio in Coronado, California. In fact . . ." She let her words trail off, reminding herself that it was best not to disclose any information that was not required.

"Finish," he ordered.

"No, I'm saving some things for later."

"Why?"

"Leverage."

"You will tell me everything I want to know in due time. Do not doubt that."

"You gonna kiss me until I reveal all my secrets?"

He grinned. "Mayhap."

Oslac was getting closer. Steven reached a hand down to draw her up to her feet.

"We will continue this discussion later," he told her, putting his mouth next to her ear, "and I do not just mean about my brother."

The wench had the nerve to wink at him and say, "I can't wait," before walking away from him and Oslac, free as a bird, with both of them watching the sway of her hips.

Then they both burst out in laughter.

Beware of rogues that are prettier than you are . . .

By that evening, Rita was still reeling with shock over the kiss. Even though she had done her best to avoid the tempting lout until she could straighten out her libido, the taste of the kiss remained with her. No, forget about lust, she needed to get her priorities in order: How to go home to Coronado.

Rita had done her best all day to shrink back into the shadows, not to be conspicuous. Oh, some might say her antics, like backflips or archery, were cries for attention, but, really, she sometimes just needed to release tension, and she didn't think of the consequences.

She had to admire the way Steven and his sidekick Oslac managed the return of three hundred or so men to the estate. He was a born CEO or military commander in another time.

They'd removed and stored everything from the newly arrived longships, which would be checked over thoroughly tomorrow. Apparently, the ships had to be ready to sail at any moment. No one was talking about what had happened on their pirate mission, but it appeared to have been unsuccessful, except for their bringing back a woman who had done nothing but cry nonstop until someone, probably Steven, shoved her into a bed closet and told her to sleep it off, or he would personally toss her off a cliff.

Just then, the door swung open, and there stood the object of her distraction, all decked out in new clothes: tunic over the slim pants known as braies, like before, but this time in dark blue with a leather belt and half boots. He must have shaved and showered recently, because his hair was still wet and pulled back off his face into a queue. Pure male temptation!

She'd bathed also, in the women's bathing longhouse where the other women kept checking her out. For a tail, or scales, or web feet, she supposed. Clean though she may be now, she wasn't nearly as pretty as Steven was. Plus, she'd had to put her dirty clothes back on.

"Knock much?" she snapped out from the far side of the small room where she'd been doing exercises . . . knee bends, squats, sit-ups. There wasn't much else to do.

"Why should I knock?"

"Privacy, for one thing."

"This is Thorfinn's bedchamber."

"No one else was using it."

"Mayhap there is a reason for that. What were you doing down there on the floor?"

"Exercises. To keep my body fit." There was nothing else to do. No TV. Not a book in the whole darn place, which was truly amazing. She stood up and wiped the perspiration off her forehead with a square linen washing cloth.

He gave her body a slow head-to-toe survey, for fitness she supposed, and grinned. Enough said!

Then he narrowed his eyes at her. "Why do you need privacy?"

"Everyone needs privacy sometimes. What are you doing here anyway? Don't you have any Viking things to do?"

He smiled. "Viking things?"

"Raping, pillaging, plundering, drinking vast amounts of booze out of animal horns, going berserk."

"Your tongue . . . how has it managed to stay intact so many years? Surely there have been men who threatened to shut you up by lopping it off."

She put a fingertip to her chin and pretended to think deeply. "Nope. Can't say anyone has threatened to lop off a body part until I got here."

He continued to stand, leaning back against the closed door, his arms folded over his chest, just watching her. He probably hoped to intimidate her by staring her down, but she met his stare and refused to give in first.

Finally, boredom won. "What do you want, Steven? I've been a good girl all day. What sin did I commit now?"

"Sin? What an odd choice of words!" he said. "Dinner is about to be served. I came to get you."

"Oh, no. Thanks a bunch, but no. Really. I'd rather just slip down to the kitchen later and grab a bite to eat."

"I did not ask you. And since when are you overcome with shyness? Last I saw you, aside from when you skulked about in the shadows all day, was when you walked away from me and Oslac, twitching your arse like a dockside trollop."

Rita's face grew hot. "What a smooth talker you are, Steven! Go find some other 'dockside trollop' to eat with you."

"I did not say you are a trollop. In truth, I do not consort with trollops, and I definitely want to consort with you."

If he thought that was going to smooth waters, he had another think coming. "Why? Because of that one kiss?" she taunted.

"It was an unusual kiss, unlike any I have experienced afore. Well worth repeating, would you not say, Ree-tah?"

"I have decided not to be attracted to you anymore."

He chuckled. "One can decide such things?"

"I can, especially if you go back to your usual negative, insulting attitude. How come you're not scowling?"

"I have scowled for three days, on the way back to Norstead. My men are complaining. In truth, I am sick to my teeth of everyone commenting on my moods. Yea, I am angry, as well I should be. I am angry at the loss of my brother. I am angry that I have lost my way of life and must needs take Thorfinn's place as master of Norstead and Amberstead. I am angry at you for trying to escape. I am angry at my people for not stopping you. And most of all, I am angry with myself."

"Wow! Why don't you tell me how you really feel? All I did was ask why you weren't scowling today."

He calmed down after his outburst. "No doubt tomorrow I will be back to my normal growling and frowning."

"Good." When he only grinned at her response, she went on, "Why don't you go find your fiancée and suck face with her?"

"Fee-auntsie?"

She rolled her eyes. "Betrothed."

Steven frowned. "I am not betrothed to anyone."

"Someone better inform the merry widow. Lady Thora has you or Oslac, or both of you, in her marriage crosshairs."

"Explain yourself, m'lady."

"Lady Thora told me that you and Oslac belong to her and warned me not to interfere."

He regarded her with amusement. "A tup does not a marriage proposal make."

"Does Lady Thora know that?"

"She will. Little does Lady Thora know, but I have already made plans for her to be back in her father's Vestfold house afore winter. Let him find her a new husband."

She shrugged. It wasn't her problem.

"Tell me more about how you are attracted to me."

Typical man! Needs to have his ego stroked. She thought about asking him why he was attracted to her, but she was afraid he would tell her . . . in embarrassing detail.

As if the subject were closed, he walked over to the bed, sat down, then lay down, big as you please, with his hands linked behind his head on the pillows.

"What do you think you're doing?"

"Waiting for you to get ready for dinner. And I do not mean boy's garb." He waved a hand toward her current attire. "Not that I do not appreciate how well you fill them out. Bend over so I can get a better look at your arse."

"In your dreams!"

"Why? A well-shaped arse is an attribute to be desired for a woman. Mayhap I will order all women in my keep to wear braies so I may assess their arse worthiness."

She made a face at him, knowing that he was deliberately baiting her. Actually, she was planning on going down to the laundry area when everyone was at dinner and washing out her tunic and tights. There was a plain, faded red wool gown that she'd pilfered from a chest that once belonged to Thorfinn's first wife. She didn't take any of the finer garments, but she figured no one would notice if she borrowed a few older items. "I'm not going down to dinner."

"Yea, you are."

"Why does it matter? Do you enjoy humiliating me?"

That shocked him. "How have I humiliated . . . well, how have I done anything objectionable since I have returned? You, on the other hand . . ."

"It would be like walking a gauntlet, bare naked, if I had to walk down there in front of all those horny men."

"No man at Norstead—horny or otherwise, assuming horny means what I think it does—would take you to his bed furs without your consent."

"Oh, that makes me feel better, assent being open to interpretation, I assume."

"Besides, you are under my shield now."

"I am?"

"Until I decide what to do with you."

"That's just great. Then what? You start lopping off body parts, or toss me off a cliff like you threatened that sobbing maid, or—"

"Swive you silly."

Her face heated again, and she was not a blushing kind of woman. "That was crude."

He wriggled his butt on the bed and said, "I had no idea Thorfinn's bed was so comfortable. Methinks I will sleep here tonight."

"And where will I sleep?"

His silence was ominous.

"Maybe we should go to dinner after all."

"Good idea!" he agreed, as if that had been his intent all along.

"You go ahead. I'll meet you there as soon as I change."

"I have a better idea. I'll wait, and we will go together."

She bared her teeth at him.

He grinned. "Take something from Luta's chest."

"I already did." She pointed to the red gown.

"That gunna is fine, but you need something over it. It is so worn I would no doubt be able to see your nipples, and that would distract me from my meal. Perchance give me a stomach upset."

"Good Lord!" she muttered at his continual bluntness. "There are no aprons like I see many of the Viking women wear here."

"Luta favored all things Saxon, including their men, apparently, since she ran off with one of them. There must be a surcoat or two in here."

He jumped off the bed in one lithe movement and went over to Luta's chest. Pulling items here and there, tossing some to the bed and disregarding others, he finally ended up with a sleeveless, collarless black garment, like an open vest, except it was calf-length. The edges were embroidered in a red and gold intertwined leaf design.

She managed to change with her back to him, giving him only a tiny glimpse of skin. Then she turned and put her hands on her hips. "Does this meet with your satisfaction, your high-handedness?"

He studied her, ignoring her sarcasm. "Not quite." Digging deeper in the chest, he pulled out a gold linked belt and a braided brass hair ornament called a fillet or diadem, used to hold a woman's hair off her face with the center medallion smack-dab in the middle of her forehead. Not of much use to her with her short hair, and she would probably have a circle imprint on her forehead for days. He fixed the belt around her waist so that it hung low about her hips. She kept telling him she could do it herself, but he slapped her hands away and insisted, "Let me." He was probably aware of the oddly sensual sensations he was generating in her by "dressing" her.

"Have you ever had long hair?" he asked.

"Sure. When I was a teenager, it hung down to my butt."

"I would like to see that."

"What? My long hair or my butt?"

"What do you think?" Grinning, he put the fillet on her head then and used his fingers to feather her short hair around the band. "Perfect," he declared, standing back to survey his creation. "Now you look like a Viking princess."

"With my short hair?"

"Even with your short hair. Yea, you will do."

"For what?" she asked, suddenly suspicious.

But his attention had already wandered. "You cannot wear those boots with a gown."

"No one will notice."

He was already deep in the chest again, pulling out several soft cloth shoes. "Here," he said, handing her a pair of what looked like ballet slippers.

"I would really prefer my boots."

"I would really prefer you take them off."

Okay, the problem was, how to take off her boots without his seeing her hidden knife?

"Stubborn damn Viking," she muttered and went to sit on the opposite side of the bed, with her back to him. Without raising her gown, she toed off one boot. No problem. But when she toed off the other one, the boot slipped, and the knife flew, hitting the side of the washstand with a clunk.

Immediately, Steven was at her side, shaking his head at her. "Tsk-tsk-tsk! Just when I was starting to trust you!"

She refused to apologize. "Did you really expect me to walk around without defending myself? Women are entitled to self-defense, too."

"In all honesty, I do not know of one other woman who wears a knife in her shoe."

"Maybe I'm smarter than the average woman. Maybe I've been trained to take the offense, instead of the defense. Maybe women in your time have been docile for too long."

"May-be you talk too much." He grabbed her hand, gave her a quick, sizzling kiss, and tugged her toward the door, which he proceeded to open.

There they immediately ran into two old, cackling women with wild . . . really wild . . . gray hair, Rita's first experience with actual cackling. They could have been anywhere from seventy to a hundred, give or take.

Steven groaned and linked his fingers with hers, attempting to move around the old crones, to no avail. They were circling them, bony hands raised high, muttering strange, guttural sounds.

"*Who* are they?" she whispered to Steven.

"Kraka and Grima, the witch sisters."

Ah, Sigge's aunts.

"Tulla, tulla, aba fri! Issa, issa, frasa beil!" the one witch chanted after throwing some smooth stones at Rita and Steven's feet. The stones had sticklike scratchings on them that Rita recognized as runic symbols.

The other witch tossed a handful of white stuff over her and Steven, which she soon learned by a flick of her tongue was salt, and pronounced, "Witches' brew, flames on high, magic gruel. Scales of a dragon, bat tongues, butterfly wings. Three man-hairs, rose petal touched with women's dew. Goddess grant she be the one to lighten the Norseman's darksome life."

"I think she means you," Steven pointed out. At her frown of confusion, he explained, "You are being sent by the witch goddesses to lighten up this dark Norseman, meaning me. I cannot wait to see how you will do that." He waggled his eyebrows at her.

Noticing that several housecarls were rushing toward them, the witches tugged up the hems of their black gowns and proceeded to rush away, one of them addressing Rita,

"Come to the circle of rowen trees next full moon. Dance naked with us to fulfill the prophecy."

And just like that, they were gone.

One of the three guardsmen rushing by told Steven, "Sorry, m'lord, we tried to keep them out of the castle, but they slipped by."

Steven nodded and then smiled at Rita. "I give you my permission to dance naked in the moonlight, as long as I get to watch."

"This is the weirdest experience I've ever had. First, time travel, now witches."

"Just ignore the witches. I will protect you."

Just then, the guardsman who had come forward said, "Did ye know, m'lord, that most men spend their lives sowing wild oats, but even more time praying for a crop failure? Ha-ha-ha!"

Rita smiled at the guardsman's ill-timed joke, but Steven just glared. How unkind of him!

The guardsman scuttled off. If he had a tail, it would have been tucked between his legs.

"That wasn't nice. You could have at least smiled at his joke."

"And encourage more of the same? I do not think so. My people have taken to telling jokes to lift my dark mood."

"I don't understand all these references, not just from the joking guard, but those two dingbat witches. What do they mean about the darkness here at Norstead, and what I have to do with some kind of light?"

"Well, I have been in a bit of a black mood."

"For how long?"

"Oh, a little while."

"How long?"

"Two years. And five years afore that as I watched my brother nigh drown in his sorrows."

"Are you crazy? That's not a mood, that's depression."

"That is what I said. My brother Thorfinn and I were

very close, and when he died . . . or left . . . or whatever happened to him . . . well, I have been unable to climb out from under this weight of sadness."

"A depressed Viking," she said. "Who would have thought it? And it's not blackness. It's called the blues."

"Huh? Do you make mock of me?"

"Blues is another name for depression."

"So, I have the blues?" He grinned. "Sounds better than depression, which is rather pitiful for a Viking."

"Hey, even Vikings get the blues, honey."

Chapter 7

How much trouble could one woman be? . . .

Steven was intrigued. Nay, more than intrigued. He was smitten.

Did not matter that the woman had arrived on their shores looking like a mottled fish. Did not matter that she had hair shorter than most boylings. Did not matter that she had an attitude and flapping tongue that defied good sense. Did not matter that she was strange beyond his wide experience with her acrobatic and military skills, not to mention her talk of time travel.

Sitting beside him at the high table, her blue eyes darted here and there, taking in all the sights, which she claimed were new to her. Not just the layout of his vast hall with its central hearth fires, or the attire and demeanor of his people, or the fare placed afore them on the table . . . wild boar in persimmon sauce; brined ham hocks in heavy cream; hákarl, or cured shark; baked trout stuffed with mushrooms and onions; honey roasted duck stuffed with oysters; skyr, a cured milk dish similar to cottage cheese, served with bilberries, neeps, carrots, peas, beets, horseradish, and wild celery; manchet bread; hard and soft cheeses; fresh fruits; oatcakes; horns and mugs of ale, mead, and cold buttermilk.

Her hair fillet was tilted on her head, giving her a rather winsome look, instead of making her appear unkempt. He had seen far more beautiful women in face and form. Why she made him breathless and gladsome was beyond his ken.

"Tell me more about my brother," he urged, as two lutists moved to the front to play their music. Some of the men had already moved into small groups to dice or play the Viking board game *hnefatafl*, similar to the Persian chess, except that one player had a red army with twelve warriors and a king, while the other player had twenty-four warriors but no king. The goal was for the white player to capture the red king. Still others had wandered off with their ladies or wenches to do what lovers did. It was a peaceful scene.

She glanced down at the table where he had linked the fingers of one hand with the fingers of one of hers, his thumb caressing her wrist.

"First, you need to understand me and where I come from."

He restrained himself from groaning, knowing she was going to repeat the time-travel nonsense.

"I come from the year two thousand and ten. In my time, life is so different. People ride horses only for pleasure, in most cases. Instead, they travel by horseless carriages, for lack of a better description, or even fly in the sky from one country to another in airplanes, which resemble enormous metal birds. For example, I could go from here to London in an hour. Most people don't hunt or fish for food. They have supermarkets where everything can be purchased. I won't even try to explain televisions or radios or computers. Just know that I could communicate with someone in, let's say, Iceland, just by picking up a black boxlike device called a phone."

His eyes went wider and wider as she spoke. It was impossible, of course, but she spoke with such conviction.

"The infant mortality rate is very low, compared to your time, because of all the modern hospitals and medicines. Birth control is available to women so that they can have sex and not get pregnant. Clothing and shoes are purchased in stores, ready made.

"We have many branches of military service, including the Navy SEALs—Sea, Air, Land special operations—which is what your brother Thorfinn is training to be. And although there have been women in the military for a long time, it's only recently that a female SEALs program was started called WEALS, Women on Earth, Air, Land and Sea. I joined that a year ago and am still in training."

"Why would you want to fight?"

She shrugged. "I needed the money. My mother had been ill for a long time before she died, and I had creditors plaguing me like locusts. Plus I've always been competitive and athletic, so when they recruited me from my stunt double job, it seemed the right thing to do."

"I am almost afraid to ask. What is a stunt double?"

"It's hard to explain, but in my time we have movies, which are sort of like dramatic productions, except some are with high adventure. The stars of these productions are too valuable to risk their lives with dangerous stunts, so they send us doubles in for them."

"Seems unfair."

"It pays well."

"Define dangerous."

She grinned at him. "Jump off high buildings. Rappel up high buildings. Jump out of planes in the sky. Crash motor vehicles. Ride a horse over a deep ravine. Get shot with a weapon. And, most recently, set myself afire."

"You jest!"

She shook her head, pleased to have surprised him.

He squeezed her hand, and she squeezed back.

"Assuming I believe you, and I cannot, where does Thorfinn fit into all this?"

"Well, I don't know him well at all. He apparently came to California two years ago. Word is that his cousin Torolf was in Baghdad for a SEAL mission, and they came across Thorfinn fighting off some Arab terrorists. They helped him and then brought him back to California. No one has said so, but I realize now that the two time periods must have crossed, and Thorfinn time-traveled to the future."

"Oh, this is just too much! You are saying my cousin Torolf is involved? Torolf disappeared years ago when . . ." His words trailed off. "You are saying that Torolf time-traveled, too?"

She shrugged. "I guess so. Actually, his entire family is in California, as far as I know. I went to a party at Madrene's home recently."

He put up a halting hand. "Enough! 'Tis bad enough trying to accept Thorfinn's passing through time, but a whole Viking clan? 'Tis beyond belief."

"I agree."

"Back to Thorfinn . . . you say he has wed?"

She nodded. "Yep. About a year ago. He married Lydia Denton, a widow, who has a young son named Michael, whom Thorfinn adopted."

"Michael? Are you serious? Thorfinn had been searching for years for his missing son Miklof. Could it be . . . nay, 'tis not possible."

"Well, the little boy does resemble Thorfinn. In fact, he has the same color eyes as you and your brother."

"He does? Oh, what a wonder it would be if Finn finally found his son again!"

"There's more, actually."

He hesitated to ask.

"Your brother and Lydia are pregnant. She is expecting twins before Christmas."

"Twins?" Tears filled his eyes then. He could not help

himself. If only it were true! He could accept Finn's being gone if he knew he was happy. "Let us go there on the morrow," he said. "I would visit my brother and see with my own eyes that he is well."

"Uh, there might be a small problem."

He frowned.

"I have no idea how I got here. Nor do I know how to return."

"*What?* Does that mean you are going to disappear in a poof of smoke one day without warning?"

"I don't know about the poof of smoke, and actually I don't know if I can go back at all."

"You sound very calm about this, as if you accept your fate, no matter what."

"I'm not calm at all. Do you really think I want to live in such a primitive time?"

"I do not think we are so primitive."

"Believe me, you're primitive."

"So, you might stay here then?"

"I hope not. Don't worry. If I get stuck here, I won't be your responsibility."

"Oh, really? Then whose?"

"My own. I've been taking care of myself from a very young age. I don't need some man to take care of me."

"And what would you do here, except cause trouble?"

She stuck out her tongue at him, which he was fairly sure was an insult. Or was it an invitation of sorts?

"You think I have all the answers. I don't even know if I've really time-traveled, and if I have, why? But there are lots of things I could do. Teach children, for example."

"Teach them what? How to fall off cliffs?"

She did not laugh at his jest, which was not really a jest, now that he thought on it.

"Reading, math, history, exercise. Or, hey, how about a women's studies class to teach females that they have as many rights as men do?"

"Odin spare me!"

"I could even entertain at banquets and stuff with my acrobatic talents. I do a mean triple backflip on parallel bars."

"That is all I need!"

"Hey, I could be the official jokester here. I know a bunch of dumb man jokes."

"Do not dare—"

"Some men drink from the fountain of knowledge, but most of them only gargle."

"How about women? They no doubt sip."

"Just think, if it weren't for marriage, most men would go through life thinking they had no faults at all."

"You should have met Oslac's wife Girda. A great pair you would have made."

"Why do men find it difficult to make eye contact with a woman? I'll tell you why. Breasts don't have eyes."

He just stared at her, unsmiling. "If those were jests, I do not see the humor. I assume that making mock of men is considered good entertainment in your country."

She shrugged. "Okay, if you don't like my sense of humor, maybe I could set up a business cutting women's hair."

He could tell she was just trying to needle him. Still, he ordered, "Never!"

"Or there must be some open-minded military commander in this blasted country who could use my fighting skills."

He put his face in both hands and rubbed hard. When he looked back at her, he said, "I suspect you are going to turn my life upside down and inside out."

"Ditto, babe. Ditto."

When she began to yawn, not once but five times in a row, he told her, "Go to your bed. We will talk more in the morning."

She nodded.

"Do you want me to accompany you?" he asked, recalling her earlier words of concern about walking amongst his men.

"Why?"

"I could tuck you in."

"Hah! I know what you want to do, and it's not tuck, buddy."

His eyes went wide when he realized what she meant. Never had he met a woman with such a frankness of manner about her, except mayhap his cousin Madrene, who had been beyond shrewish. Rita's bluntness was not shrewish, however, just surprising, and, in truth, rather refreshing.

She made her way down the dais and along the outer rim of the great hall. He and Oslac both watched her progress and the several times one or another of his men stood, about to approach her, but then stopped when they looked his way and saw the admonition in his expression.

"You are different already," Oslac remarked as he took a long draw on his horn of ale.

Steven ignored his friend's remark, knowing he would not like his observation.

"Seriously, the witches are right."

"Now, that comment I cannot ignore. Since when do you give credence to those lackbrained witches?"

"Since the sea siren arrived."

Steven tossed his hands in the air in surrender. "Spill your guts. Tell me your wise words on the state of my being."

Oslac grinned. "The witches have predicted for months that a light would come to Norstead to sweep away the gloom."

"Now, see, I already disagree. Norstead is a prosperous estate. There is food, drink, and work aplenty. Why would it be gloomy?"

"Because you are gloomy. The sheep follow the ram's example."

Steven rolled his eyes. "Methinks you have your proverb twisted." He took a drink of ale, then another. He may need it if he was going to let Oslac spew his nonsense.

"I know you do not see the effect you have on those around you, but it is there nonetheless."

"Since when are Vikings supposed to be cheery all the time?"

"Actually, Men of the North do have a reputation for enjoying life."

"I enjoy life," he insisted.

"But not like you used to."

"Ree-tah says I have the blues."

"'Tis as good a name as any for ill temper."

"And now you say I am different all of a sudden, just because the sea siren has arrived?"

"Not totally different, but you must admit, you have grinned more in the past day than you have in months."

"Mayhap all the jokes are finally having an effect on me."

Oslac cast him a disbelieving look. "And I can see that you enjoy her company."

"She may leave at any moment, Oslac. Do not put too much weight on her contribution to the light or aught else here at Norstead."

"I do not understand. How could she leave if you do not allow her to?"

"Because . . . are you ready for this, my friend? She claims to be a time traveler come to us from a thousand years in the future. A place where she claims Thorfinn now resides with his new wife, her son Michael, and upcoming twins, though how she knows they are twins in the belly, I have no idea. And one more thing . . . no more swiving Lady Thora. Apparently she is setting a marriage trap for one of us, according to Ree-tah."

Oslac's jaw dropped nigh to his chest before he snapped his teeth shut. "Asabor!" Oslac yelled then to a passing maid. "Bring us another jug of ale. Nay, make that two jugs." Then he turned to Steven. "Dost believe her? About the time travel, I mean."

"Nay. Of course not. Mayhap. I do not know."

"Good gods, but it is wonderful to have you back again. You always were such fun in the old days."

"You think this is fun?"

"More than we have had lately. Uh-oh. I just noticed that your sea siren has come back downstairs and is heading through the corridor to the kitchens. Dost think she plans to fly away?"

Instead of answering, Steven stood, emptied his horn of ale, then stomped after her.

What next? he thought.

And smiled.

He realized in that second that he was, indeed, having fun, never knowing what the wench would do next.

To his surprise, he liked the not knowing.

I'm gonna wash that man right out of my heart . . .

Rita was in the laundry annex . . . an open-sided addition to the wooden castle . . . where kettles of water sat on low embers waiting for the morning wash.

Exhausted, she still worked to clean her tunic and braies, although they might not be dry by morning at this rate. What she wouldn't give for a washer and dryer! And she vowed that she was making herself some underwear tomorrow. How, she wasn't sure, having no sewing talents, but this bare butt under her gown was kind of creepy. Hey, she thought with hysterical irrelevance, maybe she could set up her very own Dark Age Victoria's Secret here. That would show that skeptical Steven of the Fjord that she could survive here, if she had to.

"What in *Blód hel* are you doing now?" Steven yelled, storming out of the keep, coming toward her.

"Laundering my clothes?"

"Why?"

She put both hands on her hips and blew an errant curl off her forehead. "Silly question. So I have something clean to wear tomorrow."

"I have laundresses to do that."

"Oh." Her shoulders sagged with relief. "Will they do my laundry, too?"

"They will do whatever laundry they are handed, or answer to me."

"Okay," she said, and just left the garments soaking in water. She was too tired to care, as evidenced by her tripping and almost falling after a few steps.

"Foolish wench!" he said, grabbing her at the last moment and putting an arm around her waist, tucking her to his side, to keep her from falling again. When she still sagged, he picked her up in his arms.

She couldn't remember the last time anyone, especially a man, had picked her up, but she had no energy to protest. In fact, it was kind of nice.

Holding her cradled to his chest, he was still able to lift the fillet off her head. "You look like an angel with a fallen halo."

"I'm no angel."

"Thank the gods for small mercies!" He sniffed deeply. "You smell like roses."

"It's the soap I was using to wash my clothes."

"Rose-scented soap?"

"Uh-huh. I found it in Luta's chest."

"Um . . . I do not think that soap was intended for laundry. It is too precious, coming no doubt from the Arab lands."

"Uh-oh!" she said weakly, her eyelids already drifting shut.

Once again inside the keep, he approached the stairs.

"I feel like Scarlett being carried up the stairs by Rhett," she said with a giggle, and she never giggled. All this time-travel nonsense and the horror of what it might portend for her future was finally catching up with her.

"Scarlett and Rhett, huh?"

"Yep. His famous words to her were, 'Frankly, my dear, I don't give a damn.'"

He smiled down at her. "Frankly, my dear, I don't give a damn."

"Oh, God! Did you have to say that? Now I have to start all over again.'"

"Start what all over again?"

"Not being attracted to you."

His smile was wider now, and he lifted her higher in his arms so he could whisper in her ear. In a voice so sexy he could have said, "Boo!" and she would have melted, he murmured, "Frankly, Ree-tah, dearling, I do give a damn."

With those words, she was a goner.

The ultimate bartering tool . . .

Steven left his bed reluctantly the next morning, having slept through the night without the usual aid of mead or female pleasuring. Not that he would not have welcomed pleasuring from the sea siren beside him, but his instincts told him 'twas too soon.

After breaking fast, he met with his chief hersirs, the commanders of his various troops, to discuss the demands made by the pirate Brodir. How dare the outlaw Viking suggest that Steven meet with him afore releasing his sister? And what did Brodir hope to accomplish by further alienating him?

"I do not like the idea of negotiating with pirates. It sets a precedent," Steven told the hardened comrades-in-arms.

"Agreed," said Sveinn the Stalwart, a grizzled, gray-bearded warrior of forty and more years. His scarred body and one missing front tooth gave evidence of his battle worthiness. The arm rings that circled his upper arm muscles were so large they would fit nicely around a child's waist. "I say we storm all of Brodir's known strongholds and take no prisoners."

"Those are wise words," Oslac said, "but what of Steven's sister, the lady Disa."

Sveinn shrugged. "The pitfalls of war."

"Mayhap you could barter for her release," suggested another hersir, a cousin four times removed, Aldin of Norsemandy.

"I do not think 'tis gold Brodir has in mind. For some reason he has some grudge against those of us at Norstead," Steven mused.

"If not gold, mayhap something else," Oslac contributed. "How about the sea siren? You could put her back in that fish garment and tell Brodir she is a mermaid."

For some odd reason, the idea of giving up the wench did not sit well with Steven. Leastways, not until he had swived her a time or twenty.

"It is not as if the wench is any kith or kin of yours or Norstead," another hersir agreed.

"I will consider the idea," Steven said, knowing it was not too much to ask in the greater scheme of things. "I have another idea, though. Methinks we should call for a Thing, a meeting of all the clans in closer jarldoms to discuss the pirate threat. Two sennights from now should be enough time."

They all decided it was a good idea, especially since an Althing had been planned for later this summer in southern Vestfold. They would just be moving up the date and changing the location.

Still, Sveinn persisted, "Does that mean you will not offer the sea wench for barter?"

Steven knew his standing amongst his men was being tested. Would he be swayed on this important decision by the lure of a strange female? "We will abide by the decision of the Althing. If the council says that she should go, she shall."

As he left his council room, Steven shuddered to think what Rita would think of her fate being in the hands of a group of strange Viking men. In truth, he did not like the idea himself, and that was a sign of weakness he must control.

Furthermore, he had told her she was under the protection of his shield. His agreement to possibly barter her to the pirate felt like a betrayal of sorts.

"I think I liked my life better when it was bleak and uneventful," he told Oslac.

Chapter 8

You could say it was a Viking version of the Big Bad Wolf . . .

Rita awakened that morning to a warm bed, every bone and muscle in her body rested. She was renewed and hopeful that today she would figure out what was happening to her and how to find the key to getting back home.

Turning to the right, she saw that she was alone, but that someone had been sleeping there. Even worse, peeking under the blanket, she saw that she was naked.

Yikes!

He hadn't made love to her, though. After two years of abstinence, she would know. Besides, he was the kind of man who would want his woman wide-awake and participating.

Yikes again! Where did that "his woman" thought come from?

She noticed, on rising, that not only had her tunic and tights been washed and dried, but they were neatly folded and lying at the foot of the bed. On top of them was a new bar of rose soap.

Just then, the door opened a crack, and Sigge peered in. Seeing that she was awake, she slipped in and smiled shyly. "What kin I do fer you, m'lady? The master said I was not to wake you, but it is ever so late, and so much is happening."

"Did you put these here?" Rita asked, pointing to the clean clothing and soap.

Sigge shook her head. "Nay, the master did, and he tol' me ta do yer bidding."

If Rita hadn't already been fighting a fierce attraction to the big lug, she would be now.

"Some water to wash my face and clean my teeth?"

Sigge nodded and stepped outside the chamber, coming back immediately with a bucket of water, some of which she poured into the pottery bowl. Then she laid out a bone comb, along with several twigs with shredded tips and a small cup of salt . . . medieval toothbrush and paste, she assumed.

"While I'm cleaning up, could you find me one of those Viking apron thingees, Sigge?"

Off Sigge went, happy to do her bidding. By the time she returned, Rita had put the red gown back on with her boots. Intending to go outside, she had no intention of ruining those cloth slippers.

Sigge showed her how to attach the long, open-sided apron at the shoulders with silver brooches. "Mayhap later we could go visit my aunts. They have much to tell you."

"The witches?"

The tone of her voice must have offended Sigge, because she raised her chin and said, "I be a witch, too."

"I know that. Where do your aunts live? Here at the castle?"

"Nay. They live in the mountains where there is solitude and space to do their spells and potions."

That is just great.

"I grew up there until I was twelve and came here to the

castle to work the herb gardens. I may be an inept witch, but I have a talent with growing things."

"Maybe tomorrow," she said, hoping Sigge would forget by then.

The two of them headed out the door and downstairs, outside the kitchen, to the midden where they emptied the slop bucket of waste from her room, then went to look for food. Breakfast, or whatever they called the first meal of the day, was long over. Apparently, there were only two full meals served each day. Morning, about two hours after everyone had started work, and then in the evening after all work was completed.

"So, what's going on?" she asked Sigge as they went outside again, each with a slice of manchet bread, a hunk of cheese, and a cup of cold water, to watch all the activity. Dozens and dozens of men were scattered in this back area of the castle, setting up tents and small fire rings.

"The master has called for an Althing to be held here. Messengers have been sent to folks from all the jarldoms in Hordaland, inviting them to come for council." Sigge almost shivered with excitement.

"This is a big event, I take it. Is it a regular happening, or something special?"

"Something special, to be sure. Have you not heard that the pirate Brodir is still holding the master's sister, Disa, and he refuses to release her unless the master meets with him?" Sigge practically shivered as she spoke, as if it was all so exciting.

"No, I didn't know. I can see the dilemma he faces, though. It's never wise to negotiate with a terrorist, and I expect pirates would qualify as terrorists. On the other hand, it's his sister's life at stake. Why involve other Vikings in his decision, though?"

"Pirates have become an increasing problem for them all, and Brodir may be the needle that breaks the pustule."

Nice picture, she thought.

Having finished her breakfast, she dusted the crumbs off her apron and turned to Sigge. "Is there a room where seamstresses work? I need to find a way to make myself some underpants."

Sigge nodded slowly, probably not understanding what she meant by underpants.

"I find it really uncomfortable walking around in a gown with my bare butt uncovered. It was especially distasteful those few days I had my period and had to make do with a diaper kind of thing with rag strips. What do women do here?"

"Moss. There would not be enough rags for all women to use, even if they were washed out each time."

"Moss? Good Lord! You must all have green bottoms."

Sigge giggled. "You said something about underpants. What of the old ones who say a woman's inner parts need to breathe?"

"Hah! It was probably a man who said that."

"No doubt!" Sigge giggled some more.

"Seriously, women wear no undergarments?"

"Usually not, though women who need to go outside in the cold of winter, like dairymaids, put wool braies on under their gunnas."

"Well, you and I are going to have panties by the end of the day," Rita promised, looping her arm with Sigge's.

They arrived at one of the solars, a room off the great hall with slightly more light due to several glassless windows with the shutters open. It would be a useless room when the temperature dropped.

Eight women sat about sewing, including Lady Thora. While the others mended garments, Thora was stabbing her needle at a ring of tapestry.

The black looks she and Sigge got from all of them indicated how unwelcome they were. *So what!* she thought. Everyone had a job in this place. Today hers was to make panties.

"I need some scraps of material," she said. When no one spoke up, she helped herself to a dozen different pieces lying on the floor. Silk, soft wool, and linen. She also picked up a pair of shears, several needles, and some ribbons, even a strip of lace about a yard long.

"Come with me," she directed Sigge, whose face was red at the condemnation she saw in the other faces. They sat down at a bench at the far end in front of a low table. There was another ostracized woman there . . . the servant of Lady Disa, who had been doing all the sobbing and wailing yesterday. At least she had stopped hiccuping. She held a lady's gown in her lap and was repairing some embroidery along the edges.

Rita nodded at the woman and said, "Hi! I'm Rita, and this is my friend Sigge."

At first hesitant, then more forcefully, the woman said, "Me name is Sigvid." She shot the other women a "So there!" glare. It was an indication of how inwardly hysterical Rita was becoming that she actually likened the three of them to a society of Sneeches that before long would become the "in" Sneech group. Dr. Seuss, eat your heart out.

First Rita laid a square of blue linen on the table and cut a flat-topped vee out of either side so that it resembled a squat hourglass, which would be folded over and the crotch reinforced with several rectangular layers. Knowing she would have no elastic available, she figured she could punch holes in the four corners, which she would thread with ribbon and then tie high on the hips. The design wouldn't win any awards, but it should suffice.

"Sigge, you're shorter than I am but about the same size. Try this on before we do any finishing of the edges."

Without any embarrassment, Sigge raised her gown up to her waist. She, and all the women, watched with fascination as Rita fitted it on her, then tied the light blue linen with white ribbon bows on each hip.

Rita was pleased with her efforts, and she told Sigge to

take it off so that they could hem the edges. "You can keep that one," she told the young girl, whose eyes filled with such joy you would have thought she'd given her a pot of gold.

Next, Rita cut out red, black, and green silk, undyed muslin, and several colors of linen. The wool she would save for colder times . . . if she was still here then, she thought with a shudder. She also set out contrasting colors of ribbon and lace.

While she and Sigge worked, Rita talked softly to Sigvid, trying to find out exactly what had happened to Steven's sister.

"Truth to tell," Sigvid whispered to Rita, "the pirates ne'er attacked our longship. That *drukkinn* Captain Ulster . . . Ulster the Useless if ye ask me . . . caused the boat to capsize in a storm, and the pirates saved us. Of course they refused to return us to Norstead; so they *did* kidnap us."

Over the next few hours, Rita put together an impressive six pairs of panties for herself, a second for Sigge, and even one for the plump Sigvid, who protested that she really didn't want any but took it readily enough. The whole time, Rita plied Sigvid for information about her pirate adventure.

Turned out that the pirates rescued them but had no interest in doing any favors for Steven or anyone else at Norstead. They were a "fearsome" lot, according to Sigvid, except for the leader Brodir, who was golden-haired and beautiful as the god he was named for, Baldr, who was apparently the Norse god equivalent of Jesus to Christians.

Even more enlightening, Lady Disa and the pirate got great enjoyment over insulting each other. One verbal battle after another, Sigvid related.

It sounded to Rita like elementary school where boys and girls hit the person they liked. In other words, maybe Disa wasn't as unwilling a prisoner as her brother thought.

Why exactly Brodir was demanding a meeting with Steven before releasing Disa was unclear.

"Is there an attraction between Brodir and Disa? I mean, could it be that Brodir wants to marry Disa?" Rita had asked.

"Pfff! If that was all 'twas about, he would take the lady and be done with it. Pirates do not ask for permission."

Like Sigvid had all that much experience with pirates!

One clue Sigvid did give was a hint from Brodir that the reason for his being outlawed two years past was somehow connected with Thorfinn.

Rita should discuss this with Steven but decided not to seek him out. He would show up soon enough.

In the meantime, while Sigge went off to do her herb gardening, having nothing to do, and knowing Steven probably wouldn't appreciate her showing up on the archery fields, she gathered up some of the young children who had been annoying the men erecting the tents. She led them to a grassy meadow beyond the castle yards to tell them some stories.

First off, she tried interactive ones like "The Itsy Bitsy Spider," "Pat-a-Cake," "London Bridge Is Falling Down" which was coincidentally based on some Viking takeover of London, "Ring Around the Roses," and "Knick Knack Paddy Whack." After that, she convinced them to sit down around her for some quiet time, and she searched her brain for children's stories she might remember. Their favorites soon became "The Three Little Pigs," "Jack and Jill," "The Old Lady Who Lived in a Shoe," and "Humpty Dumpty," the last of which caused them to roll over with laughter. Like children everywhere, if they enjoyed something, they wanted it repeated over and over.

She was just finishing up another telling of "Red Riding Hood," where she described the wolf as looking a lot like Steven, and Red Riding Hood a lot like herself, when she glanced up and saw Steven leaning against a tree, staring at her. She couldn't tell by the expression on his face whether he was annoyed or amazed at her activity. Probably both.

"Go to your mothers," she directed the children, who groaned at their playtime being interrupted. "If you're good, I'll tell you some different stories tomorrow."

"Nay, the same ones," several of the children yelled.

Within moments, they had scattered like seeds on the wind.

Looking up at Steven, she sighed. "Okay, what did I do wrong now?"

Kiss me once, and kiss me twice, and kiss me once again . . .

Steven had left the keep in a rage when he had discovered Rita was missing, his first thought being that she had somehow popped herself back to the future. Not that he believed all that time-travel nonsense. Still, he had panicked with alarm when he had thought her gone.

First place he had searched was the area down by the fjord, figuring that if she came here from water, she would return the same way. No one working on the longboats had seen her.

But then he had discovered her here in the meadow, surrounded by little ones . . . one on her lap, two leaning on her shoulders, the others at her feet . . . and he could only stare. What was it about her that she could charm children as well as full-grown men?

"A wolf with black fur and silver gray eyes? Red Riding Hood of the short blonde hair?" he inquired as he sank down into the grass beside her.

"A good storyteller has to picture her different characters." Her face flushed prettily with embarrassment at being caught making mock of him.

"And now you are a storyteller, as well as a sea siren, soldier, and stunt person?" He picked a piece of grass from her hair and flicked it away.

"Don't be so picky. I was just telling the children stories I recall from when I was little. Is that a crime?"

"Nay, but telling all the women in my keep that they should wear chastity belts *is* creating turmoil amongst my men."

"Give me a break. I don't even know how a chastity belt works, let alone how to make one."

"You did tell them that they must cover their arses."

"I *never* told anyone else that they should wear panties. I just used some old scraps of cloth to make some for myself. Where I come from, women . . . men, too . . . wear undergarments. It's sanitary."

"Actually, I concur. Even the bed furs need airing out on occasion. A woman's pelt more so."

"That was crude, even for you." She shook her head at his hopelessness. "Are any of those children yours, by the way?"

His head shot up with horror. "Nay! I have no children."

"Kind of hard to carry on your lordly line without heirs, isn't it?"

"Lordly line?" He chuckled. "When the time comes, I will do my duty . . . reluctantly. I have seen firsthand, through my brother Finn, what having a babe . . . and losing it . . . does to a man's soul. I would as soon avoid that kind of attachment to another being."

"Well, that's a great way to live. Not! Besides that, you already care deeply about someone . . . your brother."

He nodded. "And his death has cut deeply."

"Good luck with the no babies rule. I assume you have normal male urges, and as far as I can tell, birth control doesn't exist at this time."

"Coitus interruptus."

"I beg your pardon?"

"I spill my speed outside the body to avoid planting my seed."

She began to laugh.

That irritated him. "What is so funny?"

"If you only knew how unreliable that method is!"

"Dost have an answer for every bloody thing in the world?" he griped. "Besides, I am in a rare good mood today." Leastways he was now that he had found her. "Do not spoil it for me with talk of babies."

He leaned back on his elbows and studied her. She was wearing Viking attire today . . . the red gunna covered by a blue, open-sided apron that was rumpled and grass-stained. Her face had a light golden color from the sun. And his heart was racing like a warhorse afore battle, just perusing her. "Show me," he urged in a voice husky with sudden lust, waving a hand toward her nether region.

"No way!"

"I will see eventually."

"I am not going to lift my gown and show you my panties, so just forget about it."

"As you say," he agreed . . . way too easily, if her suspicious eyes were any indication. "I will put aside my wish to see your pant-hes." *Believe that, and I have a fjord to sell you in the Arab lands.* "Still, you owe me a boon," he said, changing the subject. 'Twas always good to keep women on their toes, ne'er knowing what you would do next.

"For what?"

"Sleeping with you without tupping." *My ballocks are no doubt blue today from lack of release.*

"Jeesh! What am I? A barrel or a keg to be tupped?"

"'Tis just another word for—"

"I know what the word means. Anyhow, your restraint is admirable, but I wonder how you took my clothes off without touching me. Hmmm?"

"With great skill." *With great pleasure.*

"I am not showing you my panties in exchange for your not *tupping* me."

"Why so shy? You are not a virgin, are you?"

She made a tsking sound. "I'm twenty-eight years old, and I've been married."

That got his attention . . . and his anger. Steven did not have many scruples when it came to bedsport, but one hard-and-fast rule was not to stray onto another man's property. "You are married?"

"No, I'm not married. I *was* married. I divorced the jerk three years ago."

Divorce was rare, though not unheard of in Viking society. "You divorced him? On what grounds?"

"That he was a serial adulterer."

"Ah," he said. Infidelity was a hard nut to swallow for men as well as women. He waved a hand dismissively. "Back to your pant-he display. Not to worry. I had another boon in mind anyway."

"Why am I not surprised?" She arched her brows at him.

"A kiss." When she shook her head as if he were a hopeless lackwit, he added, "A mere kiss, that is all."

She snorted her opinion.

Did she not know that snorting was not an attractive female trait? Not that he was dumb enough to tell her.

"Steven, there is nothing *mere* about your kisses, and you know it."

Of course I know it. Did it not take me years to perfect my techniques? "Oh, really?"

"I'm still tingling from your last kiss, and—"

"You should not tell me such things. I will use it against you."

"You could try. I'm still determined not to be attracted to you, so keep your—"

Before she could finish her thought, he grabbed her by the waist, flipped her over onto her back, and was leaning over her with his lips nuzzling the curve of her neck. "You were saying?"

Instead of shoving him away, she arched her neck for his

better access and moaned, "I swear you are more tempting than a Krispy Kreme doughnut."

Steven had no idea what a dough-nut was, but the moan was what sealed her fate, as far as he was concerned. That, and the fact that she had arched her back up so that her breasts brushed against his chest. Even through their layers of clothing, the friction felt like wildfire igniting his senses.

He gritted his teeth at the sheer ecstasy, and his blue ballocks nigh burst with anticipation. He had not even kissed her yet, and he was as aroused as an untried youthling.

"Heed me well, wench," he advised, nipping at her bottom lip. "She who puts her head . . . or other body parts . . . in the wolf's teeth must proceed carefully."

Did she heed his warning? Nay, instead she used the tip of her pink tongue to lave his lips from side to side, bottom and top. "Kiss me, you tempting wolf," she ordered, her warm breath fanning his face.

He was about to protest that he was the one in charge here, but then he decided it did not matter. In truth, he liked her taking charge . . . in this matter, leastways.

At first, he just rubbed his lips against hers, shaping and adjusting to get the perfect fit. He could not help smiling as he did so because slowly, his long-dead senses were coming to life, which was a revelation to him. Oh, he had had his share of women during these dark years, before and after Thorfinn's disappearance. And he had enjoyed the bedplay immensely, but he realized now that parts of him had been uninvolved, parts that made even the merest lover's touch or merest kiss that much more pleasurable.

Which was untenable. An attraction this strong could be perilous. Whoever or whatever she was, Rita was passing by on her way to the gods only knew where. And a kiss did not a lover make.

"This should not be happening," she groaned.

Precisely! He raised his mouth to gaze down at her. As

he saw the sensuous flame in her blue eyes, and as there was a sudden tightness in his chest, he thought, *"Should not be happening"* be damned! "You are trembling."

She nodded. "I don't understand what's happening to me."

Steven decided understanding was overrated as he reclaimed her lips, this time with a searing hunger. Desire roared in his ears, and his blood thickened. And Rita . . . thank the heavens . . . was meeting his kisses with equal fervor.

Somehow he found himself atop her and was grinding his hips against her womanhood whilst plunging his tongue in and out of her mouth . . . Or was that her plunging her tongue in and out of his mouth? . . . when he heard something other than her soft mewling sounds of desire.

"Ahem!"

He levered himself up on straightened arms and at first was not able to see through the haze of his erotic enthusiasm. When he was able to focus, he saw Oslac standing with hands on hips and a smirk on his face. Steven snarled, "There best be a good reason for your interruption."

"There is, m'lord," Oslac said, the *m'lord* an indication that he was enjoying his discomfort. "Didst settle the chastity belt issue?"

"Not yet. I give you to the count of three to give me one good reason for this interruption."

"Someone ought to put a chastity belt on you Viking men," Rita remarked to Oslac. "That, I would be willing to work on."

"It would have to be a really big belt." Oslac winked at Rita, then turned back to Steven. "Brodir has sent another messenger. He wants to attend the Althing."

Steven shot to his feet, a remarkable feat, considering the state of his remaining half erection. "He dares to suggest such! I swear the man is looking to die."

"Uh, I think I might have something to add to this conversation," Rita said, rising to stand in front of them and giving them both a little wave to garner attention.

"What?" both he and Oslac exclaimed with exasperation, not appreciating the interruption.

"You don't have to yell." She was dusting specks of grass off her rump, which disconcerted him, but only for a moment. "This is man business, Ree-tah. Go back to the keep."

She bristled at his order. "Sure thing, your lordliness."

Then she began to stomp away. Over her shoulder she added, "I might have some information regarding Brodir, but, hey, I'm only a simpleminded woman. Why should you listen to little ol' me? What do I know?"

He and Oslac looked at each other.

"It appears as if big ol' me is going to listen to little ol' her."

Chapter 9

If women ruled the world . . .

As she walked back to the castle between Steven and Oslac, Rita, still reeling under the impact of her almost-lovemaking with Steven, explained everything that Sigvid had told her, ending with her own personal opinion, "I think you could settle the whole problem by letting Brodir marry your sister."

Oslac gasped, and Steven's face turned red.

At first Steven appeared too stunned to speak. When he did, it was in an even, extra-calm voice. "Go. Away."

"Huh?" *Is this steely faced man the same one who was making sweet love to me a short time ago? Talk about morphing from Jekyll to Hyde!*

"That is the most lackbrained idea I have e'er heard. You best go back to the keep and do woman things, because clearly you know naught of the workings of fighting men."

Yep. Definitely split personality, Mr. Hyde.

"I told you that you should just drop her off a cliff," Oslac inserted.

Now it was her turn to go red in the face. "It's true, I've only been in military training for a year, but every good soldier knows that in the most successful battle no lives are lost."

"Is that female illogic or time traveler illogic?" Steven ridiculed.

Oslac was grinning as if Steven had told a great joke.

She'd like to bop them both over the head with a brick to knock some sense into their thick skulls. "Listen, isn't it better to prevent a war, instead of waging one without proper planning?"

"And who says there has been no proper planning?" Oslac demanded to know.

"Brodir has been a plague on my house for years now. I think I know better than you what needs to be done," Steven explained with obvious reluctance.

"Not if you don't have all the facts."

Steven gritted his teeth before speaking. "I am a fair-minded man. Speak your piece, then leave us to men's work."

She swore under her breath but tried her best. "Sigvid says that your brother Thorfinn and Brodir were good friends at one time."

"That is so."

"Whatever grievance he has against your family started about the time your brother disappeared, right?"

Steven nodded, unsure where she was going with this line of questioning.

"Why was he outlawed? What made him turn pirate? Why do you hate him so?"

"I do not hate him. He is a *nithing*, a worthless man."

"Why is that?"

"Because of all the despicable things he has done," Oslac answered for Steven.

"For one thing, he attacked a nunnery, where he and his men raped and pillaged at will," Steven added.

"You know that for certain?"

"What? Why would you ask that?" Steven was not happy with her query.

"Because so many times wars or battles or feuds are carried out based on misinformation. Sometimes the two sides just need to sit down and air their grievances. If women ran the world, believe me, there would be more peace."

"If women ran the world, men would all move to Valhalla," Oslac quipped.

"So, you think I should meet with this miscreant?" Steven asked.

"Yes, I do. And maybe you should think about going into such a meeting with an open mind."

"Do not give offense when you know not all the facts."

"I apologize, but maybe you don't have all the facts, either."

He gritted his teeth. "And what has all this to do with marriage betwixt Brodir and my sister Disa, anyway?"

"Sigvid thinks they're attracted to each other." Well, she hadn't actually said that. In fact, she'd said that they insulted each other constantly. It was Rita who was putting a romantic cast on their squabbling.

"And attraction is enough to warrant wedlock?" Oslac hooted with laughter.

"Oslac is right. Marriages are arranged for many reasons, none of which is attraction." This was Steven's ridiculous assertion.

"What about love?" She couldn't believe she'd asked that corny question.

"Love! Love is just a honey-coated word women use to cover lust." Steven actually looked as if he believed his words. Yeah, her question had been hokey, but his response was almost insulting . . . to women anyhow.

"My marriage was a good example," Oslac added. "A finer, more biddable woman there ever was in Girda, but once the vows were scarce spoken, she turned into the Lo-

ki's favorite shrew. Thank the gods she is no longer with
us. Otherwise, I might have killed her myself."

"That observation added nothing to this conversation,"
Rita said. "And, frankly, it's not nice to speak ill of the
dead."

"In Oslac's defense," Steven said, "I must say that Girda
was more than nagsome. She nigh begged to have her
tongue slit to stop her incessant criticisms, just as Boris the
Braggart did with his wife."

Rita tried to steer the conversation back to the subject at
hand. "The proposed meeting with Brodir?"

"There will be no meeting . . . lest the Althing elders
deem otherwise," Steven decided.

"We are warriors. We know best how to handle pirates,"
Oslac proclaimed.

"And unruly, overopinionated ladies," Steven added,
smiling and waggling his eyebrows at her, as if a smile was
going to turn her all warm and cuddly again.

"You two boneheads would be good candidates for the
Moron Hall of Fame."

You could say it was a golden thong . . .

She was wearing a chastity belt. *A chastity belt*, for the
love of Frey!

After removing his clothing and flipping the blanket off
of Rita, who was attempting to ignore his arrival in the
bedchamber by staring at the far wall, Steven stared down
at the wench with disbelief. Over the yellow silk pant-
hes . . . which he, incidentally, liked very much . . . she had
wrapped one of Thorfinn's long chain-link belts around her
waist and down through her female channel, twice over,
with a small link at the end welded together.

"You best be the only woman in this keep wearing one
of those things," he warned her.

"I am."

I have an erection that could spear a stone, but not a metal chain. This is ridiculous. "My blacksmith needs a good talking to."

"Don't blame him. I kind of tricked him into doing it."

He did not want to know how. It would no doubt make him angrier than he already was. "I am not going to sleep next to a woman wearing a chain up her arse."

"It's not up my ass. Just along my bottom, like a thong."

Same thing. "It looks uncomfortable."

"It is, but if it keeps the wolf away . . ." She shrugged.

"If I wanted to swive you, no chain would stop me," he declared as he studied the situation. "How am I supposed to sleep next to someone wearing cold chains? I could get a chill."

"Well, you could always sleep in your own bed." She rolled over to look at him. "Oh, good Lord! You're naked."

"Of course I am naked. 'Tis time for bed."

"Well, don't think you're prodding me with that thing in this bed." She squeezed her eyes shut tight so she would not have to look at him.

He was fairly certain she was tempted by his manly enthusiasm. Shifting some more from hip to hip, waiting for her to give in, he said, "Dost think you can hide anything from me in that little *shert*?"

"This is one of Luta's night rails, according to Sigge. I cut it into a sleep shirt. Any objections?"

"Yea, I object. Take it off. And the chastity belt, too."

"No."

"You were willing enough to be with me this afternoon."

"That was before you turned into a jerk and told me to go away."

"I can see your nipples."

Her eyes shot open, and she glanced down her body. Immediately, her face heated with color.

"Must be some part of you likes my enthusiasm."

She looked at him again. "Oh, my God! You're even bigger. Go take a cold bath or something."

He blew out the candle on the bedside table, slid into the bed beside her, and pulled the cover up over them both. "Do not worry, m'lady, I will take care of the matter myself." Then he proceeded to make some lackwit whispering sounds.

There was silence for a moment before she burst out, "Don't you dare!"

"What?" he inquired sweetly. "I was just talking some sense into my cock. What did you think I was doing?"

"I swear, I don't know what I did to deserve this. Either God decided time travel back to you was to be my punishment for some past sin, or else he has a great sense of humor."

"Methinks both God and Odin enjoy a good joke. Yea, they are no doubt up in heaven, or Asgard, sharing a horn of ale, and laughing at us."

"I wasn't serious."

"Are you looking cross-eyed?"

"How did you know?"

"Every time you lose an argument with me, you cross your eyes with frustration. 'Tis rather adorable."

She made a growling sound.

"Hey, I thought I was supposed to be the wolf. I must tell you, I do not look good in red. Nor do I have a hooded mantle. Plus, I have big teeth. Do you want to see?"

"I can't hear you," she said, putting her hands to her ears.

Steven smiled to himself and shifted his body to get more comfortable. With his hands folded behind his head, he prepared to fall asleep. "Good night."

"Yeah. Sweet dreams to you, too."

Just before he fell asleep, he said, "Oh, by the by, I have decided to meet with Brodir afore the Althing."

Rita jerked to a sitting position. "What did you say?"

He pretended to be asleep. In fact, he let out a little snore. Betimes a man had to get the last word in any way he could.

Witching is in the eye of the beholder . . .

In her long list of "What was I thinking?" Rita added "visiting a witches' lair," right below "marrying a serial adulterer," "agreeing to wrestle an alligator," and "joining the female SEALs."

Lordy! She'd thought she was in good shape, but several days later, trekking uphill through a thick forest in badly fitting boots, always on the lookout for wild boars or other medieval creatures, for the past two hours had been insanity. And all this punishment was so that she could meet two old biddies who claimed to be witches . . . witches with a special message for her, according to Sigge.

Surprisingly, Sigge, who wouldn't know an inclined sit-up from a mile run, wasn't out of breath at all. In fact, she kept skipping ahead, then coming back for Rita to catch up.

It must be the altitude, Rita decided. It couldn't be the ten-year difference in their ages.

"I thought you said it was only a short distance from the castle," she huffed out.

"'Tis up ahead. Smell the air."

She sniffed. Yep. Woodsmoke. Of course, her next thought was, *What are they cooking? Eye of newt? What is a newt, anyway? Pigeon tongues? Human hair? Animal blood? Body parts?*

Letting her imagination run away with her wasn't helping anything. Besides, they'd reached the edge of a clearing, where she found not the hovel she'd expected, but . . . oh, my God! There stood a Hansel and Gretel cottage. It didn't have gingerbread or a candy roof or sides, but it was

neat as a pin with a red stain to the log sides, green shutters, and a yellow thatched roof through which a stream of
smoke reached up to the sky through a crude stack. In the
clearing, there was a small vegetable and herb garden, a
chicken coop, one cow grazing on whatever grass it could
find among the trees, some animal skins stretched onto a
wood frame, and, of course, a black cat.

On closer inspection, she saw all the woo-woo signs.
Runic symbols carved around the front door, windows,
and eaves. Colored stones on long strings hung from limbs
of trees, along with miniature leather bags bulging with
things she chose not to discover. The world's largest spi-
derweb was in a place of prominence between the stripped
lower trunks of two tall evergreen trees . . . at least fifteen
feet in diameter. Charlotte would be so proud! On a bench
in front of the cottage sat a wooden box heaped with what
were either dead bats or mice or birds. Maybe all three.
Yeech!

The biggest surprise came when the twin witch aunts
emerged from the cottage to welcome them. Their gray
hair was pulled back off their wrinkled faces and braided
into coronets covered by white caps, sort of like the Amish
wore with loose laces on either side. Maybe they saved their
pointed witch hats for special occasions, like when they
flew about on their brooms. And, yes, that was a broom
propped against the side of the cottage. Their matching
gowns—one blue, one green—were covered by pristine
white Viking aprons. After they'd exchanged greetings,
Sigge explained that Grima always wore blue and Kraka
green to distinguish themselves . . . when they wanted to
be distinguished, that was.

Rita shook her head with continuing amazement. "You
don't look at all like witches now."

"They need to play a role when they go down to the
castle," Sigge explained. "Dost think anyone would take
their witchly arts seriously looking like old grannies?"

Rita wasn't so sure they took them seriously, even with the screeching and cackling and scary appearance.

"Come inside, dearling," Grima said to her. "We will have a warm drink afore showing you around."

I should probably take only a sip until I find out what it is. Could be poison. Could be I'll wake in an oven. Could be . . . oh, good Lord, get a grip, Rita.

Kraka shivered with apparent excitement. "We are so happy you finally came. We have been doing the rituals for you ever so long."

For me? Come on!

"Now, Kraka, 'tis only been six months since we started," Grima corrected her sister. "Astral projections take time."

Astral projections? They think the stars shot me here? She considered the idea for a moment. *Hey, that's as good an explanation as any I've come up with so far.*

"That they do. That they do," Kraka agreed, then confided to Rita in a loud whisper, "I feared you would be channeled to us in some other life-form."

"Like a cat?" Rita laughed.

Sigge giggled. "I swear Aunt Kraka has been checking all the chickens and birds whilst Aunt Grima has taken to eyeing trees and bushes in a certain way."

"Tsk-tsk!" both aunts chided Sigge.

"She is jesting," Kraka said with a loving smile at her niece. "We knew you would come in human form."

"But I had not expected you to be so beautiful," Grima remarked.

"Now, Grima, you know she has to be beautiful to lure Jarl Steven and fulfill the prophecy," Kraka said.

Lure? What lure?

"The hair might be a problem," Grima said to Kraka, who nodded, both of them looking at her short hair curiously.

"Wouldst like to have long hair?" Kraka asked her.

"Someday, I suppose."

"Nay, we mean now," Kraka elaborated.

"Instant long hair." She laughed, but no one laughed with her. She could only imagine Steven's reaction if she arrived back at Norstead with hair down to her butt. He would really think she was an alien creature, not that he didn't already think that. "No, I think I'll go with short hair for now." She feathered her sweat-dampened hair nervously, wary that they might grow it long without her permission. And God only knew what form it would take. Curly, straight, corkscrews, a different color?

"I expect she can lure the master without long hair," Sigge offered. "He is already half-smitten."

If smitten means horny, you've got it in one. And I've gotta admit, I'm a bit smitten myself.

Both Kraka and Grima stared at her expectantly. Then Kraka took her hand and led her into the cottage. Behind her, Rita heard Grima ask Sigge, "Have you been practicing your seer trancing?"

"I have, and I even heard the speaking trees one time, but I still cannot levitate."

"Now, now, child. It takes time," Grima told her niece.

Inside the cottage, there was a cozy atmosphere. Sort of.

A cauldron bubbled over the fire in a large hearth. Rita wondered if it might be some odd witchly brew, but it smelled more like chicken soup. The fireplace surround had more runic symbols, and there were rune stones heaped in several baskets around the room. Wide benches, like low, shallow platforms, lined two walls, which Rita presumed were used for sitting during the day and for sleeping at night, as they were in the castle great hall. In front of one of the benches were a table and two chairs, all very rustic and unpainted. Bunches of herbs hung from the ceiling rafters to dry, resulting in pungent but not unpleasant scents.

Seeing her staring at a pile of ropes cut to various

lengths with odd knots and a large number of candles, Sigge explained. "They are used for casting circles when performing a spell or a meeting of the coven."

Coven? Oh, boy! That means there are more witches.

Rita and Sigge slid onto the bench behind the table while the two sisters bustled about. "Would you like a soothing herb drink or a bowl of chicken broth?"

Rita figured she was safer with the chicken broth and said so. While a sort of green tea was poured into small wooden cups for Sigge, Kraka, and Grima, a wooden bowl and wooden spoon were placed in front of Rita. In the bowl was a hearty broth containing small slivers of what she hoped was chicken, leaves of parsley, bits of onion, and tiny carrots.

Rita was about to pick up her spoon when Sigge elbowed her to indicate she must wait. The three women linked hands and bowed their heads, chanting in some strange language. Occasionally, Rita recognized a word and figured this was just some Norse variation on saying grace.

When they were done, Rita dipped her spoon into the broth, took a sip from her spoon, then another. "This is really good."

The ladies smiled at her, recognizing that she'd been expecting just the opposite.

"What's in it?" she asked Kraka.

"That tough old rooster Harry; some wild garlic, onion, and mushrooms; carrots from my garden; parsley; and various herbs."

"Have you ever put spaetzles in?" During the on-again, off-again periods of her mother's debilitating depression after her father's departure for greener fields, as in younger, more voluptuous women, Rita had become quite a good cook, even as a child. Oh, nothing gourmet. Mostly nourishing soups, which were cheap and hearty.

The sisters stared at her with interest.

"Do you have flour and eggs?"

"Yea," Kraka said. "Oat flour and fresh eggs."

"Well, I suppose oat flour would do. You just mix a beaten egg with enough flour to be the consistency of wet dough . . . not dry enough for bread or noodles."

They didn't seem to understand what she was saying.

"Would you like me to show you?"

They nodded, trusting souls that they were, and Rita was soon dropping little dough balls the size of dimes into the bubbling broth, where they doubled in size. A short time later, all of them took small amounts in their bowls for testing.

"This is wonderful," Kraka declared, apparently as surprised at her cooking skills as she had been at theirs.

"What did you call them?" Grima wanted to know. "Spit-cells?"

Rita laughed. "Close enough."

"Tell us about yourself," Kraka encouraged.

Rita told them her life story, starting with her early years with a mother devastated over a divorce, her various occupations, and why she'd joined WEALS.

They listened attentively, but she could tell they didn't understand. How could they?

"The thing is, and I know you will find this hard to believe, but I come from the year two thousand and ten."

Rita expected scoffs of disbelief, but the two witches, instead, looked at each other and smiled.

"It worked!" Sigge beamed at her aunts. "You actually managed to channel a person through time to help us at Norstead."

Kraka and Grima nodded their heads and gave each other a medieval version of high fives, clapping both palms against each other.

"Uh, you're supposed to say there's no such thing as time travel," Rita pointed out.

Kraka shrugged her shoulders. "Who is to say what is possible when the gods are involved?"

"So now the gods brought me here? I thought witches were supposed to be pagans. Good heavens! You're not Satan worshippers, are you?" That's all she would need, the devil being involved in her life.

Grima stiffened with affront. "We have naught to do with Lucifer and his minions." She pointed to the amulets around her and her sister's necks, as well as the birthmark on Sigge's neck. "Notice that the pentacle stands upright, the point of one star northernmost. In evil witches and those who worship the fallen angel, there are two points of the star northernmost, and the single point aimed downward."

Kraka reached across the table and patted Rita's hand. "You are forgiven for misreading us, child. Many people make the same mistake."

"Betimes I overreact," Grima said, no longer insulted.

"Truth to tell," Sigge elaborated, "we consider ourselves Christian Norse witches."

There had to be at least two oxymorons in there.

"Many of the old witches were pagan, before the Druids and wizards wielded magic and such," Kraka explained. "And we do give homage to the Norse goddess Asatru, as well as the Christian One-God. In fact, 'tis our belief that many of the Norse and Christian gods are one and the same."

"Okay, now that's a stretch." Rita folded her arms over her chest and stared at each of them in turn. "Let's start over here. You say that I time-traveled here by some astral projection. Why?"

"Because you are needed to bring light where there has been darkness." Kraka stared at her hopefully, wanting Rita to accept what she was saying.

Rita rolled her eyes.

Sigge put her arm over Rita's shoulder and squeezed.

"I was but a child when the pall first came to settle over Norstead."

Kraka nodded with sadness wrinkling her face more than usual. "First, the jarl Eric and his wife died. Then their son Jorund's wife and two twin daughters died. One by one, the sons and their children left Norstead, never to be heard of again, except for Katla, who married a prince of Norsemandy. Katla had many children, including the younger sons Thorfinn and Steven."

"Everyone thought the dark pall would lift when Thorfinn wed and bred a babe on his wife, Luta," Grima interrupted her sister. "But Luta was ne'er happy here, and she ran away with a passing trader, taking the babe, the light of Thorfinn's life. Neither was ever found and were presumed dead."

"I was old enough to understand then," Sigge said, shaking her head dolefully. "Those were the darkest times when Jarl Thorfinn raged and wept, then searched and searched in vain for his lost son. His wife he cared not a whit for, but the babe was his reason for living. Then he, too, was killed, and Steven became jarl."

Well, not quite killed.

"Still the pall lingers," Kraka concluded. "Can you not see why Norstead needs a light to lead the master and his followers to a new and better life?"

"Yes, I can see that, but the light is not me."

The three women just stared at her, as if she was too thickheaded to understand.

"Hey, I just thought of something. If you guys are responsible for getting me here, can you send me back?"

"Why would you want to go back?" Sigge asked.

"Um, for starters, cars, airplanes, telephones, toilet paper, tampons, indoor plumbing, electricity, computers." She saw that her words meant nothing to these ladies, so she tried a different tack. "Listen, I'm just an ordinary lady, both in appearance and background. Yeah, I've had some far-out jobs, but still I'm nothing special. Certainly not some character destined to change history in a medieval Viking fortress." She smiled at them.

No one smiled in return.

"When we did the circle spells exhorting a champion for Norstead, we did not know what to expect," Kraka related. "Male or female, it mattered not to us, though a female would do the most good. We expected to conjure a person of our time to come to Norstead. Mayhap from another country, but ne'er did we expect a time traveler. Not that we are not pleased by the notion. Truly, our names will go down in the sagas as the greatest witches ever known."

"What is it you're trying to say?"

"My sister is trying to say that we could do another circle spell trying to send you back," Grima explained, "but we could not guarantee where it would send you. Back to Roman times? For all we know, you could land in a gladiator ring with the lions."

"Only if Russell Crowe is there to protect me." *Jeesh! My brain is splintering apart here if I can joke about being in a confined space with hungry lions.*

"A crow to protect you? What crow?" Sigge wanted to know.

But Grima was on a roll. "Or you might project forward two years or two decades or two centuries. I doubt we have the skills to control the process to that extent."

"How about if you did this circle thingee near the spot where I arrived here, by the joining of the North Sea with Ericsfjord?"

Kraka shrugged and looked to her sister, who also shrugged.

"This is just peachy," she concluded. "I've heard of 'lost in space' but 'lost in time'? Okay, here's another thought. Suppose I reconcile myself to being stuck here. No, no, don't get bent out of shape over my choice of words. If I'm not able to leave this time period, how can I be sure

I wouldn't suddenly bop back one day? That's a question Steven put to me, by the way."

"The master wanted to know if you would stay?" Sigge asked with a hopeful smile at her aunts.

"That's not what I meant," she tried to say.

But Grima was already answering her question. "I do not think it happens that way. I believe there would have to be a concerted effort on your part, or ours, or both, to send you away."

With that grim news, Rita settled into a silent snit and spent the rest of the afternoon in a tour of the witches' retreat. First, there were the talking trees, which were, not surprisingly, silent in her presence, but Grima claimed were nigh singing a welcome to her. *Okaaay!* Next, they walked a short distance to an eerie cave where many of the ingredients for their potions could be found. *Think bats.* The cave was also a cool place for storing perishable food products. The stream's bed contained many oddly colored and shaped stones . . . tears of the goddesses, she was told. Giving equal opportunity to the Christian religion, Kraka pointed out the dogwood trees . . . supposedly the wood used to build Christ's cross . . . on which drops of blood could be seen on the cross-shaped flowers. The streambed also offered an unending supply of leeches. *Yeech!*

Then there was the seeing pool, where Kraka and Grima claimed they could see the future amongst the ripples. All Rita saw was water, clear and cool, which she cupped into her hands and drank greedily, only to glance up and see the others staring at her in horror. "What? Is it poison or something?"

"Not poison. Just another sign," Sigge told her.

"A sign of what?"

"A sign that you are the one."

She groaned. "Not that again."

"Only the chosen drink from the well of knowledge."
Grima beamed at her.

Rita hated to break the news, but she didn't feel any
smarter or chosen. In fact, all she felt was really, really hot,
baking in the summer sun. "I'll tell you one thing. If I'm
stuck here, I'm going to invent deodorant." At the sisters'
urging, she explained.

"You think people here smell? Dost not know how
fastidious the Vikings are about cleanliness? They bathe
every Saturday night." Kraka was personally affronted,
Rita could tell.

"You . . . anyone . . . could shower . . . or bathe . . . every
day, but the normal person perspires in the heat or from
physical labor. Sweat is a fact of life, but deodorant is a
necessity."

"And body odor is a bad thing?" Grima asked.

"Are you kidding? BO is a major pee-you." She pinched
her nose with a thumb and forefinger. "Although I guess
you could get accustomed to it."

The three women were skeptical but encouraged her
to experiment if she wanted. The sisters took her to their
herb garden and loaded her up with sage, lavender, and
thyme, along with various oils, rose petals, pine needles
and cones. They even took her to a witch hazel tree . . .
yes, there really was a tree with that name . . . where she
obtained leaves, bark, and roots. She was pretty sure witch
hazel was an ingredient in some homeopathic remedies.

By the end of the day, Rita's head was buzzing with all
that she had seen and heard that day. All she could think
about was Steven and how she wanted to be back at the
castle to discuss all these alarming ideas with him. Why,
she wasn't sure. He probably had no better idea than she
did on how she could escape from this time warp. Still, she
was convinced her being here was linked to him.

Unfortunately, it was evening before she got back to

Norstead. Muddy, sweaty, and bone-tired, she wanted nothing more than to sink down into a bed and sleep for a week. Maybe when she woke up, the nightmare would be over. But she couldn't go to bed as filthy as she was, so she headed for the woman's bathhouse, which would surely be empty this time of night. She asked Sigge to find her a clean garment.

She was already washed when Sigge returned carrying a plain, well-worn muslin gown, the type that would be worn by a servant, or maybe it was a nightgown. No matter! Even if she had to put it on over the same panties and wear boots with no socks or stockings, she was at least clean.

"I am returning to my aunts' house for a few days," Sigge told her.

"Huh? Tonight?"

Sigge nodded. "I must needs help them prepare goods to sell in their tent at the Althing. Will you be all right without me for a few days?"

Rita had to smile at that. Hadn't she been on her own for the most part all her life? "Sure."

"M'lady, I must forewarn you. I passed Elof on his way to the garderobe. He told me the master was in a fury over your disappearance. Did you not tell him where you were going?"

"Ooops!" Technically, she owed nothing to Steven, but she supposed it would have been polite to tell him where she was going. Truthfully, though, she had expected to be gone only a few hours.

"The master thinks you have gone back to . . . to wherever you came from."

So it was with trepidation that she walked through the mostly quiet keep, approaching her bedchamber. The few people she passed, men dicing or sitting about drinking ale, stared at her in the oddest way. Geirfinn shook his head at her, as if he pitied her.

Rita wasn't afraid. Fear had never played a big part in

her life. Danger was just another name for obstacles to be mastered.

Still, with a sense of foreboding, the fine hairs stood out on the back of her neck. She knew . . . she just knew . . . she was about to be thrust headlong into another major turning point in her life. As if time travel wasn't enough!

Chapter 10

Should he wring her neck or swive her silly? . . .

Steven's moods swung from hurt to rage like a pendulum, and it had been the same way since early this afternoon when he had discovered that Rita was missing, and no one knew where she had gone.

"Bloody damn woman. I should have lopped off her head when I first saw her in a fish garment.

"But she makes me smile.

"Hah! I could bring a jester to Norstead, if humor is what I want.

"I am bored, and she is . . . was different.

"What about her connection to Thorfinn?

"Bloody damn woman!"

Suddenly he realized that he was talking to himself! Son of a troll! Pitiful, that is what he was. Mooning over a fish woman who might or might not be from the future.

He had searched the keep and immediate surroundings, to no avail. When asked if he wanted troops to ride to the far reaches of his estate, even onto Amberstead, he had snarled, "Search be damned! If the woman wants to be gone so bad, then so be it!"

Still, the emptiness crushed him. How could that be? Over a woman he had known only a few weeks? One who was bizarre to say the least?

He now knew how Thorfinn must have felt when he lost his precious babe. Not that Rita was precious to him, but he suspected she could have been, given time. And that was untenable. No person, especially not a mere woman, would ever dig their claws into his heart. He was not like his brother. Yea, best that she was gone.

On the other hand, his people at Norstead believed that Rita was some kind of light . . . well, they would just have to look for another flame to burn off his blues. That is what the wench had accused him of . . . having the blues. Well, now he *really* had the blues. And it was all her fault.

Worse, he no longer had the leverage of a hostage exchange with Brodir . . . Rita for Disa . . . which he had promised his hersirs that he would at least consider. Another reason why it was good that she was gone.

The humiliation was something else. He would have to live with the rumors for days, even unto the Althing, where men from far and wide would be hearing about the sea woman who had come to Norstead and left, rejecting its master.

Tonight, after trying to get *drukkinn* on ale and mead, and only succeeding in turning bitter and foul-tempered, Oslac had suggested he go sleep afore he found himself in the midst of a brawl of his own creation. Steven had actually liked the sound of that. Hitting something would have its own rewards.

Finding another woman to share his bed furs was not even a possibility for him in his present frame of mind. In truth, his stomach roiled biliously at the idea.

But he had taken Oslac's advice nonetheless. To bed he had gone . . . hours ago.

Sitting on the side of the bed, elbows on knees, chin braced in his hands, he pondered his dismal state. Mayhap he needed to marry, after all. Mayhap King Olaf's daughter wouldn't be so bad, especially if he taught her to hold her tongue on occasion. Isrid did not strike him as a woman with wanton ways. In fact, she'd nigh bolted any time he got close to her. He could tell her that excess talking caused excess lust in men, that he would want to tup day and night. That should shut her up. And she *was* beautiful. They would make beautiful children. *Oh, gods! I think I am going to hurl the contents of my stomach.*

He heard someone in the hall. Without raising his head, he turned to the right and watched as the door handle turned. If it was Oslac come to offer him more lectures, he might very well have to dump his good friend off the nearest parapet.

But it was not Oslac.

It was the source of all his misery. Or latest misery. Rita.

"You!" he accused as he jumped to his feet and glared at her.

She closed the door quietly behind her, big as you please, as if she were not in so much trouble she ought to be shaking in her . . . yea, she was wearing boots with a night rail and carrying a large cloth bag. Her short hair was wet and spiky. *While I sat here stewing, she took the time to bathe?* Mayhap he should drop her *and* Oslac off the nearest parapet. "I thought you were gone."

"I can explain."

"I doubt that."

"I went—"

He raised a halting hand as his heart began to race so fast he could scarce breathe. In fact, he began to pant, trying to get more air into his lungs. Was he going to choke to death now? Would it be the ignominious straw death for this warrior . . . to die in his own bed straw?

"You're hyperventilating. Sit down on the bed and put your face between your knees," she advised, shoving him to sit back down on the edge of the bed and pushing his neck down betwixt his thighs.

Caught off balance and surprised by her reappearance, he had allowed her to shove him, but now he was back in control, and his panting had slowed to a regular inhale and exhale. He raised his head. "I was not high-pair anything. I am just so bloody furious I fear what I might do to you."

"I have a perfectly good explanation," she said, backing away from him as he stood. Smart wench!

But, instead of advancing on her, as she had expected, he began to remove his clothing, one item at a time.

"Wha-what are you doing?"

"Preparing to have sex with you." *And it is the best idea I have had in months, mayhap years.*

"Wh-why?"

"Why? Are you daft, woman? Because I want to." *So much you would be shocked.*

"Well, sex . . . making love . . . should be a two-way affair, don't you think?"

He waved a hand airily. "When I thought you were gone, the thing I regretted most was that I never tupped you."

"I hate that word."

"Tup, tup, tup." *Wouldst rather I said fuck?*

"That was immature."

"Therefore, I intend to swive you so many ways you will lose count. I am going to bring you to peak a dozen times, then start over again. When I am done with you, you will scarce be able to stand on buttery legs. So, I will lift you onto my lap and spank your arse for putting me through what you have today." *Good gods and goddesses, that sounds good even to me.*

"Wow!"

He was not sure if wow was good or bad. No matter!

He was nude now, and his enthusiasm stood out from his body like a brainless flagpole. He would be embarrassed at its larger-than-usual size if he were not so brain-melting excited by the woman before him . . . the woman who was studying his manpart with arched eyebrows. "A blue steeler? For me?"

He almost choked on his tongue, so surprised was he by her observation. Blue veins. Steely rod. "Take off the sleep rail."

"Shouldn't we talk first?"

"We most definitely should not talk first." *If I wanted talk, I would have wed Isrid long ago.*

Still leaning against the door, she dropped her bag and began to raise the hem of her night rail, but he was too impatient. He grabbed the neckline of the gown and ripped downward until her entire body was exposed. Without hesitation, she arched her shoulders until the gown fell from her shoulders to puddle at her feet.

"Merciful heavens!" he murmured, one of his mother's favorite expressions. How he could think of his mother at a time like this was indicative of his crumbling mind.

She stood staring at him, her breasts high and full and already rose-tipped with arousal. Down below she wore the infamous pant-hes . . . a scant garment of red silk trimmed in black lace.

"Merciful heavens!" he murmured again. For the first time, he smiled. "I give you permission to make as many of those silk chastity belts as you wish, but for now . . ." He reached down and untied the bows at either hip.

Forget about choking on his tongue; he almost swallowed it this time as he beheld the wench's latest surprise. She had no nether hair on her mons, just a slight blonde fuzz, like a peach. Pointing, he asked, "What is that?"

The wench had the nerve to grin at him. "It's a Brazilian wax. Lots of women remove body hair in my time. The last time I had it done was weeks ago, so it's already starting to grow back." Her rambling explanation told him loud and clear that she was as nervous as he was.

The question was, why? Nay, the better question was: What have I done lately to get me in such good odor with the gods? "Why?"

She shrugged.

And didn't she look ridiculous and adorable at the same time, propped against the door, nude as a newborn . . . in all ways . . . except for a pair of boots? Boots, for the love of Frigg! "Cleanliness. Appearance." She grinned some more. "And some people claim it makes sex more intense."

That got his attention. *More intense sex?* He studied that part of her anatomy by tilting his head this way and that, trying to figure how it would work to their advantage. Once he understood, he grinned back at her.

"Of course, I wouldn't know for sure about the more intense sex, since I haven't had sex since I got my first wax two years ago."

"Two years?" he sputtered, lifting her in his arms, one hand at her nape, the other cupping one cheek of her buttocks. *Thank you, God or Odin, whoever is responsible for this gift.* Immediately, she looped her arms around his neck. As she raised her legs to straddle his hips, he heard the boots drop behind him. "Oh, Ree-tah, we are going to be so good together."

"Ya think?" She nuzzled his neck, which caused her breasts to brush across his chest, which caused his cock to stand even taller.

"I am still angry with you," he told her.

"I'll make it up to you."

Before he could ask her how or tell her not to bother, she arched her hips and pushed forward, taking him inside her tight sheath. Once he managed to still the roaring in his ears, he asked, "What do you think you are doing?"

"Swiving you."

I swear, this woman is like none other in the world.

What did I do to deserve this? "You? Swiving me? It is supposed to be the other way around." He was only halfway teasing.

"Ooops. Should I push you out?"

"Do not dare!"

He glanced downward and saw that his cock was imbedded only halfway inside her female channel. He was a big man and ofttimes needed a different angle. Bending his knees a bit, he put his hands on her buttocks and arched her outward. With shallow thrusts in her hot, moist channel, already spasming toward a first peak, he finally worked himself all the way in. Only then did he look upward and see her lips parted and her eyes, darkened like the bluest sapphires, betraying her ardor. Was there anything better to whet a man's appetite than seeing his woman's pleasure?

The only thing she said was, "Gaaaaaa!"

He was fairly certain that was a signal he was doing something right.

"We should slow down," he murmured against her ear. "This first time should be a savoring. It should—"

"Shut up and move," she grunted out.

Who knew a grunt could be so sexy? A chuckle came out of his mouth as a choking sound.

Then, to his great surprise, especially at her strength, Rita grabbed hold of his arse with the tightened fingers of both hands and locked him against her. He would no doubt have finger marks on his buttocks on the morrow.

There was only one thought in Steven's mind then, and for the next hour or more. *I will never let this woman go.*

The erotic tale of Red Riding Hood and the big bad wolf . . .

"This is such a bad idea," Rita said as she followed Steven, groaning with ecstasy . . . an ecstasy she shared . . . to the floor where his knees folded on him.

"Ouch!" he said, but only halfheartedly. He was too busy arranging their bodies to suit his purposes.

She straddled him and continued her death grip on his butt so he couldn't pull out. His unique gray eyes were almost silver with a hazy arousal. His lips were parted and plumped with anticipation.

"This is such a bad idea," she said when he rolled her over onto her back. She would probably have straw in some unmentionable places come morning.

"Dost think so, sweetling?" He flashed her a quick smile that would melt the hardest heart and began to torment her with long, slow strokes into her continually convulsing inner muscles.

"This is such a bad idea," she said when the force of his thrusts moved them across the floor and knocked over a chair.

Flat on her back, she stared up at him as he braced himself on his elbows.

"Don't call me sweetling."

"Why?"

"It makes me tingle."

"Where?"

"You do not want to know."

"Yea, I do. I definitely do." He inserted a forefinger between the place where they were joined, then fluttered it. "Could it be here?" he inquired with the innocence of a wolf in Red Riding Hood's bedroom.

Where the hell is Grandma? Her moan was her answer. But then she persisted. "This is such a bad idea, Steven. It only complicates things."

"This is the best idea, and I forbid any more protests to the contrary." He rotated his hips in such a way that her eyelids fluttered, and she catapulted into what had to be her third orgasm.

"Like that, do you, m'lady?" he whispered against her mouth as he did the hip rotation thing again.

"You know I do," she gasped, "and you are going to pay for tormenting me like this."

"I cannot wait."

She tried to move, but she was pinned to the floor by his erection impaling her, his hips pressed against her belly, and his hands linked with hers above her head.

"I am not going to kiss you or touch you this time because I cannot wait. My ballocks are afire. I cannot wait. But later . . ." he promised.

Little did he know that she shared his decision. She loved his kisses. That, combined with her already heightened excitement, would have been too much. She wanted to concentrate on one sensation at a time.

"One more thing," he said as he licked, then blew on her ear.

She bucked up against him, and although he didn't move, she felt his erection swell inside her even more. "I don't think I can stand one more thing, and if you don't start this party for real—"

"One more thing," he repeated. "I must needs pull out at the end. Do not try to stop me."

For a moment, she was confused. "Oh, didn't I tell you? I'm wearing a birth control implant. See, right there under my left armpit. It's good for two more months."

He frowned. "Are you saying that my seed cannot breed with your eggs because of *that*?"

She nodded.

"Truly?"

"Truly."

He closed his eyes for a moment, as if saying a silent prayer of thanks. Then, in one fluid move, he withdrew from her and stood. Before she could blink, he tossed her onto the bed and crawled up over her, making growling noises.

Was that a Viking thing? Sex growling? Good Lord, maybe she'd fallen into one of those sexy werewolf romance novels, as well as time travel. If he started to sprout hair in unlikely places or do weird wolf mating things, she was out of here.

But no, she'd misunderstood his growls.

"You wanted the party to start? Welcome to *my* party, Red Riding Hood."

He tortured her with pleasure . . .

Steven had no time for the niceties of bedplay, which was embarrassing, really, because Viking men were known for their sexual prowess . . . he above most others. Instead, he was on the beguiling wench like a starving dog on a juicy bone.

Before he could tell her of his need or apologize for his haste and promise better later, she spread her legs, raised her knees, and raised two hands to beckon him with wagging fingers. "Come here, Steven." Her voice was sex-husky.

He thought about resisting, but only for a lackwit moment. Still, he recognized that she was a woman who liked to take control. That could be a blessing in some cases or a bane when it got out of hand.

For now, he mounted her, sinking into the wet depths of her sheath all the way. Having passed the point of long-and-slow foresport, he began to pummel her with thrusts that brought him flush against her bare mons, over and over. Usually, he could tell when a woman was approaching her peak, but Rita's inner muscles were grasping and ungrasping his cock in an almost continuous friction. Rita had her eyes closed, fists clenched at her sides, her chin arched high, her breathing rapid, and still her hips kept pace with his rhythm, meeting him stroke for stroke.

Despite his far-famed stamina, he could not hold off his raging enthusiasm any longer, and with one final lunge and a roar of completion, he lodged himself to the hilt, spilling himself inside her womb, something he had not done for fifteen or more years. And what a glorious feeling it was!

"That was amazing," she said, opening her eyes to look at him. "It appears that the Vikings earned their reputation as good lovers."

"Was that a compliment?" He was braced above her on extended arms, not wanting to crush her with his weight.

"You're conceited enough without my praising your talents as a lover. Let's just say you were satisfactory."

"Satisfactory? You will rue that word, m'lady." He pulled himself out of her with a groan of sheer pleasure/pain. Rising from the bed, he pointed at her. "Do not move."

Behind the screen he relieved his bladder, then used a soft, wet cloth to cleanse himself. When he went back, he was not surprised to see that Rita had moved to a sitting position with her back propped against two stacked pillows and a bed fur pulled up nigh to her neck.

"A little late for modesty," he remarked as he went to the bottom of the bed and began to search Thorfinn's old chest.

"I was cold."

He gave her a look of such skepticism that she blushed. "Well, maybe a little shy. You have to know, Steven, that I don't usually do this kind of thing."

Dost mean blood-flaming, bone-melting, mind-exploding sex? "What kind of thing?"

"Hop into the sack with a guy I hardly know."

You know me now, lady. "So, what do you do instead?" Not that he really wanted to know. Meanwhile, he was tossing items right and left. Who knew Thorfinn had so many braies and belts? But soon he came to the hose. At the bottom, of course.

"We go out on dates. You know, have dinner. See a movie. Walk on the beach. Go to a concert. You don't understand those words, do you? Suffice it to say, we get to know one another before screwing each other's brains out."

He smiled at her choice of words. "Like putting the cart in front of the horse, as my mother ofttimes says."

"Exactly."

"Well, we cannot erase what has already been done. And I for one have ne'er had such amazing sex, ever, and, believe you me, I have engaged in every kind of sex imaginable."

"Nice to know. Hey, what are those for?" She was staring at the two pairs of Thorfinn's hose.

"I have noticed that you always try to take control of things, even in bedplay. Turnabout is fair play, is it not?"

She was edging toward the other side of the bed, but he grabbed her foot before she could bolt. "Oh, no, buddy. No bondage for me."

He had already wrapped one of the stockings three times around her left ankle, then tied it to one of the footboard posts. "I do not know what bondage is. All I want to do is try a little experiment."

"Experiment be damned." She was slapping at him as he tried to grasp her left wrist.

He had her left side restrained and moved to the other side of the bed.

Resigned, or pretending to be, she asked, "What kind of experiment?"

"I just want to see what you are like when you do not hold the upper hand, so to speak, in bedplay. Plus, every Viking likes to explore new territory, unimpeded."

"I could just lie here like a loaf of bread."

"Not what I have in mind." He was busy now, lighting another eight fat candles he had found in Thorfinn's chest. He did not want to know why they were there.

After he had her tied loosely, spread-eagled on the bed, he lit each of the candles, arranging them as close as possible to the bed.

"What are the candles for? Some kind of ritual?"

He laughed. "Nay. The better to see you, my dearling."

"That damn Red Riding Hood story is coming back to bite me in the butt again. You had this all planned, didn't you?"

"I would have if I had thought of it, but nay, this is my creative impulsiveness at work." Just then, he thought of something else he had seen in Luta's chest the other day. With what he hoped was an evil grin, he was soon waving an exotic feather fan, which had once belonged in a sultan's harem. Thorfinn had given Luta the fan for a betrothal gift before he realized the kind of perfidy she could commit. The fan was composed of various colorful feathers . . . peacock, goose, swan, and others he did not recognize.

"What the hell are you going to do with that?"

I have no idea. "It will be a surprise." *To us both.*

"You're punishing me for leaving the castle without telling you where I was going, aren't you?"

He pondered a short while. "Mayhap a little."

"I was only visiting the witches' cottage."

"And you think that makes it better?" He raised a hand to halt her next words. "Do not tell me now. Later, you can disturb me with tales of all your intrigues, but I will not let you ruin my good mood now."

"I thought you were supposed to be a Viking with the blues."

"Usually I am, but at the moment I am . . . um, yellow."

"You mean mellow."

"That, too. I was just picking a light, sunshine color."

He arranged himself on the bed then, on his side. He was already half-hard, but that would have to wait. He had other plans.

She stared up at him warily, even when he only outlined her lips with a forefinger.

"Dost know what I intend for you, my sex slave?" *As if I know!*

"Sex slave? In your dreams!"

"I repeat. Dost want to know my plans?"

She frowned at him with wariness.

Well she should be wary!

"First I intend to kiss you. Many men do not like kissing, but I consider myself an expert in that foresport. Dost like kissing as much as I do?"

She nodded, still wary.

"Well, first I will kiss you endlessly, in so many ways we will lose count, until you reach your first peak."

"That's great, Steven, but this would be so much better if you would release me." She struggled against her ties.

"Remember, Ree-tah, this is all about control. Mine."

She said a foul word that he chose to ignore.

"After the kissing, I will move down to your breasts, where I will experiment with each of the different feathers. Then I intend to fondle and suckle until your second peaking." At that promise, he could see her already hardened pink nipples engorge even more. "After that I will move down to your bare mons, which I have saved for last. I must say I have heard of such, but ne'er seen it afore. So, I will have to examine it thoroughly. Not just by looking, but by touch and taste as well. With my fingers as well as feathers."

She whimpered.

"After that exercise, which I expect to result in another peaking or two, I will take my own satisfaction inside your female channel, which by then I expect to be hot and dripping with your woman dew." *If I can survive that long.*

"In other words, you intend to torture me."

"Yea, I do," he murmured against her lips. "Sweet torture."

Chapter 11

Kissed to death . . . the little death . . .

Steven hadn't even begun to make love to her, not really, and already Rita was so aroused, she could barely breathe.

"You are trembling," he remarked.

"Must be I'm cold."

He laughed, not at all fooled. "Not for long, sweetling."

If that was meant as a threat, she wasn't frightened. Somehow, she knew that he wouldn't hurt her and that he was no more into Sadie and Maisie than she was . . . sado-masochism, that was. Still, she was finding her restraints difficult to accept. Maybe Steven was right that she needed to be in control . . . that submission spelled weakness to her. She would have to think about that later. Right now, she was having trouble concentrating on anything other than, *"Oh. My. God!"*

His warm breath fanned her face before his mouth descended on hers. "Ree-tah," was all he said. It was both a plea and a demand, both of which increased her trembling. The only place he touched her was the pulse point in the curve of her neck where his fingertips rested lightly. Lying on his side, his other arm rested above her head on the pillow.

At first, his kisses were as gentle as the flutter of a butterfly's wings as he explored and tested her mouth with wet lips, tongue, and even teeth. Many men went through the motions of kissing, but only as a prelude to the good stuff. Other, wiser men recognized that kissing could be the good stuff, as well. Steven was obviously of the latter persuasion. Without a doubt he enjoyed every little nuance as the intensity of his kisses took her gradually from one level of pleasure to another.

Rita had doubted Steven's earlier boast that he could make her come just by kissing. She wasn't so sure now. Each step he took displayed an expertise in the art of kissing. Exploring. Teasing. Persuading. Demanding. Then he would backtrack and start all over again. It was driving her crazy, and she nipped at his tongue on its latest withdrawal, attempting to keep him where she wanted him.

His chuckle vibrated his tongue, which triggered the beginning of an orgasm. But wait, the brute stopped. "Not yet," he murmured thickly. Lifting his head, he stared down at her. His thick black lashes swept half-mast over eyes that were illuminated to silvery desire. He used the fingertips that had been at her neck to trace the moisture on her lips. Then he did the same with one of the stiffer feathers.

"Release me, Steven. I need to . . ."

He pressed a forefinger into her mouth, then took it in his own mouth and suckled.

She could swear her vagina lurched.

"Need to what?" he asked, licking her ear.

Oh, my! Oh, my! Ooooh, my! "Touch you. Kiss you. I don't know. Just something."

"In other words, you would take control, even of something so simple as kissing."

"There is nothing mere about your kisses, and you damn well know it. I swear, if I were free, I would smack you."

"That is not very loverlike of you."

"I'm not feeling loverlike."

"How are you feeling?"

She couldn't answer, because he was back to French-kissing her. Hard, fast thrusts of his tongue that caused ripples of pleasure to slingshot from her mouth to her nipples to her clitoris, all of which were swollen with her rising need.

She fought it, hating to come alone, under his scrutiny, but in the end, she jerked her head to the side, arched her hips up as much as she could, which was only a few inches, and fell into an orgasm that started inside, then moved in waves out to her slick folds, in fact to all the extremities of her body. Even her fingertips and toes felt sensitized.

When she flopped back down to the bed, her lips burned in the aftermath of what felt like a sexual possession. She glared up at him. "That wasn't fair."

"How so?" he asked, giving her a fleeting kiss.

"It was one-sided, dammit."

"Best you watch your language, m'lady. And, for your information, that was not one-sided at all." He pointed downward, where his penis was rising to the occasion, already dripping pre-come.

"Release me. The next time I come, I want you inside me."

"Nay, we do it my way."

"Yeah, you and Frank Sinatra. I mean it, release me. Right now. Aaarrgh! I'm going to have my witch friends put a spell on you. Your penis will probably shrivel up. You might lose all your hair. Who knows . . . if you don't release me right now, you might get struck by lightning."

He laughed. "I enjoy your fierceness. Yell at me some more."

"Okay, let's make a deal. You get ten more minutes to do your thing, and then you release me."

"I am not exactly certain how long ten minutes is, but it sounds too short to me. How about two hours?"

"Are you crazy? What are you going to do for two hours?"

He smiled down at her. A wicked, wicked smile. "I told you afore, Ree-tah. I plan to go exploring." He waved the fan in her face. Then his gaze swept her body from scalp to toes, especially taking note of the Brazilian wax, which seemed to fascinate him. Noticing that she noticed where he was looking, he told her, "I am saving that exploration for last."

Taking a deep breath, she exhaled whooshily and said, "Okay, Marco Polo, do your thing. Let's see if your *long*-boat is going to be able to go the distance."

She went a-Viking in a whole new way . . .

Steven prided himself on his staying power in the bedsport, but Rita was right when she questioned whether his "long-boat" would be able to stay the course. Hah! He would make sure that it did.

Bracing himself on his left elbow, he began to examine her body. For a soldier, or soldier in training, she had no battle scars. Instead, her body was smooth and soft, even those areas where she had muscles, like her upper arms, abdomen, and thighs.

A sex flush heightened the color of her cheeks, neck, and chest. Whether it was from the peaking she had already experienced or anticipation of the next, he was not sure. Who the hell cared! By the time he was done with her, the flush would no doubt be deeper and brighter.

He used the fingertips of his right hand to trace her up-raised arms from wrists to underarms, which were also bare of hair. She shivered at his light caress. Assuming she was sensitive there, he repeated the caress.

She closed her eyes and seemed to be bracing herself against another arousal.

"Open your eyes, sweetling, I would see your pleasure."

She told him to do something very crude to himself. And she declined to open her eyes.

We shall see about that, you stubborn wench.

He used a feather to vibrate against one of her pale rose nipples, which was already standing to attention or rather begging for his attention.

Her eyes shot open.

Definitely an erotic spot for her.

And so he began a thorough exploration of her breasts, which were not overly large, but they were not small, either. The areolas surrounding the pert nipples were a slightly darker shade of dusty rose. He palmed them from underneath. He traced them with his fingers. He flicked the tips with his tongue. On and on he fondled her until her whimpers became almost cries. When he judged her ready, he took one nipple into his mouth and began to suckle rhythmically, playing with the nipple of the other breast with his free hand. The whole time he watched her face for reaction.

Even so, he was surprised when she screamed.

He was about to rise, not wanting to hurt her, when she hissed at him. "Don't you dare stop now."

And he didn't. Giving equal attention to one breast, then another. Alternately licking and suckling. The intensity of her peaking was a joy to watch and almost his undoing. He took his cock in hand, near the base, and squeezed, hoping to forestall his own peaking.

"You are killing me, Steven," she finally said when her breathing slowed down to a pant.

"Good killing or bad killing?"

She smiled at him, which he took for a good sign. "Is there such a thing as a good killing?"

"In the bedsport, yea, I think so."

"Would it do any good for me to ask you to release me?"

"Not yet."

"Even if I said please?"

"Even then." He rose up from his reclining position at her side and knelt between her widespread legs. Leaning forward, he kissed her flat belly and was pleased at the instinctive clenching of the muscles there. He had feared she was too depleted of sensation for him to continue his journey right now, but, praise the gods, apparently not. "Tell me again how you did this?" he asked, examining her bare mons up close.

She explained some procedure involving hot wax and stripping of the hair out by the roots.

"Did it hurt?"

She nodded. "Especially the first time. Not so bad after that."

He could not fathom why a woman would put herself through such agony, but then he knew a Viking, Evin One-Eye, who had his second wife shave the hair on his buttocks betimes. With a shiver of distaste, Steven decided that he would no doubt do the same if he had hair *there*.

He put his hands under her buttocks and raised her slightly so that he could see where the hair had been removed along her cleft as well, a cleft that was slick and glistening with her woman dew. He could not wait to touch her there.

"Oh, good Lord! Do you have to be so close?" she complained.

"Yea, I do. The better to see you, my dearling." He sat back on his heels, letting her lie flat again.

"That Big Bad Wolf routine is getting old."

He grinned at her, then began to explore the entire area with his calloused fingertips. With fascination, he discovered that a woman's mons had so many nerve endings ripe for a man's touch, which were not discernible under the usual woman-hair.

He was not sure he preferred his women this way, but it certainly was different.

By the time he dipped his fingers in her moist cleft, she was keening her arousal with one continuous, "Aaaaaahh-hhh!" He had never seen a woman be so wet for him, but then he had never tied a woman to his bed and pleasure-tortured her to the point of madness. And she was weeping, as well.

"Dost cry, Ree-tah? Am I hurting you? Shall I stop?"

She opened her eyes, which had been clenched shut. "Yes, I hurt, you idiot. I hurt so good."

"Oh," he said, sounding as idiotic as she had called him.

He touched the moistness experimentally at first, then with more relish. He could actually see how plump the folds were, and near the top, that bud of a woman's pleasure stood out like a pearl nestled in silk. "I had no idea it would look like this," he remarked. "Truly, more men should get this close-up view of a woman's parts. 'Tis fascinating."

She made a choking sound around her keening. He was not sure if it was because of his comment or because he now had one, then two, then three fingers inside her body.

"Methinks you are ready," he observed.

"Methinks you are the moron of the ages. I was ready about an hour ago."

"Savor the anticipation, sweetling." He waggled his eye-brows at her.

If her hands had been free, she would no doubt have hit him. In fact, she appeared about to tell him to savor something entirely different, except he had arranged himself on braced elbows above her, and without warning, thrust into her female portal where her spasming muscles gave him a hot welcome. The next thrust brought him in more. On the third thrust, her body expanded to accommodate his size, and he lunged in totally.

Was there any pleasure in the world greater than this?

He gritted his teeth and tried not to move, despite the clasping and unclasping of the channel that attempted to milk his cock. Nature's way of ensuring that the man's seed erupted in the right place, he supposed.

"Open your eyes, Ree-tah," he urged.

When she did, he saw that her blue eyes were unfocused with excitement beyond anything he had ever seen before. In truth, she was almost delirious with her need for completion. Mayhap it was due to the long period of self-denial she had alluded to earlier. Or mayhap it was just him. He hoped so.

"Soon, dearling," he murmured. "Soon."

The only sounds in the room then were the wet slapping sounds of flesh upon flesh as he rode her hard, plunging into her with punishing slams as his raging lust took over. He might have keened himself then, so intense was his pleasure. He lost count of how many times she peaked.

In the end, when he ground himself against the heart of her, spurting his seed into her womb, they peaked together . . . a peaking so powerful he could swear their hearts beat as one. Every sexual experience he ever had in the future would be measured against this high standard.

Once his breathing slowed, he gazed down at her. She was staring up at him with equal wonder at what had just happened to them.

"Heartling," he whispered. That one word expressed all his emotions.

Where's Spot? . . .

In the middle of the night, Rita awakened from a warm slumber to find herself unrestrained and Steven making sweet love to her. A gentle stroking and rocking that was no less potent than his other erotic assaults.

"Shhh. Do not move," he crooned. "I will do all the work."

"Hah! That's got to be one of the most famous lines of men through the ages. Right up there with, 'You can't get pregnant if I put it in just a little bit.'"

He stilled for a moment. "You can? Get pregnant when . . . what you said?"

"Of course."

He looked horrified, then shrugged, resuming his previous activity.

"Besides," she continued breathily, "it's not like I could lie still when you do . . . yikes! What was *that*?"

"The Viking S-Spot. Have you ne'er heard of it afore?" He looked up at her from where he was doing something unusual down yonder. "Nay, of course you have not, since I am your first Viking."

And hopefully the last.

"It is a special spot on your body that only a skilled Norseman can find."

He was skilled, all right. And not even a little bit humble.

Rita wondered if a woman could die of too many orgasms. But then she thought, *What a way to go!*

Steven was fascinated with her body, like a boy with a new toy, partly because she was still a mystery to him . . . her appearance, where she'd come from, her uninhibited enjoyment of sex . . . but also because of the no-risk of pregnancy. "You mean I can do whatever I want, and my seed will not take root in your womb?" he asked several times.

"Define 'whatever I want,' " she inquired.

And he told her. In graphic detail.

This boy is far ahead of his time. Perhaps too far.

Afterward, he carried her, wrapped in a linen sheet, out to the bathing house, where he carefully washed both her and himself, followed by another bout of sex. Rita wasn't usually so passive, and, energized by her short nap and the bath, showed him what a modern woman could do when she wanted to.

"I did not know that women could do that," he exclaimed as he panted like a quarterback attempting to catch his breath after being sacked by five two hundred–pound linebackers.

She looked up at him and arched her brows, unable to speak at the moment.

"Well, I knew they could. I just did not know they would."

She disengaged. "So, you think I'm a slut."

"Must we talk now?"

"Yeah, I think so!" She attempted to stand.

He pulled her back. "A slut?"

She explained.

"Ah, a wanton. Yea, you are a wanton. The best kind. A lady wanton. And do not get all huffy. That was a compliment."

"A left-handed compliment, I suspect."

"Left, right, the best," he assured her. "Now, resume your wanton acts." Afterward, he said, "I am not sure I can walk." Immediately followed by, "Can you do that again?"

Later, they lay in bed, she on her side, with him tucked behind her, spoonlike, a light blanket over them both. He kissed her shoulder and said, "We still must needs talk."

"*Now*. You want to talk *now*?"

"Not now, sweetling. In the morning. I cannot wait to hear where you were all day and why you are associating with witches."

He yawned loudly, and, like many men after sex, fell into a deep sleep, his warm, even breaths feathering against her hair, one arm on the pillow they shared, the hand of the other arm pressed against her belly.

She kept her eyes open for a long time, too hyped up

to sleep. So many questions. So many problems. And the biggest one was plastered against her back, snoring softly in her ear.

How could so much have happened to her in such a short time? Had she really time-traveled? If so, was it a God miracle kind of thing, or some wrinkle in the stratosphere science kind of thing? And what if she couldn't go back? That would take a huge readjustment for her, and she wasn't sure she could ever accept such a destiny.

That brought her back to her biggest problem.

She wasn't sorry she'd made love with Steven. It had been too delicious, and that was an understatement. Despite his chauvinism and primitive thinking, she felt an odd, irresistible connection with him. Not love. Of course, she wasn't in love with him. She barely knew him. But what if he was "the one"? Presumably there was a soul mate for every person on the planet. And what if she had to leave him? Or worse, what if she was given the choice to either stay with him or go home?

Wiggling her body to get more comfortable, she decided to take one day at a time. If this day had turned out so well for her, she couldn't wait to see what was in store for her tomorrow. Their lovemaking had to be a turning point in their relationship.

Would he waken her with kisses?

Or would he want to stay in bed all day?

Turns out, neither was on his damned Viking agenda.

Chapter 12

He en-thralled her . . .

Steven was sated and happier than he had been in years. That's why he hated what he was about to do, but it had to be done.

Besides, it was important for a man to let the woman know what was what, right from the beginning . . . to start as he intended to go on. There were rules of conduct, unwritten but important nonetheless. A woman did not make a man look the fool in front of his comrades without some repercussions.

Rita was a visitor to his land. It would be difficult for her to understand their ways. So he must be gentle in enforcing his will on her.

For about the thousandth time, he wished that Thorfinn were still here, master of the Norstead jarldom. In the old days, as a follower rather than a leader, Steven had been free to do as he wished with no thought to how it would look to others.

Truth to tell, it was lonely at the top.

"Time to get up, sweetling," he said, nudging Rita's foot from where he stood near the bottom of the bed.

She opened her eyes slowly, still not fully awake. And what a sight she was! Lying on her back, with her unrestrained arms raised above her head, she had puffy lips, swollen from his numerous kisses . . . very numerous kisses; there were whisker scratches on her face and neck and no doubt other body parts, and her short hair was sleep-mussed . . . or was it sex-mussed? Anyone who saw her would know what she had been doing not once but throughout the night.

Perverted though it might be, he liked putting his mark on her. That puzzled him until he came to a conclusion. *'Tis an outward sign that she is mine.*

"You're up," she said sleepily, stretching with a yawn that caused the linen sheet to fall and expose her breasts, where there were more signs of his possession.

He had to restrain himself from crawling back into bed with her, but he had much to do today. Duties that could not be postponed.

"And you're dressed. Not only dressed, but you shaved," she accused him. "What's up? Is it late?"

"Nay, but I must needs be below stairs afore my men break fast. With the Althing in only a few days, much needs to be finalized. Then I have to supervise a short jarl court. Horses need to be prepared for my meeting with Brodir on the morrow. And my men must do their daily exercises in war skills. All that afore noon."

She nodded her understanding. Then, smart woman that she was, asked, "What about me?"

"You will be at my side this entire day."

"That's nice," she said, smiling. Her smile soon faded. "Why? Because you think I'll run away?"

He shrugged as if that were a possibility, though it was not the main reason.

"Let me assure you, Steven, I will not leave Norstead without informing you first. That is a promise."

You will not leave Norstead at all. That is my prom-ise. 'Twas not the time to raise that particular issue, he decided.

"What's that?" she asked, pointing to the garment laid out on the bed.

"A gunna."

"It looks like burlap. You're giving me a burlap dress to wear?"

"'Tis homespun."

"I'll wear my tunic and tights today."

"Nay, you will not."

She tilted her head to the side, studying him. "What are you doing?" She had just noticed the leather necklet in his hand, which he was attaching to a long, thin chain.

His face heated, but he could not be weak. This must be done. "I am fixing a leading string . . . leading chain, actu-ally . . . onto a thrall collar."

"Thrall? That means . . ." She frowned with confusion. ". . . slave. Doesn't it?" As understanding seeped in, her face fell, and she gasped as if he had punched her in the stomach.

He could not be moved.

"You intend to put a slave collar on my neck and lead me around like a dog?" Her voice was shrill with hurt and outrage.

"'Tis just for one day."

"No!"

"'Twill not be so bad. Mostly, you can hold the chain yourself when I am otherwise occupied." *Like when I visit the garderobe.* "'Tis symbolic, that is what it is."

"Symbolic of what? Your domination? You, the big bad Viking? Me, the lowly servant?"

"Nay, 'tis not that at all. You left Norstead yestermorn and did not inform anyone of your whereabouts."

"I told you. There's an explanation. Sigge took me to visit her aunts, and it was farther away than I realized."

He ignored her words. If he started discussing those half-wit witches with her, they would be here all day. "Listen and listen well, m'lady. All of Norstead and surrounding jarldoms watched and speculated. Everyone thinks you deserted me, just like Luta, the traitorous bitch, did Thorfinn. They whisper that I have no control over a mere woman. Therefore, my leadership will be questioned."

"You have no idea how chauvinistic you just sounded."

"If I knew what shove-nis-tick meant, I might be offended." Now he was getting frustrated. Why could the woman not be sensible? Why must she be at cross wills with him at every turn?

"It means unfeeling, woman-hating pig."

"Dost really think insults are wise, Ree-tah?"

"Steven, don't do this. Not after . . . not after all that we just did."

"That would be even worse . . . if I let my cock rule my brain."

"What else is new? That's the case with most men."

"Your sarcasm is ill-timed."

"Okay, I can see that your pride is in question, and that you need to show you're the big chest-thumping caveman, but isn't there some other punishment? Put me back in the cage again."

"You burned the cage."

"Build another one."

"No time."

"Lock me in this room all day."

"You would just sleep the day away. What punishment is that?"

"I would be bored to death with nothing to do. Not even a book to read."

"Nay, it will be as I say."

"I won't do it. You'll have to force me."

"I could do that, but I would rather not."

"If you do, I'll scream insults at you all day. I'll say you have the sexual prowess of a slug. I'll tell everyone that you have a needle dick."

He barely stifled a grin. "Then I will put a gag in your mouth."

"You wouldn't!" Her eyes welled, and one fat tear slid down her face, which she swiped with the back of her hand.

"For the love of Thor! Stop with the tears. Weeping will gain you naught."

"I'm not crying. Don't you dare think I'd shed a tear over you. I'm just so mad, venom is leaking out of my eyes. It will probably be bubbling out of my ears and nose pretty soon."

That was the most outlandish thing he had ever heard, and this time he could not help himself. He threw back his head and roared with laughter. "Ah, sweetling, can we not at least compromise?"

"Do not call me sweetling. I am not your sweetling or dearling or any other endearment."

"Yea, you are." *And heartling, too, come to think on it.*

"In your mind, I am a slave."

You are the damnedest slave I ever met. "Just for today."

"First bondage. Then slavery. What next?"

How would I know? I am as much a puppet in this time-travel charade as you. "You forgot making love until my eyes rolled back in my head and my cock nigh melted from your heat. You cannot say you did not enjoy our bedsport."

"You are crude."

"Good sex can be crude." *In fact, the cruder the better.*

She made a growling sound of frustration.

Going to Luta's chest, he pulled out a gown, one of the ones she had ordered from the Franklands: blue silk edged with gold braid. "Wear this then. No one will think you are a slave in this gunna."

"Would I still be wearing that dog collar?"

He nodded. *Would that you were a dog . . . a docile dog . . . just for the day!*

"No."

If my men heard her refusal to do my bidding, they would be suggesting I lop off a body part. "We are wasting time here. Do as I say."

"No."

Enough! He picked her squirming body up off the bed and was about to dress her himself while she screamed and scratched. "You will hurt yourself, Ree-tah. Desist!"

"I would rather die."

"You are not going to die, and you are not going to leave me again."

"I did not leave you. I told you—"

"Stop! We will not rehash that tale of your transgression. Have you no room for compromise?"

She stilled. "Let me wear the tunic and pants."

"And then you will accept the collar?"

"I will never accept the collar, but you can force it on me without my scratching your eyes out."

"How will this be any different from wearing Luta's gown?"

"The boy's outfit is mine. My choice."

"Ah, an act of defiance."

"Whatever."

When she had donned her boyling attire and he had attached the collar, he opened the door and began to lead her by the chain out into the corridor. Her prideful chin was raised so high, she might very well get a nosebleed.

He tried once more to appease her sensibilities. "Ree-tah, you have to understand that it is our way here in the Norselands. If a man does not have his reputation, he has naught."

"And a woman? What about her reputation?"

In truth, he had never thought on that.

"Just so you know, Steven, I will never forgive you for this."

"Never is a long time."

He could only hope he would have a long enough time to seduce her, winning himself back into her good graces.

The man really yanked her chain . . .

Rita was devastated by Steven's turnabout from lover to master and humiliated beyond belief. So, when the first person they ran into was Oslac, she was not in a good mood.

Oslac looked first at her face and neck exposed by the collarless tunic, where he probably saw whisker burns and a hickey, if the smirk on his face was any indication. If he could have done a high five with Steven, he probably would have. Then he took in the slave collar and chain and broke out in gales of laughter.

"Oslac," Steven warned.

But Oslac just continued to laugh. "Oh, this is perfect. Your very own pet sea woman on a chain. Will you show her off thus at the Althing?"

"'Tis only for today." Steven's face was turning red. Why he should blush was beyond Rita. She was the one who was embarrassed and getting madder by the minute.

"You know, Oslac, I've developed some witchy friends," she said. "I'm thinking I should call your beloved wife back from the dead to get your life back in shape."

"You would not!" Then, glancing at Steven, he added, "She could not, could she?"

Steven shrugged.

Oslac told Steven then, "I think you should let me take my sword in hand and stab her black heart. Be done with her once and for all."

"I think you should let me take your sword, Oslac," she said sweetly, "and stick it where the sun don't shine."

At first, he didn't understand, but Steven did, because he was grinning like she was his very own performing monkey as he did a bit of mock tsking at her.

She didn't know when her language had deteriorated into the gutter so badly. It wasn't her norm, and she didn't like it one bit. She vowed to clean up her act, in that regard anyway.

Oslac walked beside Steven, with her trailing behind the two of them, like a squaw. Or a slave. She gritted her teeth, warning herself to pick her battles, of which there were sure to be plenty this day.

As they moved down the center aisle toward the high table, dozens of men were coming into the great hall, some engaging in jaw-cracking yawns, a few breaking wind, others scratching intimate body parts, as if all were manly morning rituals. Serving women were bustling about putting trays of flat bread, mounds of butter, small pots of honey, slices of leftover meats, hard cheeses, porridge, stewed fruits, and pitchers of milk as well as ale on the long trestle tables. The men carried their own cups or horns for drinking.

Her slave collar and chain caught all their attention. Some of the men nodded their approval to Steven, some chuckled and made lewd remarks amongst themselves, some looked downright angry, considering her punishment too lenient. Not a one was on her side, not even the women who passed by on their daily business.

And especially not Lady Thora, who was swanning into the hall like a queen, followed by two of her minions, women Rita had seen in the sewing solar. Rita just knew the bitch . . . *Oops, I vowed to clean up my language* . . . the mean-spirited lady would have something to say to her, and it wouldn't be nice.

When they sat down at the high table, her bracketed by Steven and Oslac, Thora on Oslac's other side, Steven asked, "What would you like to eat?"

He was being overly polite, but then he ought to be. The brute!

"Orange juice, coffee, a Spanish omelette, buttered toast, and home fries."

He blinked at her, then slapped a hunk of the flat manchet bread on a wooden platter, a slice of bloody meat, probably lamb, but it could be venison, and a beverage. "Eat," he ordered, the glare on his face intended to intimidate her.

She took a sip of the beverage, then spat it out. "Beer for breakfast? Warm beer at that."

Steven just turned away from her and spoke to the man on his other side, Arnstein, the steward, who was discussing work to be done within the keep in preparation for the Althing, the open-air assembly of free men from many districts called to settle disputes. "Hunters will go out today for fresh game. Reindeer were sighted near the north peak yestereve, and there are always wild boars in the forest. Some of the boylings will check traps for rabbits and other small game. Fishermen will surely have good catches at this time of the year . . . turbot, sea trout, bass, lamprey . . . and Cook has asked for a goodly number of eels for her eel pies."

Steven nodded and patted Arnstein on the shoulder. "Well done, my friend."

"Bed linens and furs have been prepared for those who will sleep inside, both in the chambers and the bed closets," Arnstein added. "But . . . um, I was wondering. Will you be staying in Thorfinn's room? May I offer your bedchamber for King Olaf?"

A king was coming here? Holy cow! Rita was impressed but zipped her lips, not wanting Steven to think that anything he did was impressive to her.

"I will be staying in Thorfinn's bedchamber with Reetah," Steven replied, which caused those who overheard to stare at her.

There seemed to be some hidden message in his words. Could it be he was warning them to show her some respect? On second thought, she decided he was just staking his claim.

She turned to see Geirfinn walking by. The old man winked at her, showing his support. At least she had one friend here. Well, that wasn't quite true. She had Sigge and the two witch aunts, which weren't doing her much good at the moment, being in their mountain home.

Just then she realized that Steven had noticed Geirfinn's wink, and he was not pleased. To give Geirfinn credit, he did not quake under his master's glowering stare.

"Geirfinn," Steven growled in warning.

"Oh, get over yourself, Steven!" Rita said, giving Geirfinn a thankful smile. "Geirfinn was just showing that not all men . . . not all Viking men . . . are vicious brutes."

"You think I am a brute?"

"If the name sticks."

"You tread a fine line, m'lady."

"What? I'm not even allowed to speak my mind now?"

"Not when it shows insolence for your betters." Lady Thora was leaning forward to speak around Oslac from where she sat on his other side.

Rita was about to tell the bi . . . lady . . . who was better than whom, when Steven yanked on her chain, forcing her to look his way. "You may speak your mind, within reason."

"Reason being, as long as I bow and scrape to praise you and your mistress at every turn?"

"A little praise would not be unwelcome." He smiled at her, probably hoping she would melt in return. Not a chance! "And Thora is not my mistress," he said, for her ears only.

"Hah! Since last week, you mean?"

His face flushed with embarrassment.

She continued to glare at him and said under her breath,

"One more thing: yank that chain again, and I'm going to shove it down your throat."

"Ah, I thought you might shove it the same place as Oslac's sword."

"Good idea."

"Do not issue threats to me. You will not win."

"So, you want me to agree with everything you say. Should I bow down on my knees and beg for permission to speak at all?"

"You may go to your knees, especially if it is to do what you did last night."

She gasped and then went red with mortification when she realized that there had been a momentary lull in conversation, and practically everyone at the table had heard his disclosure.

"I did not mean to—" he started to say.

"Shut up!"

He flinched as if she'd hit him. It was probably the first time anyone had ever cut him off so rudely. At this point, she didn't care.

"I will let you get away with that just once, and that is all. I should not have said what I did in front of others, but that is no excuse for insolence."

Blah, blah, blah. "Was that an apology?"

"Do not push me, wench."

"Wench now. You've gotta make up your mind, Steven. Lady or wench."

He smiled, probably figuring that all was forgiven. "Both."

Inhaling and exhaling to tamp down her temper, she finally said, "We've got to come to an understanding here. You are bigger and stronger than me. I am in your enemy territory. Therefore you can put a chain around my neck or flog me or even kill me. But there are some things you cannot dictate."

She could almost see his brain grinding as he considered her declaration. In the end, he just arched his brows at her to continue.

"Sweetheart," she said with exaggerated sweetness, "you got lucky last night. You are not getting lucky with me again."

"Sweetling," he replied with equal exaggerated sweetness, obviously understanding the modern meaning of getting lucky, "every man makes his own luck. And I am far-famed for my woman-luck."

"Not this woman. You cut all your bridges when you put this around my neck." She tapped the leather collar with distaste.

"We shall see," he said, then added, "And, by the by, I am not your enemy." *Yet.*

Chapter 13

Some men are dumber than dirt . . .

Steven enjoyed having Rita with him, even in her sullen mood. And that was unusual for him. He enjoyed women . . . their comeliness, their softness, the wooing, the eventual and inevitable bedding . . . but he rarely had an interest in them beyond the bedsport. What sane man did?

Rita was maintaining a stubborn silence, refusing to react to his good-intentioned remarks or to their surroundings, except on those occasions when she felt compelled to speak. Like right now, with the second case before his jarl court, where Karr Half-Ear, one of his farmers from Amberstead, was asking for permission to set aside his first wife, Frida, so he could take on a third wife, Halla, perfectly acceptable under the rules of *more Danico*. In this case, however, he suspected that the first wife, who had no living parents, would be abandoned to Steven's household, where he would be required to give her work or find her a new husband. Sitting behind the standing Karr were the two women, one not unattractive but clearly having seen close to forty winters, the other young, blonde, and very buxom.

Karr was a total dunderhead, in Steven's opinion. While he could see the need for one wife to gain legitimate heirs, two was asking for trouble. Three was more than excessive; it was insanity. But that was beside the point of this petition.

"Why would you set aside Frida?" Steven asked. "Has she been unfaithful?"

Karr's jaw clenched before he admitted, "Nay!"

"Has she slandered your good name?"

Karr shook his head slowly, not at all happy to be questioned thus.

"Has she voiced a desire to end the marriage?"

"Nay, but what has that to do with aught? I have a right to take another wife if I want to."

"That you do, Karr, but our laws also say you cannot set aside a wife without good reason. She is your responsibility from the day you said your vows."

"Good reason? Good reason? I will give you good reason. I cannot support three wives, eight children, and another on the way."

All eyes turned to a preening Halla, who must be with child, although she showed no bump yet. The second wife was not present.

By the huffing noises coming from his side, he could tell that Rita was about to break her vow of silence. She had an opinion she would like to express. Surprise, surprise!

"What say you about this case, Ree-tah?" he asked. "Perchance you could give us a woman's view."

Karr sputtered his protest, and a number of men around the hall raised their heads from whatever they had been doing. Women were rarely given a voice in court, especially not a slave woman.

With deliberate care, Steven unwound his end of the chain from around his wrist and laid it on the table, indicating Rita was free . . . for the moment, leastways. He did not detach the chain from her leather collar, though. Fool he may be, but not that much of a fool.

She stood and addressed Karr's first wife. "Frida, how old are you?"

Startled, Frida sputtered out, "Thirty and nine, m'lady."

Odd how his people were unsure how to place Rita in their society, so they mostly opted for "lady," even with the thrall collar.

"And how long have you been married to this . . ." Rita's lips curled with distaste . . . lips that were still swollen from his endless kisses ". . . this man?"

"Twenty-four years. Since I was fifteen."

It was Rita who was startled now. And enraged. "Perfect!" she muttered.

"Fifteen is a perfectly suitable age for a girl to wed, with many childbearing years ahead of her."

"Why not ten or eleven?" she asked, her voice reeking with condemnation.

"That would be ridiculous. Girls do not have their courses yet and are therefore unable to get pregnant."

"You can't be serious."

"Why not? Stallions are put to mares to breed, but only when the mares are of proper age and able to come into standing heat. Only a foolish horse breeder would put a stallion and young filly in the same pen. A waste of the horse's man seed. 'Tis the same with human mating."

He thought he had made a perfectly logical explanation, but apparently not to his stubborn Rita. She shook her head at him as if he were hopeless and turned back to Frida. "How many children do you and Karr have?"

"Ten. Five boys and five girls."

"Some men should be castrated," Rita said under her breath.

"Because we are virile?" he couldn't help but ask.

"It takes only one male sperm to make a child. It takes a

real man to be a father. Do you want to be defined by your sperm, Steven?"

He had no idea what she had just said, but he was fairly certain it was a slur on his manhood.

"Are any children still at home with you?" Rita was back to grilling Frida. "I mean, are there any young ones still needing parental care?"

Frida nodded. "Three. Ota, who is ten. Maerta, who is eight, and Gunnora, who is five."

"All girlings!" Karr spat out. "What good are they to a farming man?"

"Karr, do you feel no obligation to care for your first wife and three remaining children?" Rita asked the question with as much civility as she could manage, considering her fists were clenched and her teeth gritted.

"I do not have to answer any questions from the likes of you," Karr spat out. At the glare from Steven, he added, "But, nay, I do not. A man has the need to ease himself on a young body betimes. Frida ne'er regained her strength after birthing Gunnora. She can scarce push a plow these days."

Push a plow? The dimwitted sluggard. A real man would never admit to such. Putting his wife to the plow. Shameful! But he has a point about young women. They have more energy for the bedsport.

At the rough sounds Rita was emitting through lips puffing like a blowfish, Steven figured it was best he intercede. "Karr, you may set aside Frida and your three daughters. Take another wife or twenty, for all this court cares, but Frida is due a wergild for loss of a husband, same as if you died in my service. Frida and your daughters may come to Norstead where they will be given work, if they choose, but you will set aside one-tenth of your fall harvest for their upkeep, in addition to the one-tenth that comes to me. That will continue until the three girlings are grown and wed, at which time your payment to Frida will be reduced to one-twentieth, unless she has remarried. That is my judgment."

Steven's aide indicated to an angry Karr that he should leave now. His young bride-to-be was none too happy, either. Steven predicted that she would not be exchanging vows with this older man. She would be looking for greener fields to plow. And Frida, she was staring at Rita as if she was an angel come to earth. In fact, she walked up to the dais. Standing on the lower level she looked up to Rita, who still stood, and said, "Thank you, m'lady. If not for you, me and me daughters would be beggared. If there is aught I can do fer you, I am yer servant fer life."

Interesting that she was thanking Rita and not him.

"Sorry I am to see any man reward fidelity in this manner, Frida," he said. "Mayhap I should have ordered him to keep you as wife."

Frida looked horrified. "With all due respect, m'lord, are ye daft? I have been sick of that old fart fer a long time."

On those wise words, Frida swaggered away, giving a gloating sneer as she passed Karr and the weeping Halla, who was moaning out something about not wanting to plow.

When they were gone, and the next case was being brought forth, Steven turned to Rita, who was staring at him in an odd way. "You intended to rule in that way the entire time, didn't you?"

He shrugged as if that were a possibility. "Impressed, are you?" When she declined to answer, he remarked, "I am not as insensitive or lackwitted as you thought, am I?"

Finally, she nodded, but was quick to add, "You are still not getting lucky again."

They weren't Reva and Josh, but there was a guiding light . . .

The more PO'ed Rita got, the more Steven enjoyed her jibes. And the more he dug in his deep Viking heels.

He didn't even react when she taunted him with all the things she would have done for him in bed if he hadn't been such an ass. Things that only modern women would know about. The Butterfly. The Popsicle. The Swing. The Back-bend. Diving for Treasure. The Double-Jointed Twist.

The twitch beside his flattened lips and the movement of his Adam's apple were the only betrayals of his being affected by her taunts. She had to give him credit for his quick comeback. "Ah, well, I guess I will have to satisfy myself with Rocking the Longboat, Scissoring the Sword, and Whiskering the Nether Lands."

Her jaw had dropped open, which she'd quickly clicked shut, but not before he waggled his eyebrows at her. The dolt!

She had stumbled along after him all morning, to the amusement of every living soul at Norstead, until he had committed the ultimate sin. So he could practice military maneuvers with his men, he'd attached her chain to a hitching post on the sidelines. She couldn't move more than eight feet away. The final indignity had been the big cup of water he'd left with her.

A dog . . . that's all she was to him.

Or a pet.

An amusing sexual toy to be taken out or put aside as the mood hit him.

He was across the field from her now, bare-chested, as were many of the men, wearing only boots and braies. They were engaged in sword practice, but not like any fencing demonstration she'd ever seen. No thrust and parry of rapiers. Nope, the broadswords were so big and heavy that all these men, strong as they were, could do was swing in a wide arc, right to left or left to right, hoping to cleave shields or the enemy by either lopping off a head or limb, or better yet, cut the enemy in the vulnerable area between neck and groin known as the *fat line*, where all the vital organs were located.

Others were practicing lance throwing, mace swinging, and archery. Still others used daggers to come up behind an enemy and give him a blood ring about the neck. No one said the Vikings weren't bloodthirsty fighters. In fact, it was considered a great honor to die in battle, rather than a straw death.

In the midst of it all, some soldiers rode destriers, huge warhorses, zigzagging through the melee, training them to be acclimated to the sounds and smells of battle, she supposed.

Some of the boys Rita had been teaching the other day asked Steven if she could give them more instructions. Steven had seemed to consider the request, but then refused, saying they could get instruction enough from his own archers.

Another black mark in her book of Steven crimes against her.

When the younger children crept slowly toward her, hoping for more stories, Arnstein, the steward, yelled for them to come back to the keep and help their mothers. Probably on orders from Steven the Meany.

At first, the kids pretended not to hear Arnstein.

"I can't tell you any stories right now, but I can teach you a trick."

That got their interest.

"Can you all stand on your heads?"

The older ones said yes, but the little ones just stared at her dumbly.

So, being careful of her chain and already barefooted, she stood on her hands, and not just that, she proceeded to walk around the pole. It was something she'd learned to do as a child, probably one of the early indicators that she had an athletic bent.

The children were giggling and laughing, rolling in the dirt, as they tried unsuccessfully to do the same.

"Have you lost your mind?"

Because she was surprised by the sharp voice behind her, she lost her balance and fell, almost choking herself in the process.

Steven stood, hands braced on hips, glaring at her as if she'd committed some great crime. Meanwhile, the kids had scattered like scared chickens.

"Are you trying to kill me?" she complained, rubbing her neck where the chain had yanked at her collar.

"Are you trying to kill yourself?"

"No, but I'm bored just sitting here pretending to admire your studliness. What's so wrong with playing with the children?"

"Studliness?" he sputtered. "You are being punished. You are not supposed to be enjoying yourself. And stop looking at me like you are a cat and I am the bowl of milk you cannot wait to lap. Much more, and you will find I am luckier than you think I can be."

She shook her head like a wet dog, realizing that she had been gaping at his bare chest. "You stink," she blurted out.

"Of course I stink. I have been sweating like a boar in heat."

"Did I tell you I am going to discover deodorant?"

"Huh?"

"In my time, men and women wear deodorant under their arms so that they don't smell. My witch friends gave me a bunch of ingredients to experiment with."

He put his face in both hands and appeared to be counting. When he glanced up again, he said, "Please, I beg you, do not be going around telling people that they stink."

"You mean, like your King Olaf when he arrives?" she asked sweetly.

His eyes widened with alarm. "Do not dare! Or you will find that collar and chain a permanent fixture."

Talking to him was like talking to a brick wall. So she

turned her back on him and lay down on the ground, curling herself carefully around the pole.

"Now what are you doing?"

"Taking a nap."

There was silence behind her for a moment before he said, "Mayhap we should both go indoors and take a nap. I am feeling lucky."

She thought of so many rejoinders, cute ones, insulting ones, but she decided to settle on just giving him the cold shoulder. Expecting him to stomp off, she waited.

Instead, he said, "I like your arse."

"What?" She jerked, hitting her forehead on the pole.

"In those braies, your form is clearly delineated, especially your plump arse. Very nice!"

If he thought that he was going to gain himself points by saying she had a fat behind, he had another think coming. Coming back to a sitting position with her back against the pole, she said, "You've got a pretty nice butt yourself. Too bad you're such an ass."

Chuckling, he went off to play more of his war games.

She soon had another visitor. Sigvid, who was well into another bout of hiccuping. "Can you—*hiccup*—help me—*hiccup*?"

"Me? I don't know anything about hiccups. Maybe when Sigge comes back tomorrow, she can get a remedy from her aunts."

"Her aunts—*hiccup*—the witches—*hiccup*?"

Rita nodded.

"I would rather—*hiccup*—take my chances with you—*hiccup*."

"Thanks a bunch."

"Please. Lady Thora banished me—*hiccup*—from the keep. Says I am annoying . . . *hiccup*."

She was about to say that Lady Thora had no authority to banish anyone but decided it would be wiser not to enrage Lady Thora while she had a chain attached to her neck.

"Okay, here's one thing that I've heard works." She handed her cup of water to Sigvid. "Bend over from the waist and drink this water, but wait, you need to drink from the opposite side of the cup, so that your chin is inside. And take one long sip after another. Maybe six total."

Sigvid was unable to drink and keep her balance at the same time. She fell forward, the cup flying, and her gown flipping up to expose a pair of red wool panties covering a pair of very ample buttocks, accented by purple bows on each hip. She was still hiccuping, but instead of being angry or engaging in her usual sobbing, her back was lifting rhythmically. She was laughing.

"What in the gods' name are you up to now?" Steven asked.

His eyes about bugged out at the sight of Sigvid's red-clad bottom, which she had raised in the air as she attempted to get up. She was laughing so hard that the hiccups miraculously stopped.

"Helping Sigvid get rid of her hiccups," she said, laughing along with the woman sitting beside her now, tugging her gown down over her knees.

"You are being punished. What part of punishment do you not understand? Laughing and conversing with every single person passing by is not punishment."

She looked up at Steven's stern face. "What? Afraid your men might think you're not harsh enough with me?"

"Do not push me, woman."

"Ruff, ruff!"

"What is that supposed to mean?"

"I'm learning to be a dog."

"That is ridiculous."

"I don't know. You oughtta see me wag my tail."

She almost got a smile out of him. Almost, but not quite. "Sigvid, go back into the keep and find something to occupy yourself other than bothering my . . . my thrall."

"But—"

"You heard me."

"What she's trying to tell you is that Lady Thora banished her from the keep."

Steven put both hands to his hair and tugged on the cute war braids intertwined with clear colored beads. "Aaar-rgh!" Then he told Sigvid to give Lady Thora a message from him. It was a very crude message.

"I could ne'er say *that*!" Sigvid exclaimed.

He ignored Sigvid and wagged a finger at Rita. "Do not make me come back here again, or you will be sorry."

"It's not my fault."

"Do not talk back to me. I mean it, Ree-tah. Any more trouble, and you will not like the consequences."

So she sat, leaning against her pole, with nothing to do but think, and think, and think.

There were two scenarios that occupied her most. One: what to do if she were stuck here in the past? Today's happenings didn't bode well for her place in this society. Or two: what to do if she was able to go home? Because, frankly, she was beginning to think that WEALS wasn't her fate, either. Oh, it was all well and good as a way to pay off her debts, and she certainly had the physical capability to survive its strict regimen, and she was as patriotic as the next guy. Still, this time-travel experience marked a turning point in her life. If she only knew what it was!

No time to think any more on that, though. Here came Oslac, baited for bear . . . or rather, baited for she-who-wore-a-slave-collar.

He stood before her, arms folded over his chest, legs spread in a typical male stance of aggression. Like Steven, he wore no shirt, and sweat gleamed on his very fine body. With his blond hair, height, and Nordic features, he was pure Viking. Too bad he was such a prick. *Oops, I'm not supposed to use foul language anymore. Well, maybe it's okay when I just think bad words.*

"You better scoot away, Oslac. Steven doesn't want me causing any more trouble, and you look like trouble to me."

He snorted his opinion of her warning.

"Well, spit it out," she said when he just continued to glower at her.

"I have something to say to you, wench."

No kidding. "Did Steven send you?"

"Nay, he did not."

"Your face is going to freeze like that if you're not careful," she remarked when he still just continued to glower at her. "You have enough furrows in your forehead to grow wheat."

"You make jest of me and my people at your peril, but know this: I will not allow you to destroy him."

"Him who?"

"You know very well who. Steven."

"Destroy? Aren't you being a little dramatic?"

"This family has known too much pain, Steven most of all. One by one members of his family have disappeared or died. He carried Norstead and Amberstead during the times when his brother was too grieved to care. He nigh died himself of the heartache when Thorfinn went to the Other World."

Other World is one way of thinking of twenty-first-century America.

"And now you come here promising to lift his heavy burden."

"I never promised to lift anything. And if you bring up that light business, I just might puke. I never asked to be sent here."

"Betimes the Norns of Fate have other ideas, and who are we humans to resist what the gods ordain?"

"I'm Christian. I don't believe in gods or norns, whatever they are."

Oslac waved a hand dismissively. "One-God. Many gods. It matters not. What does matter is you, wench. Someone or something guided you here to light Steven's way."

"Me? A guiding light? Like a soap opera? I don't think so!"

"I must needs leave here soon. My father is ill and needs me back in Norsemandy. But I cannot leave lest I know your intentions."

"Here's the deal, Oslac. I respect your friendship with Steven and your concern for his well-being when you're gone, but I honestly don't know what role I'm supposed to play in his future or that of Norstead."

"The time-travel nonsense?"

She nodded. "One thing is for sure, being tied up like a slave today isn't the best way to ensure my cooperation."

He shrugged as if that was of little concern. "Just know this . . . if you abandon him, I will search you out and kill you. No matter where you are. And it will be a slow death, I promise you."

"Abandon? Abandon?"

He had already turned and was stomping away.

"How could I abandon someone who never asked me to stay?"

But what if he did?

She had no chance to ponder that question further, because she was about to have another visitor. Really, she felt like the target of the Viking Welcome Wagon. Or was that the Unwelcome Wagon?

A young man carrying a big bow and several arrows was heading toward the keep when he noticed her. Looking back to the field where Steven was busy in a huddle with several men, examining a broken lance, he hesitated, then veered to the right and came to stand before her.

"I am Armod, chief archer at Norstead." The young man

was not as young as she'd thought. Probably late teens, but he was only of mid height with a lean and wiry build. Not unattractive, if you disregarded the yellowed teeth and body odor.

She nodded. "Nice to meet you, Armod. Forgive me if I don't stand."

He sank down to his haunches before her, giving her yet another whiff of BO. She was definitely working on a deodorant first chance she got.

"I saw you teaching the boylings. You were good."

"I used to compete in archery competitions. In fact, I won several blue ribbons at the World University Games." Glancing at the broken arrow in his hand, she asked, "What's the problem?"

"No problem. I just need to have the carpenter prepare us more wood shafts and the arrow maker to attach the heads."

"I'm not an expert in aerodynamics or anything, but it seems to me that you could get more speed by working on the shafts, adding a few feathers, perhaps honing the arrowheads more narrowly."

She could tell she'd gotten his interest before he urged, "Explain, if you will."

She did, but once again added a disclaimer that she wasn't an expert or even informed on arrows or bow making. "All I would suggest is that you experiment with several different designs and see which ones give you greater speed, durability, and lighter weight. Don't make the mistake of thinking a heavier bow or thicker arrow is more desirable."

"I do not believe my eyes."

"Uh-oh!" She looked up behind Armod, at the same time the young man glanced back over his shoulder. She wasn't as concerned about the fury on Steven's face as she was by the horror . . . abject fear, actually . . . on Armod's.

"Armod, you know better," Steven seethed.

"I was just . . ."

Steven raised a hand. "You know better."

Armod ducked his head.

"No man dallies with what is mine, Armod. No matter how far the dalliance goes."

"Whoa, whoa, whoa!" Rita unwrapped her chains, which had been only loosely looped around the pole, stood, and walked up to Steven. He was so angry, his nostrils flared and his jaw clenched. "First of all, I am not yours. Second, there was no dalliance. For heaven's sake, he was just talking to me."

"Shut your teeth, wench, or you will suffer the same fate as Armod."

A cold chill ran over her spine. "What fate?" When he didn't answer, she asked hesitantly, "You wouldn't hurt him . . . would you?"

Again, he didn't answer her. Instead, he told Armod, "Go inside and wait for Geirfinn's return from the fields. We will discuss your punishment before this evening's meal."

Armod slumped off, casting an accusing glare her way, as if she was responsible for his being accused of a "dalliance."

"You are not going to punish that boy for nothing."

"That boy is a man, and he is most definitely going to be punished."

"And it's my fault?"

"Come," he said, taking the end of her chain and tugging her to follow him.

"Walk slower, you idiot, unless you *want* to choke me to death."

He slowed but did not look her way. She could see that he was fighting to control his anger as he walked along. His fists were clenched at his sides, and his neck was so stiff he could have swallowed a sword with no difficulty. Okay, that was an exaggeration, but not by much.

"Where are we going?"

Silence.

"We need to talk about Armod."

Silence.

"Why are you so angry about another man talking to me? Even if he was flirting with me, which he was not, that's between the two of us. It has nothing to do with you."

Silence.

"You know, this dark and brooding crap isn't attractive to me. Oops. I vowed to cut my bad language. Let me rephrase that. Your dark and brooding *garbage* isn't attractive to me."

Silence.

"Even if we were together, I wouldn't belong to you. Unless you belonged to me, too. No, I don't like the idea of possession. People should be together willingly. A partnership."

Silence.

"I have to pee."

Silence.

They were entering the stables now, which was a surprise to her. There were several dozen stalls to hold the warhorses, as well as riding horses. One of the riding horses was being led toward them, fully saddled with a leather bag strapped over the rump. He must have sent word up ahead.

Without releasing the end of her chain, Steven mounted the horse.

"Where's my horse? Oh, good Lord, you don't plan on me walking while you ride, using that chain as a lead? That would be the most barbaric thing you've done so far." Quickly, she reached up and untied the back of the leather collar, letting it drop to the ground. "Don't go getting bent out of shape over . . . What the hell . . . I mean, what the heck!"

He'd leaned down and lifted her by the waist so that her

bare feet dangled above the ground. "Put your foot in the stirrup and lift yourself behind me." The stable hand came over and helped her up.

"I can ride myself, you know," she said to his back, even as he began to move outside, causing her to grab for his waist. "You could have given me warning," she griped. "I could have fallen off."

"Oops," he said. "Isn't that your favorite word?"

The horse was moving at a canter now, and they were headed toward the forest where he followed a path of sorts through the thick undergrowth. She was unable to speak then until they arrived at a clearing where there was a small waterfall spilling into a pond that veered off to a stream that probably ran through the Norstead estate down to the fjord.

He dismounted and left her to get off the horse herself while he took the leather bag off the horse. Then he led the horse over to a grassy area where the animal immediately began to graze.

When he came back to her, he gave her his full attention for the first time since his overreaction back at the hitching post.

It was her turn to remain silent, and she did.

"You are a great one for wanting a choice in all things," he started out.

Uh-oh! This was beginning to sound like one of those situations where what you've said in the past comes back to bite you in the butt. "Yes?"

"I made a decision whilst riding here. It was my intention, originally, to come wash the sweat off my body . . . or the stink, as you put it so nicely."

"That sounds like a good idea."

"I am going to give you a choice."

"About bathing?"

"Either I order a flogging for Armod . . . fifty lashes with the whip . . ."

She gasped.

"Or you make me the luckiest man at Norstead."

"You wouldn't!"

"I would. Your choice."

"Some choice! You would really whip a man for no reason?"

"You misspeak me. My men, including Armod, knew not to approach you. If soldiers do not follow rules, there are consequences. Is that not so in your country's military?"

It was, and sometimes it was just as arbitrary and unfair, she had to admit. Take those soldiers court-martialed for defending themselves against civilian bombers in Tikrit. "You wouldn't enjoy having sex with an unwilling woman."

"You would not be unwilling."

The arrogance of the jerk! "Exactly what would I have to do? I mean, just for today, right?"

He snorted his opinion. "For as long as I want, as long as you are here, in any way at any time I want."

"You don't want much, do you?"

He shrugged.

"I will hate you for this."

He shrugged again. "'Tis a chance I am willing to take."

"Would I have to put on that blasted slave collar again?"

Tapping his chin thoughtfully, he finally said, "Only if you do something wrong again."

"Well, hell's bells, Steven, everything I do is wrong to you."

"Not everything," he said, taking her hand.

"Where are we going?"

"Talk, talk, talk."

"You never listen to me."

"I listen."

"No, you don't. You still haven't let me tell you about

my visit with Kraka and Grima and their ideas about my time travel. I've tried to tell you I left Norstead in all innocence, thinking I would return shortly. You won't even let me tell you what Armod was discussing with me. It's as unjust to flog Armod as it would be Sigvid, or the children who approached me."

"Do all women blather endlessly?"

"Only when they're nervous." *And speaking to a brick wall.*

Silence.

"Aren't you going to say that I have no reason to be nervous?"

"Nay, I am not." He stopped abruptly and looked at her in a considering fashion. "I do not suppose you would take off your garments for me without argument."

"Hah! What do you think?"

Then, without warning, he picked her up by the waist and dumped her into the pond, clothes and all . . . tunic, tights, and belt. When she came back to the surface, choking, she saw him toeing off his boots and shrugging out of his braies, after which he dove in after her.

When he rose like a dolphin in front of her, she asked, "Now what?"

"Now I get lucky."

Chapter 14

There are Popsicles, and then there are Pup-suckles...

Steven had never been so blistering wrathsome or so blistering lustsome at the same time in all his life.

A dunking in the cold waters of the pond should be doing him good, except the wench who caused it all was crawling up onto the bank, arse upwards, giving him an up-close view of her buttocks, clearly outlined by her soaking-wet braies.

She glanced back over her shoulder to see if he was following her, then looked again when she noticed the object of his gaze. She made a tsking sound of vexation that women perfected through the ages and muttered something that sounded like "Men!"

"Do not put a rump of boar roast in front of a starving man if you do not want him to salivate," he called out.

"A pig is a pig is a pig," she called back.

Whatever that means!

She stood now on a huge flat-topped boulder, the lip of which protruded over the pond. With her short hair flattened to her head, her eyelashes clumped together, and the sodden clothing plastered to her slim body, she looked more like a boyling than a full-grown woman. But she was more desirable to him in that moment than the most voluptuous beauty.

Which was amazing to him, he thought, as he looked downward through the clear water to his raging enthusiasm, undaunted by the cold. Weren't men supposed to shrivel under such circumstances? Somehow, his body had gotten the signals mixed.

Apparently she saw what he saw, because her face flushed, and she made another of those tsking sounds.

"Get me a bar of soap from the saddlebag." Then to soften the tone of his order, he added, "To remove the stink you so colorfully described earlier today."

She walked toward the grazing horse tethered to a tree, got the soap, then tossed it out to him where he stood waist deep in the pond.

"Take off your garments, Ree-tah. There on the rock where I can watch."

Her chin shot up with resistance.

He'd expected no less. "I refuse to play these games with you. Either you agree to my terms regarding Armod, or you do not. I will not warn you at every turn. It is not fair to me or to Armod." In truth, this would be the only day for some time that he would be free to take his leisure, what with meeting Brodir on the morrow and the Althing mere days away. He intended to take advantage of every second of the freedom.

"What about me? What's fair for me?"

He began to soap his body . . . his chest, arms, underarms, and neck, then his hair. The harsh lye soap did not lather much, but it did the job. Without answering her question . . . he was done discussing a completed deal . . . he ducked under the water and swam a short distance to the shallow end, where he soaped the rest of his body.

When he finally turned around, he saw that she was standing in the middle of the rock, totally nude. She did not look like a boyling now.

Many women would blush with humiliation at being so exposed. They would attempt to cover themselves with their hands. They would beg for mercy, accompanied by leaking eyes and sobbing mouths.

Not his Rita.

Nay, she held his gaze, challenging him. Then she executed a perfect dive into the water, swam underwater like the fish he had originally thought she was, and ended on the far side of the pond, where she pulled herself up onto a ledge just below and in front of the small waterfall. With cascades of water spraying around her, through which sunlight was being filtered like a full-bodied halo, she resembled nothing more than a water sprite. A wicked water sprite.

With a shake of his head, he swam over and lifted himself to sit beside her. "Are you ever biddable?"

"If biddable means a doormat, no."

He nudged her bare foot with his bare foot for no reason other than he wanted to touch her. "I ne'er asked you to be a doormat."

"Just a slave."

"Symbolic only. To make a point." He ran a fingertip from her shoulder down her arm to her fist clenched on the ledge, and watched with fascination as goose bumps rose in his wake.

"You made your point, all right. Bondage, slavery, flogging, blackmail. I'm not sure I even like you, Steven."

He noticed that her nipples were engorged and rosehued. Was it due to rising arousal? He suspected so. If he did not miss his guess, Rita was fighting her own body's overstimulation as much as he was his, which incidentally did not have the good sense to deflate until the right moment. "The bondage was bedsport, pure and simple, and you liked it, you cannot deny that. But I will not defend myself anymore. Favor me or not, I want you."

She arched her brows toward his unbridled enthusiasm, which rose from his man-hair like a lance. "No kidding. And do you always get what you want?"

He shrugged.

"Even if you have to use devious methods to get what you want?"

He shrugged again. Wise to her ploys, he would not let her guilt him into releasing her from their pact. "Are you an honest person, Ree-tah?"

She bristled, as he knew she would. "Yes, I am. To a fault sometimes."

Gently, he pushed her backward until she was resting on her elbows. The short waterfall hit the ledge like a curtain behind her head before spilling forward on the ledge into another small waterfall. Water splashed all around them, the cold alleviated by the warm sun.

Leaning over her, he blew against the golden fuzz that covered her mons. Her stomach went inward as she inhaled sharply.

He used a forefinger to trace the line of her cleft between her closed thighs. "I do not suppose you would like to demonstrate your Pup-suckle for me?"

"What?"

He was not sure if her shriek was in response to his repeated stroking of her cleft or to his question. "Pup-suckle. Remember Pup-suckle, Butterfly, Swing, Backbend sex?" It gave him immense pleasure to see that even though she deliberately closed her sex to him, a glisten of her woman dew seeped through. One of the advantages . . . or disadvantages, depending on one's viewpoint . . . of having a bald pate down there. No secrets.

"You mean Popsicle." She burst out laughing and kept on laughing until her eyes were misting with tears of mirth. "You have an incredible sense of humor."

"Is that good or bad?" Either way, it did not matter to him, because in the process of laughing, her legs had spread slightly, giving him a foothold . . . rather a handhold . . . to heaven. The heel of his hand was now pressing against her most erotic place, his middle finger in its own hot sheath.

"It depends on whether you've given up on blackmail sex."

Good gods! How can she be grasping my finger and talking at the same time? It must be a talent future women develop. But blackmail sex? That subject was dead to him now. He refused to discuss it one more second. "You are so sexy I could peak just looking at you."

The parting of her lips and the arching of her breasts told him without words that she was in the same condition. Still, he could almost see her brain working. Should she yield to him? Or should she continue a futile struggle?

As if reading his mind, she said, "A good soldier knows when to pick her battles." With those words, she sat up and swung herself sideways to her knees, straddling him.

"And this is a battle you concede?" he asked with a husky growl. His hands swept up and down over her back, over her waist, palming her buttocks.

She nodded. "The battle, but not the war," she murmured against his mouth. And then she bit his bottom lip to emphasize her point and raised her hips before lowering herself onto his rock-hard staff.

She still thought she controlled their sex play. Well, let her. For a while.

His groan had to be interpreted as a concession of sorts to her, seeing the small smile of satisfaction on her face.

No matter.

The war talk aside, this was now one man, one woman, pleasing one another in the most exquisite way.

She was the one pushing him back to his elbows now where he could watch her take her pleasure of him, thus giving him even more pleasure. And what a glorious sight she was!

Slim. Much slimmer than he preferred his women to be. Leastways, he had in the past. But because her frame was so slender, her breasts appeared bigger, though they scarce filled his cupped hands.

Another difference was the muscle definition in her shoulders and upper arms, her abdomen and belly, her thighs and calves. She must do some vigorous exercising to keep her body in this condition. The female soldiering business, he supposed. Well, that was good. Mayhap she would be able to keep up with all he had planned for the next few hours.

She was undulating her hips forward and backward, causing his cock to almost slide out each time, abraded by the most amazing friction. Watching him watch her, she said, "Wanna see something I'll bet none of your other women have done?"

Was she daft? Of course he wanted to, whatever it was. "Only if you really want to," he demurred.

She clenched and unclenched his cock like a fist, but inside her woman channel. He had to grit his teeth to restrain himself from howling.

Leaning forward now, with himself fully imbedded and unmoving . . . damn it all to Niflheim and back, she stuck one forefinger in her mouth and sucked. At the same time, she used the other forefinger to trace his lips, then stuck the same finger inside his mouth, where he sucked to hold it there. Of course, contrary wench that she was, she pulled it out and resumed her upright straddle.

Then she did the most outrageous, spectacular thing.

Using the wet forefingers, she teased her own nipples. Tracing the areolas, then the nipples themselves. Flicking the tips to even harder points. Pinching. Tweaking. Flicking again. With each touch, an echoing ripple passed inside her body, caressing his manpart.

If that were not evidence enough of her ability to arouse

herself, she moved one hand down her body to the place where they were joined. Lifting herself slightly, she began to strum that protruding pearl of a woman's pleasure.

She was panting now, and her eyes were half-shuttered. He could tell her peaking was imminent.

"Nay!" he roared. Grabbing her hips, he began to raise and lower her hips onto him with a rhythm she soon caught. They peaked together, and it seemed like forever that her woman's bliss milked every drop of his man seed into her womb. He said a silent prayer of thanks for her birthing control device. He did not think he would have been able to pull out at the last minute, no matter the consequences.

After their breathing returned to normal, she lay half-splatted over him, their hot bodies being sprayed from splashes of the waterfall.

His thoughts were in turmoil regarding Rita and what she had just done. Her lack of inhibition was a gift, of course, but she did push the bounds.

"I've shocked you, haven't I?" she asked, kissing his chest where her face now rested.

Caught! "A little," he admitted.

"You bring out the wanton in me."

He liked that idea. "Methinks it is your taking control of sex play that disconcerts me a bit."

"You don't like that? Many men claim that they wish their partners would take the initiative."

"Oh, I did not say I did not like it. I like it, all right, but Viking men like to lead."

"Don't you mean dominate?"

He smacked her rump lightly.

A companionable silence followed, but only for a short while.

Running a hand up and down her back, loving the feel of wet silk skin, he kissed the top of her head, then put his mouth near her ear. "Dost think we can try the Pup-suckle now?"

She began to laugh . . . he could tell by her soft chuckles and the shaking of her chest against his chest, though what was so funny, he did not know.

When he rolled to his side, she raised her head and glanced pointedly at his now half-flaccid erection. "Honey, I think your pup has had more than enough for now."

She got up then and dove into the water before he could reply. If she had waited, he would have told her his "pup" had had nowhere near enough. Not of her, leastways.

Better yet, he should show her.

He was the Donald Trump of the Dark Ages . . .

There was something to be said for two physically fit people having wild, breath-stopping sex, but this was ridiculous.

They'd made love up by the waterfall. Then he'd taken her against a tree down below. Moving to the flat boulder, where they'd had a small picnic of apples, hard cheese, and flat manchet bread that Steven had had the foresight to pack, she'd gone down on him showing just how a Pupsuckle could be done. Then he'd gone down on her, showing her the famous Viking X-Spot, not to be confused with the Viking S-Spot or the modern-day G-spot. All she could say in that regard was, "You can play tic-tac-toe with me any day!" And, now, with late afternoon approaching, she was lying flat on the grass with Steven lying heavily atop her, having taken her doggie style.

"You're killing me," she said on a moan, not altogether sure she was going to be able to stand . . . or walk.

He rolled to his back but would not release her, even now. Instead, he tucked her under his arm with a hand of the other arm lying possessively on her stomach.

"Did I hurt you?" he asked with absolutely no apology in his voice.

"No, but, holy moly, Steven, what are you trying to prove? Are all Vikings this insatiable?"

"Nay. Just me."

She smacked his chest.

"Well, of course all Viking men are known for their sex prowess, but I am better than most."

"Humble, are you?"

"Truth to tell, sweetling, I am little inclined toward meekness. In this case, though, I wanted to put my mark on you so that in the days ahead when I may not always be around so much, you will remember this, and not run off to . . . wherever."

She could tell that he still had difficulty mentioning the future or time travel. "Steven, I've told you that I won't leave unless I tell you first, if I am able."

"'Tis a comfort," he said in a tone clearly saying it was not. "Tell me more about this future time."

"Well, I've already told you about telephones, automobiles, airplanes, and birth control. There's also motorboats . . . running hot and cold water indoors, not to mention toilets . . . heat and air-conditioning . . . restaurants . . . military . . . wars . . . women's equality." With each thing she mentioned, she had to give an explanation, to which he just stared at her with increasing incredulity.

"And Thorfinn lives like this? And does all these things?"

She nodded. "I wish I could explain computers to you and how they have revolutionized the world, just as the invention of the printing press did in the fifteenth century, but frankly I don't understand it myself."

"All this in a thousand years!"

"You never did let me tell you what Kraka and Grima had to say about my time travel."

He groaned. "Do you have to tell one and all these fantastical stories?"

"Actually, they already knew. Sort of."

That got his attention. He raised his head to stare down at her. "Explain."

"It's all related to this gloom business and how some mysterious light—"

"Meaning you?" he interrupted, tweaking her chin playfully.

"—is supposed to come here and change everything for the good."

"And the two witches are involved how?"

"They claim to have conjured me here."

"And you believe them? You have to understand, Reetah, that they are not known for great success in the witchly arts. And their niece Sigge is even worse. She nigh drowned the well digger one time when he was trying to locate a new spot for a well. Claimed she was trying to help, she did. Instead, we had gushers of water all over the place."

Rita had to smile at that. "I like them, and they know a lot about herbs and healing. You should visit their cottage sometime. You would be surprised."

"Nay, thank you." He shivered, probably picturing cobwebs and bats. But then he seemed to think of something else. "Does that mean that they can conjure you home as easily as they brought you here?" She could tell that the idea held no good news for him.

"That's the problem. When they prayed me here, or whatever you call the conjuring business, they weren't specific about where I was to come from. Could have been from across the fjord, for all they knew. In fact, they never even considered the fact that they might be pulling someone from the future or from the past. Heck, Steven, you might have had some prehistoric cave woman, for all they would have been able to control their magic."

"Those two should be locked up. Really. They are unsafe to themselves and those around them."

"They brought me."

"There is that," he said, kissing her forehead.

"Bottom line: they're afraid if they try to reverse the time travel, I might end up somewhere entirely different.

Like in the middle of the lion's ring at a Roman coliseum, or in a futuristic spaceship."

He smiled.

"What? You think it's funny?"

"Not funny. Just . . . I like knowing that you cannot jump off into the future, at will."

"You'd rather I leave when you're ready, right?" She saw the heat of embarrassment color his cheeks. "I know perfectly well that you tire of your women in short order, and that you think the same will happen with me."

"But not for a long time, methinks. Leastways not until your birth control device wears out."

"Thanks a bunch. To tell you the truth, I can't accept any logical scientific explanation for time travel . . . maybe someday far in the future . . . but not today. And I'm skeptical about witches and conjuring. But I do believe in God and miracles. I can only think that God had some reason for sending me here."

He thought about that for a long moment. "That would mean either that you need something that you can only get here, or there is some need here that only you can fulfill."

"Precisely."

Could it be as simple as love, or destined lovers? she wondered. Not that she was in love with Steven. Not yet. But she could be.

"Right now, I have more important problems, and I do not just mean Disa and that *nithing* Brodir, and not just the Althing. Norstead and Amberstead are being over-crowded. There is not enough arable land here to sustain the five hundred or more people. And we cannot spread farther north where the living is even harsher. As it is, we must needs trade furs and amber for additional food. It has become a juggling game for me of late: where to allocate labor to the best results. In the end, I am probably going to have to send some men and their families off to other lands to settle. Mayhap Iceland."

She had thought at one point that Steven would make a good CEO. She was convinced of it now. Without paper or calculators, he managed to pretty much put together a profit and loss system for his estates. P&L medieval style, she thought with a smile.

"Maybe you need to be creative."

"Like?"

"I don't know. Goats? Aren't they supposed to be able to graze just about anywhere?"

"Goats! Those smelly creatures!"

"Hey, whatever works. And more sheep."

"Our sheep do not produce as fine a fleece, not like high-quality Northumbrian wool."

She shrugged. "So, produce lesser quality wool. There has to be a market for that, too. And I understand there are hardier breeds of cattle. The people of Scotland are known for their whiskey, or they will be. You could brew the best mead in the world. And don't forget, I intend to invent deodorant." She waggled her eyebrows at him.

He still looked skeptical.

"Oooh, oooh, oooh! I just thought of something. What do you do with all the animal intestines after you slaughter?"

"Some we use to make sausage. Others . . . I do not know. Throw away, I suppose."

"This is great. You can invent condoms."

When she explained, his mouth dropped open with incredulity.

"You expect men to put intestines on their cocks . . . at the height of enthusiasm, yet! Have you lost your senses?"

"Hey, if it prevents an overabundance of babies . . ." She shrugged.

He laughed then and squeezed her tighter to his side. "See, we work well together. You must stay."

But only for a while. That was the hidden message, as far as she could tell.

"We must needs go back soon," he told her then, rising to his feet, then pulling her up beside him.

"Thank you for a lovely day." For a day that had started so lousy . . . with her in a thrall collar . . . it had certainly ended beautifully. The kind of fantasy afternoon a girl could tuck away to pull out in the future for poignant memories of a love that might have been.

He smiled, a smile that lit the world if he only knew, and said, "Thank *you* m'lady."

Chapter 15

Of unicorns and clueless men . . .

Steven and Oslac, fully armed in chain *sherts*, nosed helmets, and sword and lance, rode horses toward the bottom of the small valley . . . more than four hours from Norstead near the North Sea, the designated spot where he was to meet with Brodir and one of his men.

He was not stupid enough to come unguarded, however. Nor was Brodir. They both had troops lined at the top of opposing hills, ready to battle, if need be. And he had to admit, Brodir's pirates were an organized bunch, not at all the raggedy band of cutthroats he had expected.

"I noticed you and the sea wench having a heated discussion before you left this morn," Oslac commented idly.

"She wanted to come with us."

"In the gods' names, why?"

"Thinks a woman's perspective would be helpful."

Oslac shook his head with disbelief. "She is a willful one."

"That she is."

"You raise her above her station."

"Hard to determine what her station should be."

"And the time-travel nonsense. Surely you do not believe that flummery."

He shrugged. "What other explanation could there be? You have not heard all her tales of modern marvels. They are too detailed and imaginative to be a fabrication."

"You are becoming too close to her, my friend."

Steven bristled, but then he relaxed, knowing Oslac only had his best interests at heart. In truth, he had been thinking the same himself. His strong sentiments for Rita were troubling and unexpected and posed all kinds of problems for the future, both hers and his.

But he had engaged in the most amazing sex play with her yesterday . . . and through the night. Best of all, she had been with him every step of the way, and ahead of him, betimes. He smiled at some of the memories. It would be hard to give that up. As for it being more than amusement, he could not think on that now.

"You will be leaving Norstead after the Althing," Steven pointed out. "I must needs have a companion to while away the hours."

"A companion. Not a woman! And do not forget, you are still betrothed to Olaf's daughter."

"That was always a tenuous bargain betwixt my father and Olaf years ago. She may already be wed, for all we know. Furthermore, what has my marriage to do with Reetah?" That last statement rang false even to him, but then, by the time he finally took a wife, she might not even be here.

But he had no time to ponder that now. Approaching them, also on horseback, were Brodir and his guardsman.

Brodir was fully armed but without a helmet. Clean-shaven, long blond hair with war braids, slightly taller than him but slimmer. A fine figure of a Viking man, most women would say.

Beside him was that giant troll of a Norseman, Gerleff the Bull, so named because of his massive height and barrel chest. The onetime berserker sported a shaggy beard and unkempt hair. He was as ugly as Brodir was handsome.

"Frigg's foot! I hope you do not expect me to take on Gerleff if it comes to a fight," Oslac said. "He would crush me just by giving me a push and standing on my chest."

Steven laughed. Oslac was an excellent swordsman, and he knew it. Size had naught to do with skill.

The four men dismounted at the same time and tethered their horses to nearby trees. Steven and Oslac removed their helmets as they sat on a boulder facing Brodir and Gerleff on another boulder. In fact, the entire flat bottom of this bowl-like valley was littered with huge rocks, carved out by glaciers aeons ago, according to the sagas. This area had been a meeting place for many over the years, even some Althings.

Steven took the initiative. "You have my sister Disa."

"I do."

"Why did you not bring her?"

He arched his eyebrows as if Steven were daft.

"If she is harmed in any way—"

Brodir raised a halting hand. "Disa is well, and as disagreeable as any woman can be. If we come to some agreement today, I will return her to you, gladly."

"I have not seen my sister in four years, afore her husband died. She ever was one to speak her mind," he admitted.

"She calls me a loathsome lout with the brain of a dwarf and the manners of a troll. And that is the least of her insults."

Steven swallowed a grin. "I recall one time, when we were young, she said I would wag my tail at a statue if it had breasts. At the time I was smitten with the swine herder's daughter." But enough of that. "What do you want, Brodir? What happened to you, a far-famed warrior of honor, to come to this pass? You have to know you are considered a *nithing* by one and all, an outlaw of the worst sort."

Brodir's cheeks heightened with color, and he put a hand to the hilt of his sword, then dropped it. "Two years past, I killed a man. A Dane named Hogar. That I admit. But the man had beaten to death a village maid who spurned his attentions and burned her cottage to the ground to cover his crime."

"So why did you get charged?"

"Elsbeth was my mistress." He gulped as if to contain his emotions. "She carried my unborn child. Hogar put it about that I was unhappy about the coming babe, and since Elsbeth was of common blood, no candidate for marriage."

He recalled then that Brodir's father had been a high jarl at one time but had been long dead, even by that time. Although of noble blood, Brodir had been landless, being a younger son.

"Did you take your case to the king?"

"Not the king himself. Even if I was believed, the wergild for a serving woman, even a free one who was pregnant, would have been mere coin, and not that much. I wanted a confession and satisfaction beyond some rich man's purse."

"Why would the Althing court take the word of Hogar's family over yours?"

"Because Hogar was a cousin of King Olaf."

Ah! "And you had no friends to stand for you?"

"I did have a witness. Your brother Thorfinn."

"That is convenient, since Finn is gone and cannot prove your story."

"He was there, I tell you. When Hogar's family started the rumor of my killing him without provocation, that it was me who killed Elsbeth, as well, I took my case to the king's advisors and was told the law court would listen to my pleas at the next Althing three months hence. But then

Thorfinn got a missive from you telling him of a sighting of Luta and his baby in Baghdad. He rushed off to meet you there, promising to be back well before the hearing."

"And that was when Thorfinn went missing," Steven finished for him. "What do you want of me?"

"I want your help in removing my outlaw status."

Steven widened his eyes at that.

"I believe there has to be at least one man in your employ who was with Thorfinn at the time, who can help prove my innocence."

"Even if that were so, Brodir, there have been so many crimes since then."

"Such as?"

"Well, you and your men raped those novices at Sudeby and put a blood eagle on the abbess, for sport."

"Pfff! If you believe that, I have a one-horned horse to sell you. Think on it, Steven, dost honestly think I need to rape a girl? Women . . . even girls . . . approach me, not the other way round. And, truth to tell, I have never blood-eagled an enemy in battle, let alone a helpless female."

"And you are accused of using your fighting skills to organize pirates and train them to attack in fleets."

"And this is a crime? Because I fight to survive, I am less than those honored men who go a-Viking for plunder in Saxon lands? Nay, everything of which I am accused is mostly false, and it all spiraled out from the death of Elsbeth and my killing Hogar. If I can have that slate wiped clean, the rest will follow."

"And now we come back to my sister."

"Investigate amongst your men for me and set up a hearing for me before the Althing to be held on your lands. I will come willingly and hand over Disa."

"You would trust me?"

"I would if you give your word."

Steven wiped a hand over his face.

"This is what Thorfinn would want you to do."

Steven bristled. That was a low blow, but it was true nonetheless.

They agreed then with a clasp of fists and after several horns of ale. Once notified, Brodir would come to Norstead with Disa and a handful of men only. He would be escorted by Steven's hersirs and housecarls to Norstead, for his protection on the day of his hearing.

As they were mounting their horses to return to Norstead late that afternoon, Brodir commented, "I hear you have a strange sea wench living at Norstead."

Brodir heard too much, Steven realized. He must have a spy in his camp.

Before he could answer, Oslac said, "I suggested we exchange the sea wench for Disa, but you might find her even more difficult to handle than Steven's sister."

Steven did not bother to correct Oslac's statement that he would be willing to make such an exchange. He had only ever agreed to *consider* such a possibility as a last resort.

"I do not think there could be a more difficult female than Disa, if you must know."

For an odd second, Steven thought that Brodir was protesting too much, and he recalled Rita's advice. "Dost know what my sea wench suggests regarding our negotiations for Disa's release?"

Brodir frowned with confusion. "Why would you be taking a woman's counsel on men's affairs?"

Steven and Oslac both laughed. As if they had any choice where Rita was concerned.

"She thinks you and Disa should marry."

Brodir started coughing as air went down the wrong passageway. His complexion was rather green when he raised his head. "You jest?"

Steven shrugged. He liked Brodir, and he honestly hoped he could be proved innocent. "Stranger things have happened."

Like time travel, he thought.

As he and his troop rode home that afternoon, more than half a day since he had left at dawn, he wondered what Rita was up to in his absence. He had told her to stay put inside the keep, and she had promised to obey his order. No doubt she was sleeping after their sleepless night. Resting for another sleepless night, he hoped.

What kind of trouble could she get into inside the keep, sleeping or not?

Men name their penises, why not women? . . .

Rita awakened soon after dawn, happier and more energized than she'd been in years, despite being sore in some intimate places. A soreness she rather liked.

The source of her soreness was gone already, off to meet the pirates. Arg! Ahoy, maties, and all that! Her first inclination was to think, *Men and their games!* But this could be dangerous, and she would worry until he returned, hopefully this evening.

In the meantime, she had deodorant to invent, she decided with a chuckle. Jumping out of bed, she dressed in an old faded gown, which she figured would be more suitable to the type of work she envisioned. Luckily, Sigge had returned and was eager to help her. Plus, the two aunts were expected to arrive later this morning with more of the herbs and oils she hoped to experiment with.

"Don't you have work to do here, Sigge? I mean, are you allowed to flit off whenever you want?"

"Certainly. I tend the herb gardens, and whilst at my aunts' cottage, I replenish stock that has died or run out. Many herbs have to be replanted each year."

First they went down to the kitchen, where Rita introduced herself to the head cook, Brighid, an Irishwoman of fifty-odd years who had come to Norstead as the child of a thrall. Both mother, Ceara, and child had earned their freedom long ago. The elderly mother sat at the other end of a long table snapping string beans.

The enormous kitchen was a bustling hive of activity, even this early in the morning. At least a dozen people worked to set out the first meal of the day . . . mostly leftovers from the night before, but already a skinned and gutted deer was being put on the spit to cook all day. Some of them introduced themselves.

One cook's assistant, Groa, was kneading dough. Another, Herdis, was baking the round, flat loaves of unleavened manchet bread. The circular bread had holes poked in the middle so that when baked they could be stored on a long, upright pole. Groa and Herdis moved efficiently, producing dozens of the wheels within minutes. Not so quick was another maid who was using a primitive quern stone to grind grain into wheat. Yet another churned milk into butter.

When she offered to help, the cook's eyebrows arched. Apparently lowly kitchen jobs were usually done only by servants. And no one was sure just how to classify her. But there was much extra work necessary to prepare for the Althing, a big assembly of Vikings to be held here in a few days, including some specialty dishes, one of which Sigge explained to her in an undertone so as not to offend anyone. The dish in question, called *sviâ*, sat on a side table, ready to be put in the cold storage room until the day it would be prepared. *Sviâ* was a sheep's head, complete with eyes, which would be boiled and eaten after pickling, Sigge told her, giggling when Rita gagged. Rita prided herself on her strong stomach and willingness to try new dishes, but sheep's eyeballs? No way!

"How are ya at skinning eels?" Brighid asked.

Rita could hear splashing noises from the eel barrel by the door. "Uhm, isn't there something else?" she asked.

Soon she sat next to Sigge, working on a virtual mountain of clean vegetables, which they began to peel. Turnips and carrots, mostly. The peelings were saved to be put in the soup cauldron, which was always bubbling over the fire.

"The reason I came down here, actually," Rita told the cook, "is that I need to borrow a bunch of pots and containers for some experiments. Oh, don't worry. I won't take up space in your kitchen. I can work out in the laundry area on the washtub fires, since today isn't laundry day."

"What kind of ex-parry-mens?" Brighid asked suspiciously, eying Sigge at the same time. "I doan want no witchy rites bein' done in my kitchens or kitchen area."

"Oh, no. Nothing like that. I want to create deodorant, and I'm not sure what combination of what herbs and oils will work best." She went on to explain what deodorant was.

"What? Are ye daft? Folks here are cleaner than any place I know," Brighid said with affront. "Better than Saxons, fer a certainty. Those folks doan bathe but once a year, I hear. In fact, some say the Vikings take too many baths."

"I don't mean to be insulting, but everyone perspires and creates body odor, especially the underarms. Even if you shower or bathe every day, there will probably be odor if you don't use a deodorant."

"And ye think that is a bad odor?" Brighid asked.

"Don't you?"

"Ya get used to it, I guess." Brighid shrugged. "Besides, I like a man what smells like a man, not a bloody flower."

Others in the room agreed with her.

"Doan get me wrong, some folks go too far and they turn ripe, if ya get my meaning."

If you asked Rita, there were a lot of ripe fruits here at Norstead, some of them in this very kitchen. But she was a visitor to this culture and should tread politely, she cautioned herself.

"Ya oughtta concentrate on bad breath," said Solveig,

who was cracking walnuts. "When my Arne has had more than two horns of ale, he 'bout knocks me out when he comes ta bed."

"Ale breath." Groa nodded.

"I know what's worse than that," Herdis said. "When a *drukkinn* man breaks wind. Phew!" She waved a hand in front of her face.

"Beer farts!" a boy who had just begun turning the spit pronounced. When his mother made a shushing sound, he hooted, "Beer farts! Beer farts! Beer farts!" and ran away when his mother tried to swat his behind.

"How 'bout moldy rushes when the dogs have been loose too many sennights?" still another woman offered.

"Didja ever smell pus when it be putrifyin' in an open wound? Before they cut off Njal's leg, the stink was enough ta gag a maggot." This from Ceara, who fanned her face in remembrance.

"Seems there are enough bad smells without worryin' on underarms," the cook said, shaking her head at what she considered a frivolous exercise. Still, she went into a storeroom and came back with several pots and pottery jars used to store honey and spices. "Would these work?"

"Perfect! Thank you very much. I'll wait to start until after things settle down here in the kitchen."

Talk moved on then to the upcoming Althing, which caused considerable excitement. Apparently, there were only one or two of these events held each year, and while serious business was transacted, it was also an occasion for visiting and entertainment. Music, dancing, games. Like a giant medieval fair.

"Wonder how many babes will be born nine months hence," Bergliot, a big-breasted woman with a twinkle in her eye, pondered while she piled bread, cheese, and slices of cold meat on a huge wooden trencher. "Last year, there musta been twenty jist here at Norstead alone."

"One of them yer little Bjorn," Brighid teased.

The others smiled, possibly at fond memories.

"I like ta visit the different booths where folks bring things ta sell," a young girl named Deidre remarked. "Remember those candle molds we found two years past," she said to Brighid, who Rita assumed was her mother, considering the bright red frizzy hair on both of them. "The ones that mark the hours of the day?"

"According to my history books, those time-keeping candles were invented by the Saxon King Alfred," Rita contributed.

They all flashed her a "Duh?" look.

"There is one whole booth that sells nothing but ribands," Sigge told Rita. "And of course my aunts have their own booth for healing and love potions."

"Hah! I bought one of them love potions and it dint do nothin' ta make Uggi marry up with me," Ceara said with disgust. "But he did join me in the bed furs afore he realized who I was."

They all turned to look at the ancient woman, who was cackling with laughter.

"Now, Mother," Brighid chided, "you are too old for love, and Uggi is twenty years younger than you."

"*What?* No one's too old fer love, and what has age ta do with it? Yer juices must be more dried up than mine."

Brighid looked at Rita and rolled her eyes.

"The Althing sounds like fun," Rita said. "Maybe I'll have my deodorant invented by then."

"Ya could always sell those chastity belts," Bergliot said, eyeing her speculatively, especially the region below her waist, as if she could see through the gown. "We heard how ya were sewin' 'em up in the ladies' solar."

"They're not chastity belts. In fact, some of them in my country are designed to entice men, not repel them." Seeing that the women didn't understand and noticing there were no men in the room, she stood and lifted her gown to demonstrate. She even turned to show them the back.

"Holy Thor!" Brighid exclaimed. "I want one of those."

Every other woman in the room echoed her request, including Ceara, who said hers should be purple with see-through lace.

After all the laughter died down, Rita said, "Actually, the best seller in my opinion would be condoms, as I told Steven . . . I mean, your master . . . yesterday." She explained what condoms were, and then, hard to believe, she had to explain what birth control was for.

"Why would anyone wanna *not* have a baby?" Bergliot asked.

Before Rita could answer, Brighid said, "I know some women who have too many. They doan care proper fer the ones they have. Plus, some women jist are not made ta bear that many children. That is why they die early."

Wow! That was some lecture from Brighid. Rita was impressed.

"But is it not a sin?" Brighid wanted to know.

"I don't think so," Rita replied. "Now, abortion . . . that's another story entirely, and I don't want to engage in that discussion. But preventing birth . . . no, I think that should be a woman's choice."

She could tell the women were divided on the issue.

"Bet some men . . . includin' my Arne . . . would object," Solveig, the nut-cracking lady, said.

She was right. Some men did object, even in her time. Irresponsible jerks!

"I still doan understand how those condoms would work," Brighid said.

"Do you have any clean animal intestines around, ones you're saving to make sausages?"

Brighid nodded hesitantly, then made a motion to her daughter, Deidre, who went down into a cold cellar and brought up a large tray covered with a damp cloth.

"Good grief!" Rita exclaimed when she saw the vast variety of widths and lengths. They must come from all kinds of animals . . . sheep, cows, bears, deer, whatever. Picking up one of the medium-size ones, she gave an explanation of how a condom would work, emphasizing how important it was that there be no holes, not even pin size, and that it would have to be firmly secured at the base. "Hey, I'm not really recommending anyone make these. It was just a silly thought."

Bergliot picked up one of the narrow ones and said with a giggle, "Eydis is about this size. A straw cock he has."

There was much giggling.

"Skarp the Blacksmith," Brighid said, holding up a huge one. "Bull cock."

Groa took one short length of a medium-width one and held it up by the middle, with both sides drooping down. "Hedin. String cock."

Herdis took the same length from Groa, held by both ends, then moved one slightly to the right. "Lazy-eyed cock."

Good Lord, the man must have a bend in his penis.

They were all laughing uproariously by the time the sausage casings were put back in the cold cellar.

"Well, I'm off to make deodorant. Anyone want to help?"

To her surprise, several of the women, besides Sigge, followed her. They probably wanted to see what outrageous thing she did next.

The scary thing was, Rita didn't know what that was going to be.

Chapter 16

The Grand Ole Opry, they were not . . .

No sooner did Rita step into the open-sided laundry shed than Kraka and Grima arrived in full witch gear . . . wild tangled hair, black gowns, "necklaces" of colored rune stones and unidentifiable objects hanging from their scrawny necks, carrying thin sticks that she assumed were supposed to be magic wands. And they were cackling to beat the band, mumbling such drivel as "Abba cre, solum met, arsk, arsk, arsk!" which they translated to "Darkness begone, light welcome, hail to the bringer of the light."

Once they settled in, though, they attended to serious issues.

"Groa, did you steep the herbs I gave you to cure your baby's cough?" Kraka asked.

"Yea, I did. And it worked after only one day. Thank you."

"And your monthly cramps, Herdis?" Grima inquired.

"I still have them, but not so bad," Herdis said. "Should I take more at one time?"

For a half hour the two witches prescribed their own brand of medicine to the small crowd that gathered. Then, almost as quickly as they'd appeared, they were off to set up their Althing tent booth.

Rita and her helpers then started the laundry fires and set out her various ingredients that would be used in her experiments. Rose, coriander, and honeysuckle oils. Rendered pig fat . . . or lard, which fortunately had very little odor. Aloe, witch hazel leaves, roots, and bark, arrowroot powder, lavender, sage, and several flowers she couldn't identify. She had no idea where to start, so she just arranged various combinations until she had two dozen piles, which she would cook together or chop together and mix with oil or lard. She wasn't sure if she was going to end up with a liquid or cream.

And it was fun. Not just the mixing, which sometimes ended with horrible results, like the clumpy combination of arrowroot powder, oil, and flower petals. Some were too oily, and some were too dry. In the end, after much laughter all around, she had ten "products" to try. She was going to put one on herself, and the others had volunteered as guinea pigs for the rest.

The most fun, though, had come from the music. When she'd complained about there not being any musical background to their workplace, she'd had to explain Muzak, radios, and CDs. Not that they'd understood. But they did begin to sing some songs, which were pleasant enough but too soft, in her opinion.

"What we need is some toe-tapping music with rhythm," she pronounced, which of course put her in the spot of having to demonstrate. Since the only songs she knew all the words to were country from a recent movie she'd stunt doubled on, *Cheatin' Hearts*, about a rodeo star, Matthew McConaughey, his two-timing wife, Martina McBride, and the daughter, Taylor Swift.

The two songs from the soundtrack she would have embedded in her mind forever were "Achy Breaky Heart" and "Boot Scootin' Boogie." The Viking women loved, loved, loved the songs and made her . . . not the greatest singer in the world . . . sing them over and over until they could sing along with her, all of them chiming in on the refrain of "Woooo-oooh!" that sounded like a train whistle.

"What we need now," she said, still laughing, when everything was cleaned up and the various jars were all lined up, "is line dancing."

History was made then. A bunch of Viking women with their gowns hiked up to their knees, along with some young girls, and even children, and, yes, that was Kraka and Grima, lined up in the back courtyard, singing their hearts out. And line dancing. They were good, too. They did the electric slide, they dipped, they wiggled their hips, they shook their butts, they heel-toe-do-si-doed. They bent their knees and did a couple of sexy pelvic thrusts. Who knew they would have such rhythm?

At one point, Rita looked down the line at all of her new friends and wished she had a camera. Even without, it would be a memory with her forever. Forget Urban Cowboys. She'd created her very own Urban Vikings.

Now, if they could only get a couple of men to join them.

Women never do what you expect them to . . .

It was approaching dusk when Steven and his hird arrived back at Norstead. Weary. Without Disa. But satisfied with the way his meeting had gone with the pirate Brodir.

Now, all he could think of was taking a bath . . . and taking Rita. Not necessarily in that order.

Geirfinn and a number of the stablemen led by Farli met the horsemen in the front courtyard. Dismounting wearily, he asked, "Any trouble while we were gone?"

Geirfinn shook his head, but a smile tugged at his lips.

He didn't need to ask, but he did anyway, "What did she do now?"

"Nothing."

Still the near smile.

He noticed that the stable hands weren't bothering to hide their grins, either.

He thought about inquiring further but decided to find out for himself.

"Really," Geirfinn said. "She has been making pit cream all day. That is all."

"Pit cream?"

Geirfinn raised an arm and sniffed his underarm in an exaggerated fashion.

Ah, the deodorant.

He dismounted and began walking up the front steps to the keep. He noticed a bunch of men and boys following him. Not a good sign.

He undid his chain *shert* and laid it on a table in the great hall, along with his helmet and gauntlets. Arnstein was at his side immediately, picking up the pieces of armor, which he handed off to a housecarl, directing him to take them into the weapons room. At the same time, Arnstein directed another housecarl to bring Steven and Oslac cups of ale.

Steven just noticed something. "Where are all the women? I do not see any female servants about."

Arnstein motioned with his head toward the back of the castle fortress from where Steven could hear music of some type. Singing. He frowned with confusion and headed in that direction, through the corridor leading to the kitchen, through the kitchen, out to the back courtyard where gardens and laundry and such were taken care of. And that's when he saw it.

A line of females of all ages, from adult to children, were singing a loud, raucous song about achy breaky hearts, of all things. And dancing, if it could be called that, most with their gowns hiked up to their knees. Scandalous, really. But they were enjoying themselves so much, he did not have the heart to stop them.

Someone pushed him from behind, and he realized that he had at least two dozen men watching the same spectacle as he was. And enjoying it immensely. In fact, they began to clap a beat in tune with the music.

Just then, the leader of this spectacle glanced his way.

"Steven! You're back."

One by one, the women noticed him and stopped singing and dancing.

"What in hell is going on?" he asked, coming up to Rita.

"We were just line dancing. Do you want to join us?"

Her question startled him. If he had expected her to grovel and apologize for leading the Norstead women astray, he was sadly mistaken. "Nay, I do not want to line dance."

"Okay. What do you want to do? Oh. Sorry I asked that. Hey, what are you doing?"

He had taken her hand and was dragging her out of the laundry shed and farther from the keep. He yelled back to one of the servants, "Clean clothing for me and m'lady." He turned to her then. "You smell like lard."

"That's just my underarm cream." She lifted an arm so that he could smell better. "Can't you smell the roses, too?"

He shook his head in wonder at the thickness of this woman's skull. Didn't she realize how far she had pushed the bounds of propriety? "Yea, I can smell the roses."

"Maybe you could try it, too."

"So that I can smell like a rose?"

"No, I have some pine-scented ones for men to try."

"Oh, wonderful!"

Her smile about melted his brain and hardening body parts. "Was your mission successful?"

"Not nearly as successful as my current mission is going to be."

She tilted her head to the side just as they'd headed toward the women's bathing longhouse. He motioned to a guard to get everyone out, the silent message being that he should stand guard and let no one else in.

"And what would that mission be?"

He just smiled. "Did you not mention at one time something about . . . diving for treasure?"

Love is no joke . . .

"You're looking grumpy-faced again," she said as he continued to pull her along like a recalcitrant child.

He gave her a look that said she *was* a recalcitrant child.

So she decided to act like a child. "I've heard that your people have taken to telling you jokes to lighten your mood."

He groaned.

"Betcha I can make you smile."

He, of course, refused to smile, though she could see the humor in his eyes.

"Odin and Thor were up in Valhalla, just hanging around, when Thor said it had been way too long since he'd swived a wench, and the Valkyries weren't any fun at all, wanting to stay virgins forever."

"Oh, good gods! You really are going to make a jest. Now?"

"Yep! Odin suggested that Thor go down to earth where there were lots of wanton wenches."

"I am not listening," Steven said.

"Next night Odin saw that lackwit Thor, he was grinning from ear to ear, claimed to have had sex with one woman twenty-one times."

"Have a caution, Ree-tah, or Thor will strike you down with his mighty hammer."

"His hammer was all worn down, if you ask me. In fact, Odin chastised him, saying that mortal women couldn't take so much sex and that he must go down and apologize immediately."

"This is the dumbest story you have told so far, even dumber than time travel."

"Tsk, tsk! Thor returned to earth and found the wanton wench, and he told her, 'Sorry I am to have used you so, but I am Thor, and—

" 'Thor? Hah! You think you're Thor. I can hardly thit down to pith.' "

When he didn't laugh, she said, "Don't you get it? The woman had a lisp. A lisp is when—"

They were at the bathhouse, and Steven shoved her inside, closed the door with a boot, and had her up against the wall before she could blink.

"I know what a lisp is," he said then.

"You're smiling."

"Not about a joke." He already had her gown hiked up to her waist and was undoing the bows on her panties. Amazing how men, no matter the time period, learned how to remove a woman's undergarments in seconds, whether they be corset or bra, no matter how complicated the fastenings were. Not that bows required a rocket scientist. Still . . .

"You missed me," she guessed, and was already unlacing the front of his braies, shoving them down where they pooled at his knees.

"Is it so obvious?" he murmured against her neck.

"Oh, yeah!" She pressed her belly against his "obvious." Then, "You've only been gone a half day."

"Seems like half a year."

"You're insatiable."

"And that is a bad thing?"

"No, that is a very good thing." She put her hand to him, then tickled his balls.

He closed his eyes and probably saw stars behind his lids. "I do not think I can wait," he gritted out.

"Does it look like I care?"

He leaned his head back to look at her.

She licked her lips, slowly, just the way that drove men wild, according to *Cosmo* magazine.

He grinned, bent his knees a bit to align their bodies, and thrust into her welcoming folds, already moist for him. Then he lifted her by the knees and arranged her legs around his waist. With his hands cupping her buttocks, guiding her, the sex jump-started into fast and furious. And very, very satisfying.

A short time later, she was half-lying along the steps into the bathing pool with Steven behind her. Her legs were between his legs, her back to his chest. He had just dropped some hot rocks, making the water lukewarm.

Snuggling her in tighter, he confessed, "I am perplexed by the hold you have on me."

That goes two ways. "You mean the insatiable thing?"

He shrugged. "That and more. I am usually bored by now with a woman."

"And you're not with me?"

"Not yet."

She pinched the hand that was resting on her stomach. She knew what he meant, though, except she knew what the problem was, even if he did not. They were falling in love with each other.

Love was scary in the best of circumstances, making a person vulnerable, even weak. Its highs and lows made a person reel, as if they were bordering on madness. But love between a man and woman separated by a thousand years, that was the scariest of all. In fact, it was impossible.

Rita turned so that she was lying atop Steven. Taking his face in both her hands, she said, "Let's just take one day at a time. Each one a gift . . ." Left unsaid, was: ". . . until we part."

But they both knew it was there.

The poignant, gentle lovemaking that followed was a testament to that inevitable end.

What's love got to do with it? . . .

The days that followed were busy ones at Norstead as folks began to arrive for the Althing. From dawn until the evening meal, Steven was busy arranging accommodations, stabling animals, sending out hunters and fishermen, greeting and visiting with Norse dignitaries. He was not averse to delegating responsibilities and did so with expertise, but still there was always something that called for a leader's hand. In particular, he had been investigating Brodir's claims that someone in his hird of soldiers had been with Thorfinn at the time the pirate said there had been proof of his innocence.

The only time he saw Rita was when he crawled into the bed furs at night where she, thank the gods, welcomed him with open arms and thighs. She was a blessing he feared would slip through his fingers if he were not careful. Nay, that was not quite true. She would definitely slip through his fingers; the question was: How long could he postpone the inevitable?

In the meantime, she was still experimenting with her deodorants, even on him. He had to admit to liking the pine-scented ones, though he was still sweat-soaked at the end of a day. Perhaps not such smelly sweat, though, he conceded.

"You are in love with the woman."

"What are you going to do about it?"

Kraka and Grima had jumped in front of him as he stepped out of the garderobe, spouting nonsense about love, of all things. Frigg's foot! They must have been hiding behind a bush, waiting to ambush him.

"By thunder! You two are enough to scare a dragon!"

"The moon is on the wane, the darkness returns, all will be lost anon at Norstead," one of them predicted with a few cackles thrown in, "lest the master open his burdened heart to the magic of the light."

The light prattle again! Their message, if that is what it was, was as clear as mud.

"Do you two ever comb your hair?" he asked. "Is that a cobweb on your shoulder? For Asgard's sake! That bag around your neck is made of snakeskin. Yeech!"

"Saba, saba, ulick, abba. Cat eyes boil and manparts coil. Ick vee, ick vee, cast thee rune rope." The other witch . . . he never could tell the two of them apart . . . had a stick raised over his head as she chanted and danced around him.

"Enough!" He glowered at the two barmies. "What exactly do you want from me?"

One of the witches narrowed her eyes at him. "Three of your man hairs?"

His eyes widened with surprise before he laughed out loud. "Not going to happen! Why would you want such anyhow?"

"For the love potion," one witch replied. "We could get none from your lady love."

That being because she was bald thereabouts, he supposed.

"Not that you are not already under the influence," the other witch added.

"We just need to reinforce the spell."

"I am not in love," he told them.

To which they both laughed, or rather cackle-laughed.

"I do not believe in love."

More cackle-laughing.

"Assuming that you are referring to Ree-tah, she will be leaving here eventually."

"Not if you convince her to stay," Kraka and Grima said at the same time.

"Me? Why would I do that?" he asked, though he could think of one or twenty reasons, all of them involving bedsport.

"Love," they both replied and were gone so quickly that he almost might believe he had imagined their conversation.

As he walked back to the keep, he pondered their words. Was he in love with Rita? How would he know, never having experienced the sentiment before? Was it a good or bad thing if he was?

What did love have to do with it anyhow? Love was not needed for good sex. Nor was good sex a guarantee of love. So, why the constant blathering of the skalds or the witches about love?

So many questions. So few answers.

Chapter 17

She refused to be the other woman . . .

If Rita hadn't been convinced before that she had time-traveled, she was now. She had never read nor seen anything like it. There was no way she could have imagined the scene before her.

In a flat valley of about five acres, tents of many sizes and colors and rough shelters made of tree limbs and thatch had been erected for the visiting Vikings and their families. They were arranged around one much larger open-sided tent where the Althing meetings would be held, starting tomorrow morning. Most of the people would eat and sleep out here, the only ones housed inside being King Olaf and several minor kings or chieftains with their families.

Booths were set up in some sections selling everything from wine to fur cloaks to roast meat and vegetables on a stick, like kabobs, to jewelry. Soapstone candleholders. Bone needles. Antler combs. And services were for sale as well, like barbers and fortune-tellers who read rune stones.

Then there were competitions . . . wrestling, archery, lance throwing, and swordplay.

It was like a huge state fair, with important business to be decided along with the fun and games.

Since Steven was so busy during the day, Rita spent her time with Kraka and Grima at their booth selling herbs or walking about with Sigge, who had developed an attraction for Sigurd, a young soldier from a neighboring jarldom.

Thus, Lady Thora was able to find her alone one day while Sigge went walking with her new boyfriend. "So, what do you think of Lady Isrid?"

"Who?"

"King Olaf's daughter Isrid. Have you not met her?"

Rita frowned, trying to remember. Yes, she recalled now. A young woman of about twenty who had been assigned one of the bedchambers with three other "noble" women. She had talked constantly, with one train of thought leading to another, nonstop. "You must be the Lady Mermaid," she had remarked amiably. "I have ne'er met a mermaid afore. Of course I have ne'er met any sea creatures either. Dost think you could make me one of those chastity belts I hear so much about? Oh, look at that adorable baby over there. Do you have any babies? Where is my maid? She was supposed to find me a blue riband. I do not like to wear yellow ribands on Thorsday, do you?" That was the way the young woman had blathered on.

"Yes, I've met her," Rita told Thora.

"What did you think of her?" The look of malice on Lady Thora's face should have forewarned her. "Since she will be Lord Steven's wife, your time in his bed furs may be on the wane. Assuming he does not set aside your mistress duties all together. Or mayhap he will pass you on to one of his soldiers or a visiting jarl."

"I have no idea what you're talking about."

"Lord Steven and Lady Isrid are to be wed. Mayhap even here at the Althing, if King Olaf has his way."

Rita froze in place, not wanting to believe Steven would betray her in this way. Even if they weren't married or engaged, fidelity was a given. Or at least she'd thought it was.

"On the other hand, it may not matter . . . if you are traded to Brodir in exchange for Lady Disa."

"Are you saying that Steven is considering that?"

Thora examined her fingernails as she spoke with a seeming nonchalance. "It was mentioned in a meeting with his hersirs afore he went to negotiate with the pirate."

Rita turned on her heel and stomped away, not wanting to hear any more. It was probably lies. Lady Thora loved to stir up trouble. There was no reason why she should believe her. Still . . .

When she saw Sigge at the witches' booth a short time later, she said right off, "Is Steven engaged to marry King Olaf's daughter?"

Sigge's face bloomed with color. "Uh . . . well, methinks they may have been betrothed when they were children by both fathers, but that does not mean—"

Rita put up a halting hand. So, it was true. He probably considered her his bit on the side until the wedding. Heck, he might even, in all his arrogance, think she would continue to have an affair with him after his marriage. Hah! He had another think coming. She was not, nor ever would be, the other woman.

Rita knew she couldn't confront Steven while he was busy around other people. Someone might accidentally, or not so accidentally, lop her head off. So, time crawled the rest of that day until it was time to go to bed. When he finally came into the bedchamber, closing the door behind him, she was fully awake, fully clothed, and so steamed her brain was probably cooked.

He smiled at her. The unsuspecting idiot! "I put your new deodorant on tonight, sweetling. The apple-scented one. Oslac says I smell good enough to eat." He waggled his eyebrows at her.

"You louse! You stinking, two-timing sonofabitch!"

"What?" He ducked as she threw a boot at him. "What in bloody hell has your bowels in an uproar?"

"You do, you lying scumbag." She threw a second boot, which he caught deftly in an upraised hand.

"Why didn't you tell me that you're engaged?"

"Engaged in what?"

She missed him with one of Luta's hair fillets, and it landed at his feet.

"Aaarrgh! Engaged to marry. Does the name Isrid ring any bells?"

She could see the flush of guilt on his face, which pretty well sealed her fate with him. She fought the tears that filled her eyes and blinked them away.

"Ree-tah!" he said, picking her up by the waist and hugging her tightly, despite her kicks and slapping hands. Only when she'd worn down did he release her slightly to sit down on the bed with her on his lap. "It does not change anything."

"It changes everything."

"I have no intention of wedding Isrid."

"You don't?"

"Not unless I have to."

She slapped at him again, and this time was successful, until he pinned her arms to her sides and kissed her neck.

"I was only nine years old when Isrid was born. My father and hers made a pact for our eventual wedding, but I ne'er agreed. And no doubt they were *blindfuller* at the time. Drunk as a lord!"

"So, it's not binding?"

"Not unless King Olaf deems it so, and he has not mentioned it for some time."

Clueless! The man is clueless! "Maybe he's waiting for you to make the next move."

"Mayhap."

Mayhap? Mayhap? I'd like to smack some sense into

the big oaf. "And if you're forced to marry her, what about me?"

"What we have has naught to do with marriage."

Forget smacking. Where's a baseball bat when I need it? "I cannot believe you said such a fool thing. Do you think I would let you touch me when you're married to someone else? Do you think I would let you boink me after boinking your wife?"

"For your information, I have not played you false. Not once. In fact, I have not *boinked* another woman since I met you." He smiled at his use of the word *boink*, probably figuring she would smile with him.

Not a chance! "Give the man a medal. He's managed to keep his pants up for a record . . . what? Three weeks?"

"Four."

"Wow! Your self-control is amazing."

"Your sarcasm ill-suits, m'lady."

"Your insensitivity ill-suits, m'lord."

"Damn your impertinence! I do not understand why you are so upset about a marriage that may or may not take place, and if it does, at some unnamed time in the future, you might not even be here."

Oh, great! Use that against me. "Didn't I tell you about my womanizing husband? Didn't you think it would matter to me that you were pledged to someone else? And there's another thing. Did you suggest trading me for your sister Disa when you met with the pirate?"

"I did not."

Well, that was something. "Lady Thora said you discussed the possibility with your hersirs."

"It was discussed, but I was not the one to suggest it."

Is he for real? "Don't play word games with me. Did you or didn't you nix the idea?"

"I said I would consider it, that is all. Besides, it did not become necessary."

"And that makes everything hunky-dory."

"Hunk of what?"

She managed to squirm out of his hold and jump to her feet.

Already at the door, she told him, "No, don't come after me. I'm going to find Sigge and sleep with her out at the witches' tent. I couldn't stand to have you touch me tonight."

"I could make you stay."

"I would hate you even more than I do at the moment."

"I am not too fond of you either at the moment."

"Well, then, we are even. Maybe this is the way it ends for us."

"Never! Methinks I have been too lenient with you. Since when does a mere woman dictate what her man should do, especially when her man is a high chieftain of his own jarldom?"

"I don't care if you are the high chieftain of hell, baby. Since when does a mere man get the right to set all the rules?"

"I will decide when our relationship ends. Do not delude yourself otherwise."

"So now we have a relationship, do we?"

"What do you call swiving each other silly if not a relationship?"

"I call it one too many booty calls."

"I would be offended if I knew what that meant."

"It means the fuck fest is over, sweetheart." She gasped at her use of such foul language, especially when she had vowed to stop.

Steven just smiled, however, as he sensed her discomfort.

He moved to the door himself then and told her, "There is no need for you to seek a bed pallet elsewhere tonight. I will leave. We both need time apart afore we say things that cannot be taken back."

It seemed to Rita that they were way past that point already.

"Once the Althing is over, we will settle this issue, but not now, not in the heat of anger."

"What issue would that be, Steven?"

"The issue of you and me. I came to my bedchamber early tonight, excited to try something new in the bed arts that came to me unbidden this afternoon, and what did I get instead? Rejection."

"You think that's rejection? I could pull a Lorena Bobbitt on you if you dared to try to screw me now." She explained exactly what that entailed.

He flinched. "The trickster god Loki must be laughing his arse off, playing with my life like this. Truth to tell, I am not accustomed to rejection, nor am I accustomed to women making demands of me. I need time to decide whether I can accept those terms. Or not. A Viking man is the head of his household, whether it be a humble or a royal one."

"What's wrong with a partnership?"

"If the woman rules, he is less than a man."

Before she could respond to that last outlandish statement, he left, closing the door behind him.

She wanted to go after him and tell him to come back, but she didn't. She couldn't. Because the one glaring elephant in the room was love, or lack of love. If a man loved a woman, he made concessions. He certainly didn't even think about being with another woman, forced or not.

There was no question in her mind now that she loved him.

The question was: Did he love her?

Or was he even capable of love?

And even if he did love her, was she prepared to stay here in this primitive time just for the sake of love?

Steven was right about one thing. Her God, or the Norse

gods, were having a grand old time playing with their lives.

Some laws are made to be broken . . .

"With law shall the land be built up, and lawlessness shall be laid waste," pronounced Agmundr, the lawspeaker for the opening session of the Althing after banging his staff on the floor of a wood platform. "Peace be to you free men of Hordaland, Vestfold, and Jutland. Come ye to act justly according to the ancient laws."

Agmundr, an ancient man with a long white beard that flowed down to the waist of his red tunic under a full-length bear cloak, would act as both the lawspeaker and the Thing chieftain today. Agmundr was wise with age and was said to have five wives, six concubines, twenty-two children, and nineteen grandchildren.

Steven could only imagine how impressed Rita would be with those numbers.

Also represented were twelve men, himself included, representing the various jarldoms on the law council. At least three hundred other men sat about the field.

Agmundr raised his arms high toward the tent roof. "In the tradition of Odin who sacrificed one eye to drink from the Well of Knowledge, I exhort you to judge wisely by a majority rule. In the name of Forseti, god of justice, I exhort you to judge fairly. This is the way of all good men.

"Order depends entirely on the willing acceptance of those in judgment, which will be shown by the *vapnatak*, or weapon clatter." All the men banged swords against shields to demonstrate the method by which votes would be cast.

Nodding his head with satisfaction, Agmundr then recited one-third of the Norse laws. The same was done every year. On the fourth year, he started over again. Since there was no written law, this was the way that Norsemen remembered the wisdom of the elders.

Witches could be stoned or drowned, Agmundr told them.

Steven made a note to himself: Warn Kraka and Grima to not call attention to themselves.

Murder could be repaid with murder, rape with rape, except that mostly a sizeable fine was levied according to wergild, or the person's worth. Agmundr recited each of those amounts. Cattle thefts, women thefts, and escaped slaves had specific punishments as well. Even wooing bees and bitter milk carried specific levies.

Smiling to himself, he wondered what Rita would think about these valuations, especially since women, even of the same class, had a wergild much lower than men, unless they were of childbearing years or proven breeders. Better yet, virgins. A high price was placed on maidenheads.

But then, he cut himself short. He was angry with Rita, had not spoken with her since he left the bedchamber last night to sleep in the stables.

A half dozen cases had been settled by mid-morning when they were about to break for the first meal of the day. Steven stood and said, "I wish to plead the cause of Brodir the Pirate. Let me tell you what has happened. Then you may ponder my words and decide this afternoon whether you will permit Brodir to come in person to tell you his story."

An uproar arose, many of the Vikings outraged that he would even suggest leniency in dealing with the far-famed Norse outlaw.

When Agmundr banged his staff for order, Steven added, "Men may differ in opinions, but it has always been the rule that both sides must be heard to arrive at a just decision. I see that some of Hogar's kin are here today. Let them speak, then let Brodir have his say. I must warn you, I have witnesses to support Brodir's claims."

Again, an uproar, mostly coming from Hogar's contingent, which included King Olaf's retinue. King Olaf glared at him as if Steven had performed some personal affront to him.

In the end, the law council, backed up by the *vapna-tak*, agreed to hear Steven's witnesses that afternoon. After that, a vote would be taken as to whether Brodir would be able to speak before them on the morrow.

Walking out of the tent, heading toward the keep, King Olaf stopped him. "Where do your allegiances lie, Steven?"

"With truth and justice."

"Even if it goes against your betrothed's family?"

Now would be a good time for him to bring up the betrothal, but he hesitated for some reason. "You must be fair. If Hogar was blameless, what harm is there in hearing Brodir?"

King Olaf sneered, but at least he did nothing to prevent the hearing. For now, leastways.

Just then he noticed some of the entertainers arriving for this evening's after-dinner amusements . . . jugglers, musicians, and acrobats. *Oh. My. Gods!* There was Rita, wearing a tunic and braies, doing a series of front flips, six in a row after a running start, contorting her body in a manner that should be physically impossible. The acrobats that he had hired watched her closely, then attempted to do the same, most of them failing after two flips.

"Is that the strange sea wench that you rescued?" King Olaf asked.

Steven jerked to attention. He thought the king had gone on ahead of him.

"Yea, that is Ree-tah."

"Why is she dressed like a man?"

How would I know? "Because it is more comfortable, I suppose."

"'Tis scandalous."

If only that were the most scandalous thing she does! He shrugged. "The customs are different in her country."

"And what country would that be?"

"America."

"Ah. Is that not the country just discovered by Erik the Red?"

He nodded hesitantly, wary of where this conversation was headed.

"Will she be entertaining us this evening?"

I sincerely hope not.

"I understand that she thinks we Vikings stink, and that she teaches your women wicked songs and wanton dances. I understand she is your mistress."

Steven narrowed his eyes at the king. Someone here at Norstead had a big mouth. First reporting to Brodir, then to the king. He did not like spies in his midst. Not one bit.

"Rita is protected by my shield. If you have any complaints about her, bring them to me. Otherwise, watch what you say. King or not, you cannot malign her without maligning me."

"You do not speak as a betrothed man, Steven."

"Well, mayhap that is because I do not consider myself a betrothed man."

The king bristled, sputtering with outrage.

And he was the one stomping toward the keep then, knowing this was not the time or place for this conversation. Not when he was so boiling angry.

Just before he entered the back door of the keep, he turned and saw that Rita now had a bow and arrows in hand and was walking toward the competition area. *Nay, nay, nay!*

"Oslac!" he yelled, seeing his comrade coming up behind him. "Go grab the wench and lock her in the bedchamber until I have a chance to talk to her."

"With pleasure." Oslac grinned at him. "Shall I tell her to remove the tunic and braies afore you arrive to *talk* to her?"

"Not unless you want a carrot chop to your manparts."

"Uh-oh! Methinks someone is getting grumpy again. Do you know what the left nut said to the right nut . . . you know the nuts betwixt your legs?"

"Oslac! Not now!"

"The one nut told the other nut, the lackwit in the middle thinks he is *sooo* hard."

"What is he talking about?" King Olaf wanted to know.

"Nothing important."

"Steven needs some cheering up," Oslac explained.

"Why?" Olaf wanted to know. "Is there something I should know about afore I welcome him to my family?"

"Well—" Oslac began, still grinning.

"Enough!" Steven turned to Oslac. "On second thought, leave Ree-tah alone. Just tell Geirfinn that she is not permitted to enter any competitions, and that includes archery, spear throwing, swordplay, arm wrestling, bear baiting, horse racing, running, or swimming."

King Olaf's eyes went wide at Steven's implication that a woman would dare try any of those activities. A few sennights ago, pre-Rita, he would have had the same reservations.

When he got to the great hall, he directed King Olaf and other nobles to the high table, and he was about to go speak with Arnstein to make sure everything inside the kitchen was ready to be served when he was approached by one of his neighbors. It was Jarl Brandr Igorsson of Bear's Lair, located far north of Norstead.

"Steven, I have something important to discuss with you."

Does not everybody?

"Have you met my wife Joy? Her name had been Joy Nelson."

He motioned to a beautiful red-haired lady in noble Viking attire, clearly with child, talking to Lady Thora a short distance away. "I would not usually bring my wife so far in her condition, but we heard some things about your visitor, and . . ."

"My visitor?" He sighed. "You mean Ree-tah. Sweet Valhalla. Word must have spread afar that I have a freak here at Norstead."

"Not a freak," Brandr said, putting a hand of sympathy on his forearm. "A time traveler."

Steven was shocked, and he moved back a step. While rumors had traveled about a strange sea siren that he had rescued, even stories about her inventing armpit cream and doing weird dances, no one knew about the time-travel tales except Oslac, and he would not be loose-lipped.

"Do not be alarmed. We can talk later, in private, but for now just let me say one thing." He pointed to his wife and rolled his eyes. "Female Navy SEAL? Uncle Sam's WEALS?"

"No way!" Steven said, repeating one of Rita's favorite expressions.

And Brandr, eleventh-century Viking to the bone, said, "Way!"

Chapter 18

Will you be my new BFF, m'lady? . . .

After being denied permission to compete in any of the games, Rita went off to the side of the palace with more than a dozen young women and children. They were singing and line dancing, some of them laughing so hard they fell on the grass with laughter.

They'd added "The Hustle" and "The Chicken Dance" to their repertoire, but their favorites were still "Achy Breaky Heart" and "Boot Scootin' Boogie."

With every stomp of her foot and every belting refrain of the songs, Rita was letting loose some of her anger and frustration toward Steven. How dare he make love to her when he was engaged to another woman? How dare he even indirectly agree to trading her to a pirate in exchange for his sister? How dare he walk away from her last night without resolving their issues?

And where had he slept, anyway? If he'd been off with some other woman, a Viking bimbo, she was going to be really, really upset. Even more than she was already upset.

She had lots to be upset about, too, and not just the little itty problem of her time travel. When she'd awakened this morning, it was to a roiling stomach, which prompted a quick rush to the chamber pot, where she hurled the contents of her stomach, over and over until there was nothing left. Then, when she'd come downstairs with Sigge, the smell of oatmeal cooking in the kitchen caused another mad rush, this time to the garderobe.

Even more telling, she'd then been famished. In fact, the *sviâ* didn't seem quite so horrific. She'd ended up scarfing up a slice of manchet bread oozing butter and honey, a cup of milk, an oat cake, and two slices of rare roast boar.

Then she'd had to pee just about every hour.

And she'd burst into tears for no reason after her last potty trip.

If she didn't know better, she would think she was pregnant.

In fact, Sigge had turned to her and said, "Methinks you are breeding."

No kidding!

Which was impossible, since she still had the implant, which should last at least another month or so. Assuming birth control implants traveled well . . . like a thousand years and God only knows how many miles. *Well, duh!* She'd felt like whacking herself upside the head for that idiocy in relying on a modern-day device in a Dark Ages setting.

Really, that would be the final icing on her cake if she found herself pregnant to an engaged man a thousand years in the past. Would she ever be able to go home then? Would she want to?

But for now, she wasn't vomiting, peeing, craving, or crying. She was singing and dancing. Like a lunatic.

That's when she noticed the small audience they'd garnered. And in the front was Steven, who stood between a tall, dark-haired Viking and a red-haired, pregnant Viking woman. The woman strode right up to them where they were singing and dancing and asked, "Can I join you?"

Huh? "Sure. Why not?" She moved aside to make room for the newcomer.

"My name is Joy . . . Joy Nelson. My husband is Brandr Igorsson from Bear's Lair. We live north of here."

Joy Nelson? The name sounded familiar to Rita. She decided that Steven must have mentioned her when talking about all the people who would come to the Althing. "I'll teach you the dance steps," she offered.

"That won't be necessary." The woman smiled at her and said, "Billy Ray Cyrus, right?"

Rita gasped . . . then fell into a dead faint.

Friends throughout time . . .

Rita awakened to find herself on her bed in Thorfinn's room, her only company the woman she'd just met. Joy Nelson.

Oh, good Lord! It just came to her. A few years back a WEALS trainee named Joy Nelson had disappeared on a SEALs mission abroad. An explosion or something. Although it had been a covert op, there had been a lot of publicity because one of her brothers had been a POW killed by al-Qaeda the year before, and another brother was an NFL football player. Still was.

Could it be?

Sitting up, she removed the cool, wet cloth from her forehead, handing it to the woman sitting on the edge of the bed, staring at her with sympathy. "Time travel?" Rita inquired.

Joy nodded.

"How is it possible?"

"Honey, I've been here a year and a half, and I still don't know why. Well, that's not exactly true. I believe I was sent here by God . . . I know, presumptuous of me, huh?"

Hey, she'd had similar thoughts.

"Brandr had been in such a dark place. A berserker, he had suffered so much that he needed someone to rescue him. Me."

"You're kidding! Everyone thinks I was sent here to lighten Steven's life. He's been in such a blue funk following . . . well, lots of things. There are two witches here who think they're responsible for my time travel, if that's what it is."

"Witches, huh?" Joy shrugged. "I prefer to believe in miracles. Godly miracles."

"Me, too." Rita swung her legs around to sit on the edge of the bed next to Joy. "Where is everyone?"

"Steven had to go down to address the Althing. Something about a pirate. He's very worried about you. In fact, he didn't want to leave your side until I assured him I would stay until he returned."

"Don't be fooled. He's a jerk."

"Aren't they all? At times."

"I only got a glimpse of you with your husband. You seem very happy."

"I am."

"I guess you had no choice but to stay here."

"I had a choice. At least, I told JAM to try to go back to the future without me."

"JAM was here?" Rita wasn't sure how many shocks she could take in one day.

"Yes. Oh, my goodness! If you know him, that must mean he got back safely. I'm so glad to hear that. We weren't sure the time travel could be reversed."

She put a hand to her aching head. "So, I could go back if I wanted to?"

"Uh. I'm not sure. All I know is that in my case . . . and JAM's . . . our portal to the past was through Hedeby, a Viking trading town that is now located in Germany. It's where my last mission took place. He planned to hang around there in hopes that something would pull him back. Apparently, it did. I suspect he prayed a lot."

They smiled at each other, knowing about JAM's priestly past.

"He's in love with Kirstin Magnusson."

"Is he? That's wonderful. I can't wait to hear all the news from the future. How's Obama doing as president? Are Brad and Angelina still together? Who won on *American Idol*? No, wait. There's probably been another *Idol* season since I left. I'm sure the show will go on and on as long as Randy, Simon, and Paula are around. What's the latest computer gizmo? Anyone interesting on the SEAL teams these days? Is Cage still there?" Tears filled her eyes then and she asked hesitantly, "Do you know anything about my brothers? How did they react to my 'death'?"

Rita told her as much as she could, and Joy was as incredulous as the rest of the country over Paula Abdul's being dumped and the boom in e-books triggered by Amazon's Kindle. Plus, the crash in the economy. Then Rita mentioned the fact that Joy's brothers had gone suddenly mum on the talk show front several months after her "death." She assumed now that it was because JAM had reported to them. That made her feel better.

"I'm really confused, though," Rita said. "Are you saying that if I go to the spot where I arrived here that I can go back?"

"No, I don't think it's as simple as that. I believe it has something to do with destiny . . . celestial destiny . . . but also choice. You have to believe that you would be better off . . . that destiny would be better served . . . by your return to modern times. It's really very simple, in the end."

"Not so simple in my case." Rita put a hand over her belly.

"You're pregnant?"

"I think so, despite my birth control implant. It's early days, but the signs are there. Wish I had a pregnancy test."

"That does change things," Joy remarked. "Whatever you decide to do, I suspect it should be soon. I'll do whatever I can to help you."

Just then, the door swung open. Didn't anyone knock here?

In strode Steven, who ignored Joy and picked Rita up, hugging her. "Are you unwell? I have been so worried. Was it bad fish? Or some other malady? Should I fetch the Arab healer from Birka? Can you walk? Should I carry you?"

"No, no, no, no, no, in answer to your questions. Why do I need to go anywhere?"

He held her at arm's length, and she saw the worried expression on his face.

"Uh-oh!" she and Joy both said at the same time.

"King Olaf wants to meet you. At dinner tonight. And he has ordered you to appear before the Althing council on the morrow. He wants you to wear your mermaid garment."

Women! Can't live with them. Can't live without them . . .

Rita was behaving very strange. Even stranger than usual.

By that evening, she had said the word "No!" to him more times than he could count.

No, she would not attend the dinner.

No, she would not sit at the high table.

No, she would not wear the mermaid garment.

No, she would not talk nicely to the king.

No, she damn well would not appear before any heathen council comprised of men only.

No, she would not show her pant-hes to the noble ladies visiting here at Norstead.

No, she would not sing and dance to entertain one and all. Actually, he had vetoed that one, as well. He did not want her turning men lustsome with her sexy moves.

No, she would not let him within an arm's length of her, even to help her dress.

And there were other strange things.

Every time he turned around she was running for the garderobe to relieve her bladder. It was probably just an excuse to avoid his company. Still . . .

And weeping! For a woman who claimed never to cry, her eyes were leaking water like a broken rain barrel.

Lady Igorsson, Brandr's wife, constantly shot daggers at him with her eyes, for what crime he was not sure. She'd probably heard about his supposed betrothal.

Brandr kept hinting to him that his wife had time-traveled, too. More than that, it seemed that Lady Igorsson had been a wheel, just like Rita, one of those female seals, for Thor's sake!

He tried to make sense of it, to no avail.

But, leastways, when Rita had adamantly refused to don the black skin apparel, he had forced her to wear one of Luta's more precious garments with a threat of the thrall collar. She wore a white, finely pleated, long-sleeved gunna, or shift, covered with a sky blue apron embroidered with silver thread on all the edges and connected at the shoulders with highly embossed gripping beast brooches. From her ears dangled sapphires that matched her sparkling eyes.

In silence, they left the bedchamber and walked down the stairs to the great hall.

"You look beautiful," he told her.

"Bite me!" she replied.

He was fairly certain she did not mean that literally.

"Are you wearing deodorant? You smell like lavender. Can I smell your underarms?"

"Only if I can break your nose."

Now they were approaching the dais where two dozen notables were already seated, including a scowling King Olaf and a red-eyed Isrid. Brandr and Joy were there, as well. Rita would not have come otherwise.

The hum of conversation died down as they passed through the great hall's center aisle. Her short hair was attracting many comments.

"I hate you for making me do this," she said in an undertone, though her chin was raised high.

"No one is picturing you naked," he assured her. "I warned them not to."

"Idiot."

He smiled. If she was insulting him, it meant she was getting back to her old self.

"Is that King Olaf up there? The one with red hair who is scowling at me?"

"It is. Behave yourself, Ree-tah."

"I don't have to bow down to the old fart, do I?"

He groaned. "Please, do not call him that."

"And that must be your sweet, virginal fiancée. How sweet! Oh, no! It looks like she's been crying. What did you do to her?"

"Me? I did nothing. Truth to tell, she probably heard about your presence here."

"Why would that bother her?"

"She probably fears you will take me away from her." Did he sound pompous? Of course he did. Bloody hell!

"Well, good heavens, Steven. You're all hers. Do you want me to assure her?"

He barely restrained himself from smacking her on her rump. He did pinch her arm, though. "Do not dare."

After introductions, Steven sat next to the king, who was indeed scowling, with Rita on his other side, and Joy and Brandr beside her. On the king's other side was Isrid, who cast a weepy smile his way. To his surprise and eternal gratitude, Oslac sat on Isrid's other side, patting her arm with sympathy. Best Oslac beware, or he would find himself betrothed, instead of him.

Dinner was an excruciatingly painful process that seemed to last forever. The only really alarming part came when Rita had begun to gag, not at sight of the *sviâ*, which was a nause-ating food offering, even to him who had been known to eat the awful gammelost on sea voyages, but at the eels, which appeared to be swimming in a dill cream sauce. They had not really been swimming. It was just that the trencher in which it was served was wobbly. King Olaf, sensing Rita's discomfort, deliberately asked that the eels be placed before him, and he proceeded to down several of the slimy buggers.

"I hear that you give safe harbor to witches here at Nor-stead," the king said suddenly.

Steven could feel Rita stiffen at his side. Reaching under the table, he squeezed her hand.

"They are good witches," he assured the king.

"Pfff! There is no such thing as a good witch. Burn them at the stake, I say. Or drown them."

"In the absence of any healing men here at Norstead, Kraka and Grima help my people. They raise herbs, noth-ing more." He crossed his fingers superstitiously at the lie.

"Mayhap we should have the Althing council decide their fate," the old slyboots suggested.

"Lest someone has a proven complaint to lay at their feet, the ladies do not have to appear for questioning." *Oh, gods, I hope the well digger is still gone. Or the trader who grew hair on the bottom of his feet after insulting them. Or the priest whose holy water turned bloody after being caught ogling a young boy. Or . . .*

I am in deep trouble.

Rita squeezed his hand in return, as thanks.

Do not thank me, m'lady, he thought. *We are not out of the woods yet.*

He could tell that the king did not really care about the witches. He was using that as an excuse to rattle him afore bringing his real issues to fore. Like the betrothal to his daughter.

As if reading his mind, the king said, "Would you like to take my daughter for a walk in your gardens?"

Huh? What gardens? But, whoa, he knew what this was about. The king hoped to put him and Isrid in a compromising situation where he would be required to offer marriage. In truth, he did not know why he resisted so. He suspected that Lady Igorsson, a fellow time traveler, might give Rita advice on how she could go home. She might already have set her departure in motion.

Home? That word struck an unwelcome chord in him, because he did not want her home to be elsewhere.

"Well?" the king prodded.

"What?" Oh, he had not answered the king, he realized. "Nay, 'tis best I stay and entertain my guests."

The king was not happy with his response. Neither was Isrid, who was pouting to Oslac with a rambling discourse. Over her shoulder, Oslac rolled his eyes at him.

"Look," Rita said, standing suddenly and addressing the king, which was not acceptable protocol. "We're all dancing around the same tree here. You want Steven to marry your daughter. Your daughter wants to marry Steven. And you all somehow think I'm standing in the way. Well, I'm not. Go for it. I for one have to go pee."

A half dozen eyebrows rose at her outrageous words, and he was left holding the bag, so to speak.

Turning to King Olaf, he said, "Ree-tah is correct. We need to talk, but not here. Let us retire to the solar with cups of mead where we can be private and honest in our words."

The king nodded.

Before he left the dais, Steven turned to Lady Igorsson. "Please, go to Rita until I am able to join you."

Lady Igorsson stood and regarded him with distaste. "She needs you, not me, you clueless baboon."

He looked to Brandr then, arching his brows in question.

Brandr just shook his head at him. "I am as clueless a baboon as you. Whatever a baboon is."

Oslac did not even wait for him to turn his attention his way. He murmured behind his hand to Steven, "Something is amiss with Isrid. I think she has a lover."

Well, that would certainly solve all his problems.

"Find out," he ordered Oslac.

"How?"

"I do not know. Seduce her."

"Whaaat? Nay. You will not shove her off on me."

As he started to follow the king, Brighid stopped him, which was unusual. Brighid rarely left her kitchen during a feast.

Face ruddy with embarrassment, she blurted out, "The maids want ta know if we will be line dancing t'night? And kin the men join us?"

Of all the bizarre things that had happened today, this capped them all. But then he laughed and gave his consent with a cheerful, "Why not?"

Chapter 19

Rock-a-bye and be gone . . .

Rita was in hiding. From everyone.

Instead of going to the witches' tent where she knew Steven and the others would look first, she made her way to an abandoned cow byre she had passed in the woods on the way to the witches' cottage last week. With her she carried a blanket and a short sword. The blanket because she knew it got chilly at night. And the sword because she had no idea if there were wild animals about.

She needed time alone to think.

With the arrival of Joy, a fellow time traveler, and her news about JAM returning to the future, she had a clearer idea of what could be done if she chose to leave Norstead. There were no guarantees, but she was pretty sure that if she really wanted to go home, the answer was to go to the joining of Ericsfjord and the North Sea, to stay there and pray until something happened. Maybe she didn't even need to go there. Maybe all it took was a decisive request to end her visit in the past.

It all boiled down to Steven.

And not just because she might be pregnant.

She loved him. She couldn't explain why. She just did.

But he did not love her in return. If he did, he would have asked her to stay and put a definitive end to any talk of a royal wedding with Isrid.

Well, he had ordered her to stay on several occasions. But there had always been the unspoken caveat, "for a while." Not forever.

She was pretty sure that if she decided to stay, there would be no chance to reverse that decision later.

Her head ached with all the questions rattling about in her brain, and every creaking branch or hooting owl had her jumping with fright. It seemed like hours before she finally fell asleep.

In the middle of the night, she was awakened not by animal noises but the feel of a cold body slipping under the blanket with her. A torch was stuck into the ground just outside the byre.

Before she had a chance to reach for her short sword, Steven said, "'Tis just me. Go back to sleep, heartling. I am cold and tired from hunting for you, and, in truth, I have drunk enough ale to sink a ship."

That was for sure. She could smell the ale on his breath as he spooned his thankfully clothed body behind her, pulling the blanket up over both their shoulders, but she welcomed his presence. She could not deny that fact.

"Steven, what is going to happen?"

"Shhh. We can discuss everything tomorrow. I must be up afore dawn to go meet Brodir and give him safe escort to the Althing. So much to be done!" He yawned widely.

She couldn't help herself. She had to ask. "What about Isrid?"

His chest shook behind her.

Laughter?

She turned in his arms. "What's so funny?"

"Isrid is pregnant."

"What?" She attempted to slap his face, but he grabbed both of her wrists.

"The babe is not mine, you silly goose. It appears that one of the king's hersirs broke the royal maidenhead. The king had hoped that Isrid would seduce me into the bed furs and be wed afore the Althing was over. Hah! She will be wed, but not to me."

"Well, that is good, then."

"More than good. Can you see me as a father? This was a close call. No weddings or babies in my future, I will tell you that."

And that sealed Rita's future.

Forget Johnny Depp, this pirate was HOT . . .

The next morning, Rita awakened early, but she was alone. When she got back to the castle, she had time only for a sponge bath and didn't even change her clothes. Sigge was so excited she could barely stand still. "Hurry, hurry," she kept urging her. The soldiers would soon be returning to Norstead with the famous pirate.

Joy met them as they left the castle proper and headed toward the crowds that lined a roadway of sorts. Already, she could see the returning troops, all on horseback.

It appeared as if Norstead troops, at least three dozen of them, protected the pirate contingent. First, there was Oslac in full military gear. Then came a black-haired woman, dressed in noble Viking attire, riding sidesaddle. She was haughty and beautiful, as Rita would have expected a member of Steven's family to be. Then came Steven, also in battle attire. Beside him rode the pirate Brodir.

Every woman in the crowd, including herself and the highly pregnant Joy, sighed. Brodir was probably the most handsome man she'd ever seen. Long blond hair down to his shoulders with thin war braids framed a face with perfectly sculpted features. Oddly, black brows and thick lashes highlighted caramel-colored eyes.

The pirate rode the horse like a Viking prince . . . back straight, staring straight ahead, one hand resting casually on the pommel, the other on the hilt of his sheathed sword.

"Oh, my God!" Joy said. "Have you ever seen anything like him before?"

"No. I've said that Steven looks like a young George Clooney, but he's nothing compared to this man. And believe me, I've been exposed to some of the most handsome men in the world in Hollywood."

Just then, Steven passed by. Hardly turning, he winked at her.

And she blushed.

Brodir, sensing the direction of Steven's attention, winked at her, too.

Immediately, she heard Steven address the pirate in sharp tones, but they had already passed by, and she was unable to hear what was said.

"I wish we could attend the Althing and hear what will be going on," Rita said then.

"I think I know a way," Sigge said, quickly explaining how they could pretend to be serving maids, replenishing the supplies of ale.

"Are we going to get in trouble for this?" Rita asked.

"Probably," Sigge said, biting her bottom lip with indecision.

"Good!" she and Joy said at the same time.

He wasn't Judge Judy, but he was okay . . .

Steven was beginning to get bored. They had been debating Brodir's case for three hours now. Everyone wanted to break for the first meal of the day, but still the king and the law council members droned on.

Just then, strumming his fingertips on the table before him, he noticed one of the serving maids at the back of the tent, carrying a tray of ale-filled wooden mugs. It was Rita. His eyes widened with shock. Did the woman have a death wish?

Brandr, on his right side, elbowed his ribs. "Can you believe that?"

"I know. Rita defies me at every turn."

"I was not referring to your wench. I was referring to my wench."

Yea, there she was, big stomach and all, laughing with some of the Bear's Lair men at the back of the tent.

Brodir grinned at both of them. "Can you men not control your women? Methinks you need to take a few lessons from a pirate."

"Meaning you?" Brandr scoffed.

"Precisely," Brodir answered.

"You are not free yet," Steven told the outlaw. "But, truth to tell, I have had enough." Standing, he interrupted the lawspeaker who was going on and on about the ancient laws of outlawing, and rescinding an outlawing, and outlawing an outlaw rescinding. "With all due respect, Jarl Agmundr, I have given you not one but three witnesses who attested to Hogar's crimes. Brodir acted as any Viking man would when his woman and child were murdered, even if that woman was not nobly born. I suggest we remove the outlaw levy, and assign a wergild for Brodir to pay to Hogar's family."

Brodir tried to stand and protest the wergild, but Steven shoved him back onto his bench, hissing, "Dost want to leave here today with all your body parts intact?"

The pirate grumbled but remained seated.

"Why do you smell like lavender?" Brodir asked.

"'Tis my underarm deodorant. Dost have any objections?"

Brodir grinned and put both hands up in surrender.

A call was made for the vote, and the weapon clatter was almost universally in Brodir's favor. They were probably just as bored as he was and wanted to get the case finished.

"Food is served in the hall," Steven called out to all the attendees. "We will meet here again at noon to settle other business. Then the competitions will begin on the north field. Archery first, then wrestling and swordplay."

Once the tent was emptied, except for him and Brodir, the pirate said, "Thank you, Steven. I owe you."

He shrugged. "I did it for my brother as much as you."

"How can I repay you, my friend?"

"I do not suppose you are looking for a wife?"

"The sea wench?"

"Nay! My sister." Disa had already nagged him for an hour afore he insisted he had to attend the Althing. Mostly, she complained about Brodir.

"I would rather be outlawed," Brodir said and stomped off.

Now Steven needed to find Rita. For once, he was the one who wanted to talk.

A forever kind of love . . . or not . . .

Rita was in her bedchamber that evening waiting for Steven. He did not arrive until close to midnight.

"Thank the gods, you are here. I have been wanting to speak with you all day but could not get away." He could not fail to note that she was fully dressed. Not a good sign.

Still, he went up to her and hugged her in greeting. To his surprise, she did not shove him away.

"I have missed you, Ree-tah."

"I've missed you, too," she said, but there was a bleakness in her eyes.

"What is it, dearling?" Mayhap he should tell her a joke,

but, nay, jokes hadn't worked to lighten his mood. Only Rita had.

"If I want to return to the future, Joy has told me what I must do. It's not a surefire method, but it might work." She explained what Lady Igorsson had told her.

He could swear his heart stopped beating for a long moment. "Do you intend to leave? Do you want to leave?"

Instead of answering, she asked, "Do you want me to stay?"

"Of course I want you to stay." He reached for her again, but she danced away.

"For how long?"

He frowned in confusion.

"How long do you want me to stay?"

"As long as you want."

She shook her head. "No, you don't understand the question. You know that you'll get bored with me soon, like you do with all women."

He was not so sure of that. "What is your point?"

"The only commitment I can see you making would be for the greater good of Norstead. As in a suitable marriage."

"If I wanted that, I would have wed Isrid long ago."

"What *do* you want?"

"You."

"I repeat, Steven. For how long?"

"Are you asking me to marry you?" He could not help the iciness in his voice as he asked the question. He did not relish being backed into a corner like this, especially not by a woman.

"And if I was?"

He shrugged. "If that was what it took to keep you here, perchance I would."

"Perchance? I'd like to perchance you." She inhaled and exhaled for patience. "You are feeling like you escaped the executioner's axe by Isrid falling pregnant to someone else, aren't you?"

"Yea, I am," he freely admitted.

"Would you have refused to marry her in favor of me?"

"That question is unfair."

"Is it?"

"Ree-tah, I am weary. We are both exhausted. So much has happened in a short time. You have to admit that it is best not to make momentous decisions under such conditions."

Her shoulders slumped, and he felt as if he had failed her in some way. Well, tomorrow when they were both rested, he would set things to right.

She let him undress her then, and when they were both naked, he snuggled up against her back. He fully intended to let her sleep, but when he tucked her closer against him, he felt a wet drop fall on his hand. She was weeping.

"Ree-tah!" he said, turning her. At first, he just kissed the tears away and caressed her shoulders and back in a soothing manner, but soon the need to connect with her in a deeper way overtook him. He made love to her. Gently. Adoringly. Beseechingly, though he knew not for what. Understanding, perhaps.

This was no fast and furious, blood-boiling frenzy to swive. It was a mutual kissing. Stroking. Murmuring. And when he finally joined himself with her, he felt an overwhelming emotion he did not recognize. In fact, its intensity frightened him.

"I love you," she whispered.

Was that it? Was it love?

Unfortunately, he waited too long to speak his mind. She already slept.

And Steven was as confused as ever.

Love hurts . . .

Rita waited until early afternoon while Steven would be involved with Althing matters before leaving.

Going out to the stables, she saddled her own horse, telling the stableboy she was doing an errand for his master. The only thing she took with her was the wet suit and flippers, a small tent, a blanket, and some bread and cheese. She would let the horse loose later to return to the castle.

It took her several hours before she arrived at the rocky shore where she had first emerged here into the past. It had been hard making a decision to return to the future, but after much deliberation, she decided that it would be best for Steven and Norstead if she went.

Truly, even if he'd said he loved her, which he hadn't, she was not the best lady to partner with Steven at Norstead. He needed someone of his culture, and probably a lady of his noble class who would bring him military alliances. After talking with Disa yesterday afternoon, she had a better idea of what kind of woman that would be. Not that Disa was unkind to her, just brutally honest. "Steven is a wonderful brother. The best. But he is a born womanizer. It is not in his makeup to stay with one woman forever. Most Viking men are the same. We Viking women learn to live with it. Not happily. I certainly do not intend to expose myself to that pain again. Still, I can see that you care for my brother. Could you live with that kind of marriage?"

Disa had been assuming that Steven had offered marriage. Not that it would have mattered. Without love, she would not marry. And even then, fidelity was crucial to her.

Her leaving would be better for everyone.

So she arranged the small tent, spread out the blanket, and waited. And she prayed, "Please, God, this is so hard. Help me get home. Wherever that is."

How deep is your love? . . .

Steven was frantic that night.

It wasn't until after the evening meal that he realized that Rita was gone. Everyone . . . Kraka, Grima, Sigge, Lady Igorsson . . . looked weepy-eyed but claimed no knowledge of where she was. Finally, his meddling sister disclosed her part in advising Rita of all his shortcomings.

"I should have left you to rot in the pirate's lair," he'd told her in the end.

She had just smiled. If ever there was a witch, it was his sister.

It was morning before he'd discovered the riderless horse returning to Norstead, and he finally figured out where she had gone. It was with a pounding heart that he approached the clearing where her small tent was erected. Had she left already? Was it too late?

He tethered his horse to a tree some distance away and approached quietly. She was on the other side of the tent, kneeling. Good gods, she appeared to be praying herself back to the future.

"Nay!" he shouted, causing her to tumble over, then quickly rise to her feet.

"You shouldn't have come," she said, brushing off the seat of her braies. Her eyes were red with weeping.

"Yea, I should have come. Well, that is not quite true. You should not have left Norstead, requiring me to come after you. But here we are." He threw his arms out in surrender and sank down to a boulder.

"What are you doing?"

"Staying with you."

"You can't stay with me."

"Why? I'm going back with you to the future."

"What? You can't do that."

"Why not?"

"Because you're needed here. Your people depend on you."

He shrugged. "You are needed, too, but you are leaving. Do you not care about Sigge and the witches? How about your newfound wheel friend? And me . . . who will turn this blue Viking into a cheerful man? I may just die of sadness without you."

"Don't overdo it, Steven."

He shrugged. "Besides, it will be good to see my brother again."

"Steven! Stop it! This is not a game. What if you come back with me and don't like it? Not that I even know if you can come back with me. Hell, I don't even know if I can go back."

He smiled at her nervous blathering.

She took a deep breath. "Why are you doing this?"

"For you. Where you go, I go."

She let out a little whimper. "Don't."

"Ree-tah, you said something last night, but you fell asleep afore I could respond."

She narrowed her eyes at him, knowing precisely what she referred to. "You had plenty of time."

"Yea, I did, but this is new territory to me." He stood and motioned with his fingertips for her to come closer.

"Not a chance!"

He smiled. Being a natural-born seducer, he knew when he was winning a battle of the senses. "I love you," he said.

"No!" she said and began to weep.

"I love you."

"No, you don't."

"I love you."

"Stop saying that."

"I love you, I love you, I love you. There is no argument that will make me change my mind."

"Yes, there is," she said. "I'm pregnant." She clamped a hand over her mouth, immediately regretting having blurted that out.

This was the time for careful words. He knew that what came out of his mouth next would determine his future.

A baby. She was going to have his baby. A snot-nosed, bawling bratling with black hair and blue eyes. Or blond hair and silver gray eyes. *A child.* A being created by the two of them. A baby!

He wanted to ask how that could happen with the birthing control device, but the whys and hows did not matter. Not really.

On the other hand, he was outraged. She would go away without telling him of her pregnancy. He could have gone a lifetime before ever knowing he had a son or daughter somewhere else.

He stepped up to her, lifted her into his arms, and said the only thing he could. "I love you, heartling."

With those words, which would have gagged him at one time, but came so naturally now, Steven's heart lightened.

He smiled against her mouth. "I want to make love with you, but not here on this rocky ground where you first came seducing me."

"Me seduce you? Hah! You told me I was an ugly mermaid."

"Me?" He put a hand over his heart and feigned innocence. "I fear we might both be tossed through time in the midst of peaking and land in some place neither of us would relish. Like the moon." Even so, he was already beginning to remove her garments, kissing every bare spot along the way.

"The moon, huh?" She had her hands under his braies in the back, on his bare buttocks—Thank you, gods, for unshy maidens—and was shoving the cloth down his hips to land at his feet. "Did I tell you that men in my time have traveled to the moon and back? Moon exploration is actually possible."

His jaw dropped open, whether from her telling him of that modern marvel or from the place where her hands were now touching him. Talking was not what he had in mind with a rising enthusiasm. Forget the moon. Now was the time for exploration of a different kind. "Come, my betrothed, and pledge me your troth in the age-old fashion."

"Betrothed? I did not hear any proposal from you. And, besides, next time a man asks me to marry him, it better be down on not one knee, but two."

He laughed. "If I am down on two knees afore you, it will not be to use my tongue to speak."

"Steven!" she said with pretend shock.

That was one of the things he loved about her . . . that he could not shock her. Well, mayhap he could. After he bared her body and whilst he removed the rest of his garments, he lifted her onto the bare back of his horse and immediately mounted behind her. "We will go to a soft forest bower not far from here where we can make love in comfort, or else . . ." he chuckled, placing a hand over her belly, "we could have horse sex if we cannot wait that long."

"That is such a myth. That sex can take place on a horse. Writers put that in romance novels all the time, but . . . yikes! What are you doing?"

"Do you not know by now that you should ne'er tell a Viking that he cannot do something?"

Her only response was a gurgling noise. He was fairly certain it meant she liked what he was doing, and the rhythm of the slowly moving horse aided his cause. Immensely.

Later . . . a way too short time later, he lay beside her on the soft moss carpet with sunlight filtering through the evergreens. She was panting for breath.

He was smiling. What man would not smile if he could make his woman breathless.

Looking up at him, she traced his jaw with a fingertip. Love shone in her blue eyes.

"Will you miss being back in your own time?"

"This is my time now. But, yes, there are things I will miss. Hopefully, you'll make up for all those losses."

"I can only try." He cast her a lascivious leer, knowing full well that sex was not what she had meant. Or not totally. He turned serious then. "Do you really think the gods sent you here because I was so sad?"

"My blue Viking," she teased. "Yes, that's the only explanation I can come up with. God sent me to you. He saw how unhappy you were and how it was affecting your people."

"The ways of the gods are deep and unfathomable." He plastered a particularly doleful expression on his face then. "Uh-oh! The flames of my good mood seem to be dying. I feel the blues coming on again. Perchance . . . do you have some other trick to refire my embers?"

Rita realized then that Steven would be using that excuse for the rest of their lives as a rationale for her to make love to him. Well, she had news for him. It went both ways.

"Baby, I have a thousand ways to light your fire, but keep in mind . . . sometimes mermaids get the blues, too."

Epilogue

You haven't partied 'til you've partied Viking style...

Everyone agreed the Althing that year was the best ever, highlighted as it was by the marriage of Lord Steven of Norstead and Lady Rita of America.

The lawspeaker Agmundr reluctantly conducted the ceremony under the decorated Althing tent with Oslac, Brandr, and Brodir standing beside Steven as his witnesses, and Rita having an amazing five witnesses: Joy, Sigge, Kraka, Grima, and Disa. No one had ever heard of witches being part of a wedding ceremony afore.

The bride was a sight to behold in a white, soft wool gown of the Saxon style, but it was covered later with a Norse apron of highly prized crimson samite silk adorned with gold braiding. Hanging from the chain betwixt her two shoulder brooches were the keys to Norstead.

Steven was just as beautiful, some said, attired as he was in a black tunic and braies of the finest wool, cinched at the waist with a gold-linked belt said to be worth a king's ransom. Presumably, it was a gift from the pirate Brodir.

During the ceremony, Steven placed his gold ring . . . the selfsame matching one worn by his brother Thorfinn . . . on the tip of his sword and handed it to Rita, saying, "I give you this ring to mark the continuous circle of our unbreakable vows, and this sword to hold in trust for our sons." He'd glanced at her flat stomach as he spoke, and tears filled the bride's eyes.

Steven promised his new wife protection under his shield, love until death, and fidelity, which outraged some of the Viking men. She promised him love, honor, and lots of some strange things called Pup-suckles, to which Steven had thrown his head back, roaring with laughter, then a quick kiss of thanks.

He'd chased her back to the keep for the *brudr-hlaup* or "bride-running." Viking ritual called for him to swat her on the arse, then lay the sword across the threshold. If she stepped over it, it would indicate that she accepted her new husband. She not only stepped, she did a front flip over it.

He had then sword-pierced one of the high standing beams, the roof tree, of his great hall. The depth of his cut indicated virility. No one was surprised that his gash was very deep.

His *morgen-gifu*, or the "morning gift," would be presented to Rita on the morrow to show his satisfaction with her bed performance. It was said to be an odd-shaped piece of marble he'd brought back from the Arab lands, but he declined to explain its significance to anyone who asked. Except for Oslac, who just smirked.

When asked by the lawspeaker if she had a *heiman fly-gia* for her new husband, Rita had replied, "Yes. All the proceeds next year from the sale of my deodorant."

Several of the Viking men in attendance were not impressed, having heard how the odd wench complained of their body stench.

There was much feasting at the wedding reception, the primary drink being mead, which tradition said should be imbibed for a month during the "honeymoon" period. Strangely, Rita refrained.

The entertainment that night amazed one and all as Viking women and men alike line danced to "Achy Breaky Heart," "Boot Scootin' Boogie," and a new ribald song, "Save a Horse, Ride a Cowboy," except the words were changed to "Save a Longship, Ride a Viking."

Eight months later, a large babe with black hair and silver eyes came howling into the world. Steven proclaimed at his birth, with tears in his Viking eyes, that he would be named Thorfinn, after his brother. And he added that mayhap his son would one day travel the world in his very own longship . . . mayhap even to America.

Dear Readers:

Well, *Dark Viking* is the seventh in my Viking Navy SEAL series. What did you think?

When writing series, even if they are loosely linked and can be read out of order, a writer eventually comes to a point where she asks: "Should there be more?"

There are many pros. When readers like a particular "world" that a writer creates, whether it be vampires, a small lakeside town, a family, or Viking Navy SEALs, they want to return to it again and again. Almost like a situation drama or comedy on TV: *Seinfeld*, *Two and a Half Men*, *Bones*, *NCIS*. They don't want the same story over and over, but they want the familiar setting and secondary characters.

I have a particular affection for each of the SEALs featured so far: Torolf (*Wet and Wild*), Ragnor (*Hot and Heavy*), Ian (*Down and Dirty*), Pretty Boy (*Rough and Ready*), Thorfinn (*Viking Unchained*), and the female SEALs, or WEALS, Joy Nelson (*Viking Heat*) and Rita Sawyer (*Dark Viking*). Most, or all of which, are still available new.

On the other hand, story lines can become stale.

Even so, I think there is a place for more Viking Navy SEALs. For example, Cage, JAM, Sly, Britta's sister Angelique, even F.U., yearn to tell you their stories. And by the way, have you checked out Scary Larry's novella, "Tomorrow Is Another Day" in the *Ladies Prefer Rogues* anthology?

What do you think?

Please visit my website at www.sandrahill.net to get my latest news, learn more about my books, view book videos, see genealogy charts, enter contests, and obtain freebies.

I love to hear from readers. You can contact me at shill733@aol.com.

As always I wish you smiles in your reading.

Sandra Hill

Glossary

Althing (or Thing)—an assembly of free Viking men from a wide area that made laws and enacted justice, forerunners of a legislative body, usually a festive affair as well, giving families and friends an opportunity to get together and share news and fun

Asgard—home of the Aesir gods

Braies—slim pants worn by men, breeches

Brudr-hlaup—the bride running, a wedding ritual in which the groom chases the bride from the ceremony site to the great hall

Brynja—flexible chain mail shirt

Companaticum—"that which goes with bread," which usually meant whatever was in the stockpot of thick broth, usually with chunks of meat, always simmering in the huge kitchen cauldron, which was, unfortunately, not cleaned out for long periods of time

Drukkinn (various spellings)—drunk in Old Norse

Ell—a measure, usually of cloth, equaling forty-five inches

Fillet—band worn around the head

Hand—four inches

Hauberk—a long defensive shirt or coat, usually made of chain links or leather

Hectares—unit of land measure equal to 2.471 acres

Heiman flygia—the bride-price consisted of three payments: from the groom would come the *mundr* and *morgen gifu*, while the bride's parents provided the *heiman fylgia*

Hersir—military commander

Hide—a primitive measure of land that originally equaled the normal holding that would support a peasant and his family, roughly 120 arable acres, but could actually be as little as 40

Hird—permanent troop that a chieftain or nobleman might have

Hirdsman—one of the hird

Housecarls—troops assigned to a king's or lord's household on a longtime, sometimes permanent basis

Knarr—a Viking merchant vessel, wider and deeper than a regular longship

More danico—practice of having more than one wife

Morgen gifu—the morning after gift a husband gave his wife to show he was pleased

Niflheim, or Hel—a dark misty region for the dead, similar to hell, except there was ice, snow, and eternal darkness

Norsemandy—tenth-century name for Normandy

Northumbria—one of the Anglo-Saxon kingdoms, bordered by the English kingdoms to the south and in the north and northwest by the Scots, Cumbrians, and Strathclyde Welsh

Sennight—one week

Skald—poet

Thrall—slave

Tun—252 gallons, as in ale

Valhalla—hall of the slain, Odin's magnificent hall in Asgard

Valkyries—female warriors who did Odin's will

Vapnatak (or weapon clatter)—at an Althing, the men indicated their votes by banging swords against shields

Wergild (or wergeld)—a man's worth

Also available from *USA Today* bestselling author

SANDRA HILL

Viking Heat

Psychologist Joy Nelson thinks things are bad when
she finds herself training in the modern-day female
Navy SEALs program. But then her life takes a turn
for the worse. Somehow she's been thrust back in
time to the cold Norselands, and is being auctioned
off as a thrall, or slave—a gift for a Viking warlord,
who would be a perfect candidate for Male Chauvinist Viking of the Centuries.

penguin.com

M699T0510

Also from *USA Today* bestselling author

Sandra Hill

VIKING UNCHAINED

"Sandra Hill has truly outdone herself."
—*Night Owl Romance*

"Ms. Hill had me rolling with laughter with every turn of the page. She breathes life into her characters and makes the reader wish they were real. I dare say anyone who reads this story will come away with a smile." —*Coffee Time Romance*

"Hill goes a-Viking again! It's a blast!"
—*Romantic Times*

penguin.com

DON'T MISS

Ladies Prefer Rogues

Janet Chapman, Sandra Hill, Veronica Wolff, and Trish Jensen

Out of time, out of place, but still searching for true love.

New York Times **bestselling author Janet Chapman** writes about a band of twenty-third-century warriors on a mission to save mankind . . .

USA Today **bestselling author Sandra Hill** plunges a woman back in time to post–Civil War Louisiana, where the poor Southern belle must make a living as a matchmaker . . .

National bestselling author Veronica Wolff tells of a seventeenth-century Scotsman who avenges the death of his greatest love . . .

USA Today **bestselling author Trish Jensen** spins a fetching fable about a woman from the Wild West who lands in modern-day Nevada . . .

penguin.com

M619T0510

Penguin Group (USA) Online

What will you be reading tomorrow?

Patricia Cornwell, Nora Roberts, Catherine Coulter,
Ken Follett, John Sandford, Clive Cussler,
Tom Clancy, Laurell K. Hamilton, Charlaine Harris,
J. R. Ward, W.E.B. Griffin, William Gibson,
Robin Cook, Brian Jacques, Stephen King,
Dean Koontz, Eric Jerome Dickey, Terry McMillan,
Sue Monk Kidd, Amy Tan, Jayne Ann Krentz,
Daniel Silva, Kate Jacobs...

You'll find them all at
penguin.com

Read excerpts and newsletters,
find tour schedules and reading group guides,
and enter contests.

Subscribe to Penguin Group (USA) newsletters
and get an exclusive inside look
at exciting new titles and the authors you love
long before everyone else does.

PENGUIN GROUP (USA)
penguin.com